PENGUIN BOOKS

THE
SACRIFICE
BOX

MARTIN STEWART has previously worked as an English teacher, university lecturer, barman, recycling technician and golf caddie. A native of Glasgow, he now lives on Scotland's west coast with his partner, daughter and a very big dog. He enjoys cooking with eggs, running on the beach, re-watching his favourite films and buying books to feed his to-be-read pile.

Martin's critically acclaimed first novel, *Riverkeep*, was short-listed for the YA Book Prize and the Branford Boase Award, and longlisted for the Guardian Children's Fiction Prize.

Follow him on

Twitter:	**@martinjstewart**
Instagram:	**martin_j_stewart**

D0654948

Praise for *Riverkeep*:

'A cracking, startlingly original story . . . It would be an extraordinary book by any author – but it is Martin Stewart's first' *Spectator*

'Relentlessly brilliant . . . Stylish, precise, limitlessly evocative of landscape, atmosphere, guilt and terror . . . That he has packed enough detail, talent and skill in there for three books can hardly be a criticism. His characters lived for me by the end' *Guardian*

'Extraordinary . . . Stunningly original' *Evening Standard*

'Completely absorbing' *The Bookseller*

'Brilliant' *Sunday Express*

'Outstanding' *Scotsman*

'Utterly compelling and masterful' *Booktrust*

'A stunning debut' *Sunday Independent (Ireland)*

'Exquisite' *New York Times*

THE
SACRIFICE
BOX

MARTIN
STEWART

PENGUIN BOOKS

PENGUIN BOOKS

UK | USA | Canada | Ireland | Australia
India | New Zealand | South Africa

Penguin Books is part of the Penguin Random House group of companies
whose addresses can be found at global.penguinrandomhouse.com.

www.penguin.co.uk
www.puffin.co.uk
www.ladybird.co.uk

Penguin
Random House
UK

First published 2018

001

Text copyright © Martin Stewart, 2018

The moral right of the author has been asserted

Set in 11.5/15.5 Bembo Book MT Std
Typeset by Jouve (UK), Milton Keynes
Printed in Great Britain by Clays Ltd, St Ives plc

A CIP catalogue record for this book is available from the British Library

ISBN: 978-0-141-37161-0

All correspondence to:
Penguin Books
Penguin Random House Children's
80 Strand, London WC2R 0RL

For Mum and Dad

I never had any friends later on like the ones I had when I was twelve. Jesus, did you?

The Body, Stephen King

0

Sacrifice: 1982

Sep knelt beside the box. The forest was tight with heat, and sweat prickled on his skin.

The clearing around him was a blanket of root and stone, caged by silent trees and speckled by dark, leaf-spinning pools that hid the wriggling things of the soil. And at its heart, as though dropped by an ebbing tide, was the sacrifice box.

Mack was hopping in anticipation behind him. Arkle, Lamb and Hadley stood on the other side of the box's stone, their sacrifices complete: a scatter of burnt dragonflies, a little mirror and a diary.

'Sep,' said Arkle, then louder: 'Sep!'

'I'm doing it,' said Sep.

'No, it's not that . . .'

'Shut up!' whispered Lamb.

Sep squeezed Barnaby. The little teddy's plastic snout was fixed in a smile, and his eyes were deep and brown.

'Are you OK?' said Hadley.

'What?' said Sep, turning his good ear towards her.

'I said, are you OK?'

He took a deep breath. 'Yes.'

'It's all right,' said Hadley, lisping through her braces. Sep could hear the wheeze on the edge of her voice. 'You don't have to.'

'Yeah, he does,' said Mack, chewing. 'We said we would. All of us. And it was *his* idea.'

'Are you eating *another* sandwich?' said Arkle. 'Pac-Man with legs, you are.'

Sep looked at Barnaby's matted fur and pudgy limbs. The teddy was a ruined thing – dragged through briar, thorn and rain until his tummy split. Sep's mum had stitched him up with an old shoelace, the summer before she got sick.

As he thumbed the lace Sep's good ear hissed with the treetops' breeze – then the wind died, and there was no sound but the pat and chuckle of the recent sunshower as it dripped, leaf by leaf, down to the earth.

'Sep, c'mon –' said Arkle.

'Shut *up*!' said Lamb. 'You're interrupting his sacrifice!'

'*Sep!*' Arkle hissed again, even though people normally did what Lamb said since her mother died.

Sep sighed, and looked up at Arkle's sweaty grin. 'What is it?' he said. The air was green and sticky, and dandelion seeds clung to their faces.

'You're kneeling in poo,' said Arkle. 'It's just there. See? There?'

Sep looked.

'Yes, thank you.'

'D'you see it? It's brown.'

'Yeah, I've got it.'

2

'Under your right knee.'

'That's my left knee,' said Sep, wiping his jeans on the grass.

'Same difference.'

'Are you putting the bear in or not?' said Lamb.

Sep looked at tall, strong Lamb – shoulders back, her mother's headscarf tied round the plaster cast on her wrist. She met his stare evenly, and he saw Arkle nod and Hadley smile, the trees behind them split by the recent lightning.

Barnaby had been a gift from his mum. Sep had tucked the bear beside her in the hospital bed when she was sleeping after the operation – and he'd wondered, on the way home in his granda's car, whether her dying would mean he'd get to stay on the mainland forever.

He'd never forgotten the way the thought had felt in his head. Hot. And guilty.

He reached out to the box's cold stone, squeezed Barnaby one last time – then tossed him after the other sacrifices and stepped towards the others.

'Finally!' said Arkle.

Mack raised his sacrifice.

'You're putting in your watch?' said Lamb.

'Why not?' said Mack, shrugging. 'There, I've stopped the hands. It'll always show the time of this perfect moment, when we did this together.'

'It doesn't matter *what* you put in,' said Arkle. 'Right? It's just a thing.'

'It does so matter,' said Sep. 'We're doing this for each other – whatever you sacrifice has to mean *something*.'

'All right, Seppy. So now what do we do?'

'Close it,' said Sep.

Mack's dark brows furrowed low as he heaved on the box's stone lid. Sep looked for Barnaby, but the box was deep, and there was only darkness inside.

He thought about the broken wrist that had kept Lamb from hockey camp, the holidays abroad that had isolated Hadley, Mack and Arkle from their usual friends; the way they'd bumped into one another on the beach, and how they'd drifted into such perfect happiness over the last couple of weeks.

'You know,' he said, 'I've loved this summer. I've never really had anyone to . . . I mean –'

The lid slipped. Mack swore and snatched his hand away, gripping his fingers.

'Are you OK?' said Hadley. 'Are you bleeding?'

'No, it's fine.' Mack flexed his fingers and swore again. Then he laughed. 'I think it bit me.'

They stood back and looked at the sacrifice box. As the lid darkened in the rain it disappeared into the forest's skin, seeming like nothing more than a small, turf-sunk boulder. The world smelled bright and fresh and green.

'It's kind of amazing we found this,' said Lamb.

'It was the storm,' said Sep, twisting his headphones. 'The box wasn't here last week. The rain must have washed it out.'

'How old do you think it is?' said Hadley.

'Hundreds of years. Maybe thousands.'

'Maybe millions?' said Arkle.

'You're an idiot,' Lamb muttered, then flicked his ear. Arkle grinned.

'I still think we should've made it into a fire pit,' he said, flipping the lid on his lighter up and down.

Sep saw Hadley watching him from under her fringe. Her tormentors, Sonya and Chantelle, had chased her to the forest and along the edge of the ravine, and her eyes were still red. He looked up through the trees at the clouds – great towers of pearl that flattened to anvils on the sky and spread out over the island. The tide crashed on to the rocks, and he thought of his mum listening to the waves through the open window of the living room.

'Now what?' asked Arkle.

'We say Sep's words,' said Mack.

'They're not really mine,' said Sep, remembering how the words had come to him, like a knife driven into his skull – a waking dream so vivid he'd cried out in the bright sunshine.

'What do you mean?' said Lamb.

'I kind of dreamed them. They're just . . . they're the box's rules.'

'All right, so we say them. Then what?'

'Then we'll always be friends,' said Sep.

'How does *that* work?' said Arkle.

'Because we're making a promise to each other.'

'And it'll be *our* secret,' said Hadley, gripping her inhaler. 'We can't tell anyone.'

'Oh, I don't think we should talk about this at school,' said Arkle. 'I mean, it is kind of lame.'

5

The rain started again, cold drops on their hot skin.

'Let's say the words then,' Sep said.

'Bagsy not stand next to you, poo-legs,' said Arkle.

They arranged themselves around the box as the rain grew heavier, draping the clearing's edge in grey sheets and closing them in.

Sep tried to peer through it.

Something was moving in the shadows between the trees. He narrowed his eyes, focused on a shifting speck.

There was a sound like someone whispering – or shouting from far away – and a long moment hung in the clearing. Sep felt his skin crawl as he sensed other figures around the box, their shadows closing in.

Then Hadley said, 'Sep?' and the moment lifted, and they were alone again.

Two crows spun through the rain. They settled on a branch high above them, shaking the drops from their feathers and shuffling their feet.

'I'm fine,' said Sep.

Hadley took his hand in hers and lifted it over the box, joined their palms to the others'. Sep felt how warm her skin was, caught her soft scent on the forest's breath, and closed his eyes.

'Ready?' said Mack. 'Remember what to say?'

Lamb nodded, her jaw muscles tight.

Something's really happening, Sep thought – then Hadley squeezed his hand, and he forgot about everything that wasn't her.

'Now,' she said. 'Before Roxburgh finds us.'

They spoke the words – the rules of the sacrifice.
'*Never come to the box alone,*' they said, hands unmoving.
'*Never open it after dark,*' they said, fingers joined together.
'*Never take back your sacrifice,*' they finished – then let go.

PART I

FOUR YEARS LATER

although I am fond of this island,

. . . so ~~greatly~~ desire ~~to leave this island, and~~ there is no

question that I am prepared for ~~(and excited about)~~ the

challenges of residential campus living.

In applying to your prestigious establishment, I have

reflected on the nature of my life and so been drawn to

who
Aristotle, ~~the great philosopher~~ believed in the power of a fruit

metaphor, claiming that 'the roots of education are bitter, but

the fruit is sweet' and that 'friendship is a slow-ripening

fruit'. Not wishing to overstep the boundaries of my middle-

about education
school education, but Aristotle was wrong ~~on both counts~~, the

which
roots of ~~education~~ are as sweet as nectar for a keen mind. ~~And~~

~~the notion of friendship as 'slow-ripening' is flawed — it suggests~~

~~the inevitability of friendship, and casts solitude as unwelcome~~

It is to my credit, I believe, that I have
~~aberration. Well, I have chosen my solitude, and~~ used ~~it~~ to

the solitude I have experienced
sweeten the roots of my education.

Yours sincerely,
^
~~Many thanks in advance for your consideration.~~

September Hope

1

Morning

June 1986

Even as the sun was creeping over the trees and lighting the sky a delicate pink, the moon's ghostly scimitar shimmered on the edge of sight. Sep thought of its dark side as he peered into his telescope, searching once again for the comet and, once again, finding nothing.

He tumbled out of bed and pulled his Pink Floyd T-shirt over his head, giving the armpits a sniff. It would do, he thought, breathing in the burnt toast and sea salt as he went down the stairs.

The house was calm – coloured by the muted dawn, gulls padding on the flat roof. But his mum was asleep in her chair again, halfway through dressing and breakfast, her patrol belt loose on her knees, coffee cold under a rainbow of oil. Her nose was twitching. Sep flicked the hair from her face, then switched on the radio.

Static hissed into the room. He frowned, then twisted the dial, trying to tune into something – anything but silence.

But all he could find was empty, wobbling noise. He clicked it off, then pressed the flashing light on the answer machine.

Hi, darling, it's Matt. I was wondering if —

'Oops,' said Sep, stabbing the delete button.

Checking quickly over his shoulder that his mum was still asleep, he opened the cereal cupboard, but the second he put his bowl on the worktop she said —

'Morning, pet. I couldn't sleep, so I got up early, but I must have dozed off. Put that down. You're not eating that rubbish on a school day.'

'I like cereal,' said Sep.

'That's not cereal, it's sugary gunk stuck together with sugar — only for weekends. You need brain food.'

Sep reread his application form under the table while she spooned fresh coffee into the pot and opened a tin of white crab, singing under her breath as she mashed the meat in a bowl.

'What's that you've got?' she said.

'What?' said Sep, turning his good ear towards the kitchen.

'I asked what you're looking at.'

'Nothing,' said Sep, folding the pages into his bag. Homework.'

'You've always got homework.'

His mum piled the crab on to boiled eggs and slid the plate across the table.

'Crab. Just remember — they can't hurt you if they're in a tin.'

Sep suppressed a shiver. 'Haha.'

'You feeling better today?'

'My head's still a bit funny, and I've got a toothache.'

'That's been three days. Four now, actually. Early night for you tonight.'

She looked out of the window, tipped some salt into her palm and tossed it over her shoulder. 'Couple of crows on the grass.'

'That's for magpies,' said Sep with his mouth full. His mum's walkie-talkie crackled, and he jumped.

'It's *crows*,' she said. 'Magpies stole it from them. We're in trouble if they go on the roof.'

Sep flexed his jaw. The crab was sweet and good, but it hurt his sore tooth. He wondered how much longer he could avoid the dentist. 'Superstitions are stupid,' he said.

'They have to come from somewhere.' She shook pepper on her egg and sipped her coffee. 'Crow on the thatch, soon Death lifts the latch.'

'What does Death do with Yale locks?'

His mum rolled her eyes.

'Save us from the cleverness of children.'

Sep watched her face. Her eyes were pink and heavy, he thought, and her skin was pale.

'Are you all right?' he said. 'You're not eating anything.'

'Of course.'

'Then it's not the same as –'

'No!' she said firmly. 'Definitely not, I'm fine. Now, remember I'm on double-shift today, so you'll need to get your own dinner.'

'I'm working after school anyway. I'll get something from Mario's.'

'Well, you can't eat chips every day, so get something healthy-ish. And I wish you wouldn't work so much. You should relax.'

'And do what?'

'I don't know. You're fifteen. Watch a film. Go out.'

Sep looked up from running a finger over his plate.

'With who?'

'What happened to that crowd you used to run around with? The boy named after the racehorse, and the sporty girl?'

'Arkle and Lamb?'

His mum clicked her fingers. '*Arkle!* I kept thinking of Shergar. Who were the others?'

'Hadley. And Mack. I haven't hung out with them in years. As soon as we started back at school they just . . . went back to their real friends. They don't even speak to me. *Or* each other. What made you think of them?'

'I don't know.' His mum shrugged. 'My dream last night . . . they knocked on the door, looking for you. And I wondered about it when I woke up. They were nice. Are they still at your school?'

'Well, yeah. We've all got English together – it's the only school on the island.'

His mum peered into her mug. 'Not everyone stays,' she said.

'It's a full scholarship,' said Sep after a moment.

'You know I don't care about the money, it's just . . . *boarding* school? You could finish high school here, then go to uni on the mainland. Everyone makes friends at uni.'

'Everyone?'

She sighed.

'I know school's been hard, my brave boy. And you've always had itchy feet. You'll go to the city and love it. You won't be back.'

Sep hated it when she called him brave. He wasn't; he just endured it – brave as a rock stuck in the tide. But, more than that, he didn't want to *have* to be brave – he wanted to live his life with effortless joy. Like everyone else.

'It might not work out,' he said.

'Oh, I know, I know.'

She shook more pepper on her egg, but left her plate untouched. The silence between them was punctured occasionally by static from the walkie-talkie, and it felt as though her effort to contain her emotions had tightened the air around the table, like a wet rag wrung in strong hands.

Sep ran his thumb over his Walkman buttons, then looked through the kitchen window. The sea's flat edge was just visible between the tops of the trees, vanishing and reappearing as the branches were tossed by the wind. Beyond the water lay the mainland, a pale smudge of green and grey, with the blades of windmills backstroking their way across the horizon's line. The city was invisible in the distance, its imagined weight pulling the landscape towards it like a stone on a sheet.

He carried their plates to the sink, tipping the uneaten food on to a napkin and folding it into his pocket.

'Do you want a lift?' she called.

'What?'

'Do you want a lift to school?'

'In a police car? I get a hard enough time, thanks.'

She smiled, and Sep relaxed.

'I could drop you off round the corner —'

'It's all right. I've got my skateboard.'

'You know I don't like you on that thing.'

'So get me a moped,' said Sep, lifting his sandwiches from the fridge.

She rolled her eyes.

'Would you at least take your bike?'

Sep thought of his old yellow Chopper, covered in an eczema of rust and four years of spiders' webs.

'No,' he said, grabbing his bag.

'Don't you be feeding that fox!' shouted his mum.

The door banged shut behind him. Morning had yet to warm the island's bones, and the air was cold despite the glow feathering through the trees. Sep felt the fresh, bright chill on his skin, and rubbed his arms.

The fox was sitting on the path, its fur haloed in the morning's gold. Sep put the napkin at his feet and stepped away.

'Here you go,' he said. 'That's all I've got. Come on, I'm late.'

He took a step forward.

The animal leaped back on scalded paws, then settled again before yawning, its sharp face tiny beneath enormous, black-tipped ears.

Sep moved again and the fox skipped back, amber eyes flashing, its little body humming with wildness. It blinked and cocked its head.

He reached out to touch the animal's ears, and it darted out of reach, balanced on the edge of its paws.

'Maybe one day you'll trust me,' he said.

The fox waited until Sep was out of sight before it lifted the crabmeat in its mouth, then trotted into the trees.

2

Late

Morning's low sun spilled round Sep as he rolled downhill. Its light gathered like caramel in the island's rock pools, burst like torch beams through the forest, and smashed hard and flat against the schoolhouse walls. The day began with the drone of flies and the rumble of working engines – and through it all time curled like a worm, bunching as it moved, alternately rushing and pausing and sometimes stopping completely.

It had settled slowly on Lamb, kneeling at her mother's cracked mirror as she brushed her hair and soaked in the past while Arkle – the hive of his mind buzzing with excitement and TV – felt it whip past in a distracted, hyper blur. It brushed lightly on Hadley as she floated through her sketches and scribbles, the coffee cooling in her mug as she sat on the stairs and inked the sides of her canvas shoes. It closed round Mack on his daily run past the river where the lost things of the town gathered: a rusting trolley, the urban scum of carrier bags, and the sack that had been full a few days before, but was now flapping empty in the flow. Minutes pressed on him like a deep-water squeeze as he ran back to a house of shouting and drink and slamming doors, where nothing ever changed and time seemed hardly to move at all.

And now the seconds slipped from Sep before he could catch them, cool air swirling through his T-shirt as he coasted down the gentle slope, in time for nothing but another detention.

The skateboard's rumble unspooled behind the music in his headphones – a mixtape of early Bowie and The Cure, one side each. 'Close to Me' started as the road leaned to the left, the squat brick and glass of the school growling into view above the bay's wide mouth and the stretching tongue of the old pier. The tide was high, the sea gripping the land. Wet stone gleamed as the waves withdrew, imperceptibly, like the shrinking of a dead man's gums.

Sep peered through the glare and found the mainland, only a green haze, but there, distant and solid – and everything the island was not. He had first been there when he was small, to visit family before his mum got sick, a few long afternoons reduced by memory to beaming relatives, tall buildings and the roar of streets. He wanted that life – the busy, vibrant anonymity, not the Hill Ford fishbowl – and the lodestar of the city's engineering college shone with a bright heat that had burned through his other desires until it was all that was left: a steel chamber in his heart that beat with a single impulse.

Leave the island.

Sep rolled into the car park just as the bell stopped ringing, then rubbed his jaw. A strange feeling filled him – like a swelling in his ear tubes; like someone breathing just over his shoulder.

He looked up at the sky. The moon was gone, the rock and ice of Halley's comet somewhere beyond the light.

Sep blinked away the pain and sucked his gum.

The other stragglers – out-of-town farm kids, sleep-ins and smokers – melted away as he flipped up his board and passed through the doors. Scanning the foyer, he went to the vending machine, dropping his headphones around his neck. Another minute wouldn't make any difference – he was already late, and he was top of the class in chemistry. Mr Marshall practically dribbled on his notebook.

He bought a can of Spike and – the *second* he popped the ring pull – a sharp little hand fell on his shoulder.

'Late *again*, Hope?' whispered a reedy voice. 'Every day this week. I'll have your lunchtime for that.'

'Morning, Mrs Maguire,' said Sep without turning. 'We really must stop meeting like this.'

Maguire plucked the can from his hand and moved in front of him.

'That smart mouth of yours . . .' said Maguire. Her glassy eyes drilled into Sep's. 'I'll have *two* lunchtimes, how does that sound?'

'Of course, miss.'

Maguire angled her head back, digging her bosom into Sep's belly.

'Why are you wearing those ridiculous "high-top" trainers again?'

'To keep my socks clean, miss,' said Sep, staring straight ahead.

'Three.'

Sep blinked.

'But it's Thursday,' he said. 'There's only two lunchtimes left till the weekend.'

'I'll have Monday as well then, won't I?' said Maguire. She leaned up until her nose was almost touching Sep's chin. 'You know what your trouble is, Hope? You have no *respect*.'

'On the contrary, miss,' said Sep, leaning away from her coffee breath. 'You've been on late-coming duty in the same school for thirty years. Of course I respect you.'

Maguire's eyes narrowed, and she moved her lips to Sep's ear.

'Let me give you some free advice, young man –'

'That's my deaf ear, Mrs Maguire,' said Sep, turning his head.

'– you might be as bright as a button, but you can't outgrade a bad attitude. Colleges want rounded individuals, not just test scores. You need to get out from behind the books, make some friends – do something interesting. I *know* your application is incomplete . . .' Maguire's voice softened, '. . . what are you going to write about if all you do is study? What will you say when they ask about the relationships you've built here?'

Sep stared past her head, towards the seniors' common room.

'I don't know,' he said eventually.

'Well, think on. Otherwise the only way you'll get to the mainland will be to row there on your inflated ego.'

'But, Mrs Maguire,' said Sep, face wide and innocent, 'the ego's an abstract psychological concept. It's not seaworthy.'

Maguire allowed herself a smile.

'Then you'll sink, Hope. Get swimming.'

She walked away, chuckling.

Sep waited until she was out of sight, then pumped more coins into the machine and ran to class.

He half dozed through double chemistry, even on the wobbly stool, his mind lulled by the familiar whisper of Bunsen burners. But third period on Thursday was history, and history meant Wobie.

Wobie was old. His immense, sagging frame was a monument to threadbare tweed – his one tie lavishly stained with coffee and eggs. A big-band clarinet player in his youth, he'd lost a finger and a dream during national service: now he read the newspaper through every lesson and smoked little cigars out the window. Wobie never kept his promises and never checked homework. His breath was legendary – there was a long-standing rumour that one of his enormous sighs had blinded two third years.

His classroom was the hottest place in the school, a painted-shut pit of brown walls and browner carpet, itchy with dust and lanced by sunbeams that burned the desks and dazzled the students. That the old man had not sweated to death was considered a modern miracle – his crimson face was permanently shiny, like a glazed pot.

Sep, swinging on his chair at the back of the class, watched Wobie turn the huge pages of his newspaper with reverential care. Each time a page swished Sep clicked a button on his Walkman, letting the tape spool through the heads, tracking the fragments of time as they died around him.

He swung forward, blinked rapidly and tried to concentrate – reread a page of his application form for the umpteenth time. The gears of his mind crunched as the words slipped past his eyes.

Tell us about yourself outside school. Think about times in your life when you made successful connections with the people around you, perhaps as part of a group or team; or when you achieved something you're proud of.

Sep looked at the blank page for a full minute, then folded the form into his bag.

Wobie was picking his teeth and ignoring Anna Wright, whose hand had been raised for several minutes. Eventually the broadsheet lowered and his poached-egg eyes dribbled over the top.

'Yes, Miss Wright?'

Anna dropped her hand and massaged her wrist.

'Sir, I forgot my textbook, sir.'

'Woe betide those who forget their textbooks,' said Wobie, returning to his article. 'If your illustrious neighbour, the Face and Hair of Stephen Ashton, has a copy, then you may share it. If not, the Corn Laws' mysteries will remain forever opaque. And that, Miss Wright, would be a tragedy – the political machine has much to teach us of society's cadence in centuries past, and of the transient nature of this fleeting bubble we call life.'

'What?' said Anna.

Stephen slid his textbook across the desk towards her.

There was a knock at the door, and the eyes of the class snapped gratefully towards the sound.

'Enter,' called Wobie.

A fair-haired first-year girl stumbled into the room, Post-it note clutched in her hand, kitten badge pinned to her jumper.

'Yes, small person?' said Wobie.

'Please, sir, it's from Mr Tench,' stammered the girl, handing over the note.

Wobie took it and read, his mouth set in a toadish frown.

'Master Hope,' he said, giving Sep a disinterested smile. 'It seems you have been summoned to the Lair of the Gangling Beast. Do you know what this concerns? Your famed tardiness perhaps?'

Somebody whispered something, and there were sniggers.

Sep shrugged.

'Could be, sir.'

'You were late this morning, I trust?'

'Of course, sir.'

'Begone then, and take your things lest you are detained past the ringing bell. Quickly now – woe betide those who disobey the headmaster.'

'Yes, sir.'

'And, Hope, stop shrugging – you look like a Frenchman.'

'Yes, sir,' said Sep, throwing his stuff into his bag. He felt the eyes of the class, but stopped at Anna's desk.

'Do you want this?' he whispered, holding out his textbook. 'Just for today?'

Her eyes widened.

'Thanks,' she whispered.

'Freak,' said Stephen, loud enough for the class to hear.

A few of them laughed and Sep felt his cheeks burn.

'A scholar *and* a gentleman,' said Wobie, as he teased a cigar from its box and hung it in his purple lips. 'So few of us left.'

Sep felt the embarrassment lodge, heavy and familiar, in his gut as he closed the door behind him – and in its last sliver of light he saw white-haired, blank-faced Hadley, staring at him through her fringe.

3

Midtown

She'd changed her mind when the rain started. Usually she walked everywhere – even in the dead of night, even in the rain, even if her swollen hip was causing its trouble – but when her long white hair had grown heavy with water she'd staggered into the subway's steamy heat and shuffled into a corner to wait for the train home.

There were only two other people on the platform at Midtown: a middle-aged white man with a weasel's moustache and a nervous comb-over, and a young black man in a sleeveless Guardian Angel T-shirt. He had enormous sunglasses stuck in his hair, and tipped them at Shelley like a cap as she sank on to the bench.

She tucked herself away behind her big coat and spectacles, feeling brittle and old as she watched the litter dance in a whirlpool of wind. After a minute or so the rusting, spray-painted train rattled into the station, howling through the dark with electric flashes that lit the graffitied walls like the swooping beams of a lighthouse.

As it screamed to a stop Shelley had a sense of time shifting around her. The train seemed somehow larger than normal, and heavier – as though it was pulling at her with gravitational strength.

Wings fluttered as she stepped unsteadily through the doors, and two crows hopped on to the waste bin behind her.

She held on to the door, looking for a seat, but they were full of sharp-lapped stockbrokers and youths in open, studded jackets. One spike-haired boy had an enormous ghetto blaster between his knees, the speakers shaking with a thrashing sound. The carriage tasted rat-fur sweet, and it felt dangerous and tight.

When the boy turned the blaster's volume even higher and started banging on the windows with his studded gloves Shelley wondered whether she should have gotten a cab instead. She turned to go.

But as she stepped from the train on to the platform her hair lifted in a gust of wind.

And caught between the closing doors.

'Oh!' she cried, her head snapping backwards. 'Oh, my! Help! Help!'

The man in the Guardian Angel shirt rushed over to her.

'It's all right, ma'am!' he shouted. 'I've got you! Just hold on to me –'

The train began to move. Shelley stumbled into his arms.

'Help! My hair! My *hair*!'

People inside had seen what was happening and were pulling on the doors as the carriage wobbled into motion.

'*HELP!*'

The boy had dropped his blaster and was heaving at the space beside Shelley's hair, trying to push it through to the other side as his friend pulled frantically on the emergency stop.

As the train picked up pace the Guardian Angel lifted Shelley from the ground, running with her in his arms as she screamed and the people inside battered the doors: then the vehicle flew into the dark, dripping tunnel and Shelley was torn from the Angel's grip. He knelt, looking at the blood on his hands as terror poured into his stomach and the sound of wings echoed on the wet tiles behind him.

A third crow had appeared. Litter swirled round the birds as they watched, the electric light shining in their eyes.

4

Tench

Mrs Siddiqui looked up as he entered the headmaster's office, but carried on typing.

'Late again, September?'

'I don't know – I just got a note to come down.'

'So maybe no trouble for you?'

'I *was* late today,' said Sep, shrugging and pulling an awkward smile.

'Don't do that to your handsome face,' she said. 'And this hair, why be having it all over your eyes? How will you see your teachers?'

'Sorry,' said Sep, lifting his fringe.

She nodded and ripped the paper from her typewriter.

'*So* much better. Cheekbones – like your mother. And how is your mother? Anwar says she has not been to the restaurant for a little while.'

'She's fine,' said Sep quickly.

'Good, good. Now go in. *He* is doing nothing,' she said. Then added darkly: 'Thinking, probably, of fishing.'

Sep thanked her and knocked.

'Come in!' came Tench's earnest voice.

Sep always forgot the full extent of the headmaster's fish mania, and so was freshly amazed by the number of flies and reels mounted on the walls. Every frame was connected by a tissue of magazine cuttings, full of smiling, rubber-clad men. The room even smelled of fishing – the chemical tang of rubber boots, the tinny smell of water and the odour of drying socks – as though Tench had just stepped from a tinkling stream.

It was odd to make your workplace a shrine to your hobby, Sep thought, stepping over a pile of *Angler's Monthly*. He wondered if the walls of Tench's fishing hut were papered with exam results and timetables.

'September!' said the headmaster, looking up, all pork-pie face and badly knotted tie. 'Good, that was quick. Caroline must have run up the stairs.'

'Caroline?' said Sep.

'Little girl with the message.' Tench held his hand about waist height to indicate Caroline's stature. 'Fair hair. Wants to be a vet actually – she's got work experience lined up, so you'll see her again no doubt.'

A spool of fishing line lay unravelled on his desk. Until recently there had been a picture of Sep's mum there too, but Sep had begged her to have it removed.

'Sit down, sit down,' Tench said, gesturing to the soft chairs.

Sep sat, holding his bag. The headmaster sat opposite, but the seats were too low so he perched awkwardly, knees halfway up his chest, like a man on a child's bicycle.

'How's your mum?' he said.

'She's fine, sir,' said Sep stiffly, then added: 'Thanks.'

'Good, good. It's a few days since I've seen her, what with one thing and another. She works long shifts, your mother. She's the best sergeant I've ever had . . . *we've* had, I mean! On the island! The best *we've* had.'

'Thank you, sir,' said Sep. His jaw was tight, the bad tooth digging into his gum.

'But I didn't call you down to talk about your mum! Haha!' said Tench, smiling widely, his wormy lips broad and pink.

'Haha,' said Sep, shifting on the seat.

'No, I wanted to discuss your school career, Sep. Is it still OK to call you Sep? I know it was when you and your mother came to dinner, but we're in school now, and –'

'Of course, sir.'

'Good. Now, Sep, it looks as though you'll be finishing your schooling away from the island, which is wonderful for you, of course, a great opportunity. We're sorry to see you go, and I'd obviously rather you stayed, but if you must leave –'

'I must,' said Sep quickly.

Tench gave him a quick, tight smile.

'Well, in that case there's a bit of glory to be had for the school: a champion's catch, you might say. The Dale Hutchison Memorial Scholarship is a prestigious award. No one from the *district* has ever won it, even on the mainland – it'll be the best thing to happen to the school since Gillian Thomson got her Blue Peter badge. You're going to be in our Hall of Fame –'

'What Hall of Fame?' said Sep.

'– you'll establish our Hall of Fame,' said Tench, without missing a beat.

Sep shuddered, remembering the assembly held in his honour when the college invited him to apply: the headmaster's long, enthusiastic presentation used so many fishing metaphors Mrs Woodbank had called it the 'I Have a Bream' speech.

'Thank you, sir,' he said. 'So, what do you –'

'I just want to make sure everything's all right,' said Tench, spreading his big hands. 'Mrs Maguire says you've not finished your application – put the final bait on the hook, so to speak. How's it all going? Your work, your focus . . . things at home?'

Sep bit some loose skin from his bottom lip.

'Fine,' he said, touching the pages in his pocket. 'I want to go so much, more than I've ever wanted anything. I can't . . . I can't not go.'

Tench looked out of the window at the island, nodded, then turned back.

'Some weather, isn't it? Too hot for you?'

'A bit, sir. I burn easily.'

'So does your mother,' said Tench, and Sep visibly winced as he imagined the headmaster putting sunscreen on his mum. 'It'll rain soon, don't worry. This heat is building up to a storm – like a kettle coming to the boil. Brings the fish to the surface, you know. Rain like that.'

'Yes, sir.'

Tench sighed happily.

'I'm from the mainland, originally, you know. Just outside the city. I miss it sometimes, but I wanted to live in a small town. I wanted that smallness, to know my neighbours. Living here you can share each other's lives in a kind of . . . family of families. In Hill Ford I really believe that, neighbour by neighbour, we can work towards a kind of shared happiness, that we can connect to the very essence of the human animal, and all the spiritual nourishment community can bring. And this island has the best fly-fishing in the northern hemisphere. Do you understand what I'm saying?'

'Yes, sir.'

'But other people,' he gestured at Sep with open palms, 'they want just the opposite. The big world. And it's yours if you want it: you've got all the bait you need in that box of yours, you just need to reach out your net and take your chance. We've never had a student as able as you. If you stayed you'd get the best results we've ever had. But this scholarship . . .'

'I understand, sir. It's all I think about. I'll finish my application tonight, after work.'

'Good, good. And please let me know if there's anything, Sep, *anything* the school can do. We all want this for you, and I'd like to think you would come and see me. I'm a friend first and a headmaster second, all right?'

'Yes, sir.'

'I suppose angler comes after that.' Tench looked thoughtful. 'And there's your mother, of course . . . I've never really thought about that list before.'

'Maybe you should write it down,' said Sep.

'Now *there's* a good idea,' said Tench, rummaging for a pad among the tackle and line as Sep left the room. 'That mind of yours! Say hi to your mum, tight lines – and think of the school!'

'I will, sir,' said Sep, and he went out past Mrs Siddiqui into the busy corridor, his application form burning like hot steel against his skin.

5

Class

The rest of the day passed like every other day: Sep finished his biology ahead of everyone else, read through lunchtime detention in a corner of Maguire's stifling office, ate a whole stick of sugary rock, and snuck on his headphones whenever he could (New Order and The Smiths, double-sided, speckled with Floyd like cherries in a fruit cake) – and spoke to absolutely nobody.

Eventually he was slumped, sweating, in his last class: English.

The room had baked in the day's heat until it was airless and tight, dust dancing in the fat beams of sun. Nobody moved, they just sat, wet-skinned and limp, breathing the tang of unvacuumed carpets and varnished wood.

'Anyone?' said Mrs Woodbank, fanning her face with a book. 'I know it's near the end of the day, but come *on*.'

Sep looked at the poem. The words shifted, and he felt a little spark in his mind as he saw the answer.

But don't ask me, he thought. *Don't ask me again*.

'September?' said Mrs Woodbank, fanning faster.

'*Septic, Septic, Septic*,' chanted the boys at the back of the class. Mrs Woodbank waved her hand for them to stop.

'It's about growing old,' said Sep. He lifted his headphones, saw Mrs Woodbank's face and let them snap back into place around his neck.

'The human condition, *yes*, thank you,' said Mrs Woodbank. The light wobbled in the overhead projector. She banged it on the side, and a little cheer went up from the back of the class as it winked out. 'Wonderful,' she said, turning to the board, chalk gripped in nicotine-yellow fingers.

'Look, we all know Septic knows the answer, miss,' said Arkle, swinging on his chair at the back of the class. 'What's the point of this? We just did exams, like, a month ago. And I won't lie, miss, I'm all exammed out. I think my brain is full.'

Mrs Woodbank looked at him over her glasses, sweat beading on the knuckle of hair between her eyebrows.

'The "point", Darren, is that we have begun our study of *next term's texts*,' she said, snapping the last three words in time as she tapped her binder on the table. 'And it seems unlikely *your* brain is full, given the mess you submitted for last week's assignment.'

'You mean my story?' said Arkle.

'I mean your story, yes.'

'What was wrong with it? I used everything on your list.' Arkle fumbled with the papers on his desk and produced a crumpled sheet that was stained with food. 'Setting, characterization, dialogue, theme, plot,' he read. 'I did *all* that, like. In order.'

Mrs Woodbank took off her glasses and pinched the bridge of her nose.

'Those are the tools of a writer's craft,' she said. 'You're not meant to do them one at a time.'

The class flickered with laughter. Arkle grinned, then frowned.

'But I always leave my plot to the end,' he said, almost to himself.

Sep shifted in his seat, felt the barrier between him and the rest of the class like a coil of wire. Arkle's puzzled face made him think about what his mum had said over breakfast, and he turned to look outside. The bay was speckled with giant rocks, nibbled by the white teeth of the inward tide.

'Back to the poem –' said Mrs Woodbank, grabbing a note as it was passed along the front row. 'What's so important it couldn't wait until the end of class, Stephanie?' She unfolded the little ball of paper and held it up to the light. ' "I really like Tony." Well, thank you for that insight – Anthony, consider yourself warned. *Now*. Let's consider the poet's use of language here, in "the children green and golden–" '

The door opened and the athletics team trooped in, vest-clad and red, socks loose around their ankles.

'Where have you been?' said Mrs Woodbank.

Lamb looked down at her running gear.

'Sports day,' she said.

'Nobody told me.'

Lamb shrugged her broad shoulders as the rest of the team, Mack among them, took their seats. 'It's sports day,' she said. 'All day. Till now.'

'Go to the office,' said Mrs Woodbank.

Lamb sighed, dropped her bag and turned to go.

'Hey, Lamb,' said Arkle, 'have you ever been mistaken for a boy?'

'No,' said Lamb, scowling, 'have you?'

'Darren! What have I told you?' shouted Mrs Woodbank as an *ooooooh* rumbled round the class.

' "Try to act like a normal human being",' said Arkle sadly. One of his yakking crowd reached over and gave him a dead leg.

As the room pulsed with another quick laugh Sep felt his barrier break and snapped his head round.

Hadley was watching him again, eyes huge in her thick glasses. She looked away, but flicked her eyes back to his.

Then he saw Mack was watching him too.

He felt their eyes burning into his cheeks, which began to redden.

Looking down at his jotter, Sep closed his mind to the noise around him and wrote: *Spring*. Then, the others' eyes still on the back of his head, he drew a circle round the word and wrote around it: *Life*. *Growth*. *Change*.

As he was packing up, Mrs Woodbank sat on his desk.

'Are you all right, September?' she said.

Sep nodded.

'Good. You seem distracted.'

Sep shook his head, felt the ears of the class bend towards their conversation like eager petals.

'Nothing to do with your scholarship?' Mrs Woodbank went on.

'I'm fine, miss, thank you,' said Sep, grabbing his Walkman.

'Well, I'm thrilled for you,' she said as he stuffed the last of his books into his bag and jogged from the room. 'There's not much on this island for a boy with your brains!'

Sep fumbled down the play button.

'September, my man!' said Arkle.

Even though he was across the corridor, Sep could smell the cigarettes and deodorant. He lifted his headphones.

'What?'

Arkle leaned forward and frowned.

'Your earphones are broken,' he said. 'It's only coming out one side, and the foam's ripped.'

'Yeah,' said Sep. 'Doesn't really matter to me, though, does it?'

Arkle grinned and thumbed his feather earring.

'Right,' he said, 'cos you're deaf and that.'

'Right.'

'I said cos you're deaf and that!' Arkle said again, louder.

Sep felt a little twist in his chest, and clenched his jaw.

'Ah, shit, I was just kidding . . . I'm sorry, don't take us wrong,' said Arkle. 'How's tricks?'

Sep screwed up his face.

'I need to go,' he said, turning into the dim-lit throat of the school's main stairwell.

'Hang on –' said Arkle.

'Why?' said Sep. 'You want to talk to me now? Today? I need to work. I've got no time for this.'

'Ah, come on, why're you –'

'Darren, you've been calling me "Septic" for years.'

'And you call me Darren.'

'That's your name.'

'Not to my pals,' said Arkle, smiling with his big square teeth.

'Right,' said Sep. 'But your pals are, you know . . . dicks. And we're not friends, are we?'

Arkle stopped smiling. He wiped his dripping brow.

'I know, it's just that –' He looked about, saw Mrs Woodbank bustling over and whispered: 'Later, right? Later. We want to talk to you.'

Then he ran off, the protruding tongues of his trainers clapping against his jeans, his long hair bouncing on his collar.

' "We"?' said Sep to himself.

As he watched Arkle go he saw Mack and his gang in the corridor beyond. The six were gathered round the lockers like wolves round a kill, their Mohawked thug-in-chief, Daniels, tripping everyone who walked past. Sunlight festered in the tight air, and violence shimmered in its haze.

Daniels, snake-eyed and beef-skinned, saw Sep watching and turned to face him – shoulders aggressively set, chin jutting. He was wearing a sleeveless shirt over a vest, and muscles bulged on his arms like sacks of flour.

'Hey! Asshole!' he shouted. Then he mouthed more words, pretending he was shouting and that Sep couldn't hear, gesticulating wildly. The rest of them laughed the noisy, fake laugh of the henchman.

Sep clicked in a new tape and turned to go.

'I'm talking to *you*, deaf-boy!' Daniels yelled, and before Sep could move Daniels was on him, pressing him to the wall and scattering the tapes from his open bag.

6

Daniels

'Can't you hear me?' whispered Daniels. 'Can you not hear me shouting?'

'Let me go, *Keith*,' said Sep, looking at the ground and gritting his teeth. A circle was beginning to form around them.

Daniels' breath was hot on Sep's cheek.

'Or what?' he said.

'Daniels, why don't –' said Mack.

Daniels grabbed Mack's arm and held it clear, the skin white under the points of his fingers.

'Can you hear me, queerdo?'

I can hear you breathing out your fat mouth, thought Sep, leaning against Daniels' iron grip, frustration and shame tearing at his guts.

Hadley was in the crowd, her lips pursed like she wanted to shout.

'Maybe you'd rather talk about your mum and Tench?' Daniels growled. 'How long's he been fishing in her stream, queerdo? Does she grip his rod?'

Sep's fists were clenched so tightly that his knuckles ached.

'Do they do it in your house? Are you in the next room, pressing your shit ear to the wall?'

Hadley looked away. The heat felt like it might split Sep's skin, and he prayed to God the tears pricking his eyes wouldn't fall down his face.

He opened his mouth to scream.

'What are you *doing*, Daniels?' said Arkle, leaning against the wall.

Daniels whirled on him, eyes wide, keeping his grip on Sep's neck.

'There he is,' he hissed, 'the boy with the teeth.'

'Killer burn, Keith,' said Arkle, rolling his eyes. 'I heard you running your mouth when I was halfway down the stairs, thought I'd pop back and check it out. It's always fun to see a monkey dance.'

Daniels' nostrils flared.

'You starting something, teeth-boy?'

Arkle grinned.

'Maybe,' he said, waggling his eyebrows.

'You really want a go?' growled Daniels. 'You and me?' He squared his shoulders and cracked his neck. 'I'm older than you.'

'Yeah, you got held back a year cos you can't read properly,' said Arkle, cocking his head sympathetically. 'Does that count as a self-burn?'

The crowd laughed, and Daniels' hand tightened. Sep choked and coughed, watched Arkle stare back at Daniels with cool, collected defiance.

Then he saw Arkle's hands were shaking.

'Why don't you just piss off?' Sep shouted hoarsely, prising Daniels' fingers away, waiting for the onslaught to start.

But Daniels ignored him.

'Are you really trying to start something? For this deaf queerdo?' Daniels asked Arkle. 'Try it. See what happens.'

'Shit, no – I don't even want to *touch* you. I'm just telling you to get your big spotty face out of here.'

The crowd gasped silently, and Daniels' face – already livid and red – darkened.

'Who are you calling spotty?' he said quietly.

'Are you kidding?' said Arkle, playing with his lighter. 'The state of your face? And, by the way, I've seen you getting changed – so I know your arse is just as bad.'

The crowd wobbled with hysterical laughter, and Daniels' face went an even more threatening purple. Sep, still pulling to free himself, began to feel light-headed, the heat pressing on his airless head.

'You been looking at me in the shower, faggot?' said Daniels quietly.

Arkle looked him up and down, then pulled a face.

'You're kind of hard to miss, aren't you? But yeah, I've been watching your arse in the showers, now I'm looking at your face and honestly, Keith? Some days I can't tell them apart. I need to remind myself your arse is the one without the nose.'

Even Sonya and Manbat laughed, but they quickly turned it into a growl and moved closer to Chantelle and Stephen, right alongside Daniels. Sep glanced at Mack – saw he'd gone pale, his eyes wide.

But underneath his red Mohawk Daniels looked scarily calm.

'You know what, *Darren*?' he said. 'I'm not going to hit you. I know what you're doing. So I'm going to hit your little deaf friend instead.'

A weight dropped through Sep's stomach, and the world began to move in slow motion.

'Wait!' said Mack.

Arkle moved as Daniels lunged forward and Sep threw up his hands, limbs blurring in the lightness of his skull; then another voice shot through the bubble and brought the world back up to speed.

'What is the meaning of this?' shouted Mrs Maguire, scattering the crowd like dandelion seeds, Mr Tench a few paces behind the battleship of her indignant chest.

Daniels dropped Sep and tried to look as though he'd never touched him, his hands loose and relaxed. Sep snapped his headphones on to his ears, but left them silent.

'How *dare* you bring this kind of unseemly squabble into my school! Your exams might have finished, but I can still –'

Daniels cut her off.

'It's got nothing to do with you, Magpie.'

'Don't you *dare* take that tone with me!' said Mrs Maguire, her eyes blazing. 'I remember you when you were a snot-nosed little boy, Keith Daniels, crying when you skinned your knees – am I supposed to be scared of you now you've got zips on your trousers?'

'*Thank* you, Mrs Maguire,' said Mr Tench, easing her aside by the elbow. 'What seems to be the problem?'

Daniels' face had gone pink.

'September, sir. He started it.'

Tench allowed his full height to loom over the corridor, and Sep saw that his face was different – its well-scrubbed gleam uncommonly hard.

Maguire reached up and grabbed Daniels' collar.

'And how many times have I told you about that haircut? It is *expressly* forbidden in the school handbook!'

'You tell him, Aileen,' said Arkle.

Maguire flared her nostrils at him.

'Don't you *dare* use my first name, Hooper. Daniels, explain. Now.'

'It wasn't me who started it,' said Daniels, lip almost trembling as he conjured a picture of innocence.

'Yes, you said it was September,' said Mr Tench. 'I find that difficult to believe.'

'It's true, sir.'

'I did not!' said Sep.

But Daniels was warming to his victimhood.

'And then Ark– Darren – called me names and made fun of my acne,' he said weakly. 'He said my bum and my face look the same because they're so spotty.'

'Is that true, Darren?' said Tench.

'Yes, sir,' said Arkle solemnly. 'Keith's face looks exactly like his bum.'

Daniels' act shattered and he lunged forward, but Tench grabbed him and turned him away.

'Another detention for that, Darren, usual time and place. Keith – go with Mrs Maguire, please.'

'*And* you'll be with me tomorrow lunchtime,' said Mrs Maguire, her heels clicking along the corridor, herding

Daniels' gang like sheep. 'Mr Hope has already booked himself a slot with his lateness and cheek, so you can sort out this *ridiculous* squabble then.'

Daniels turned to Sep, his face lit with glee. Mack turned as well, with a look Sep couldn't decipher.

'Sure,' said Daniels, fixing Sep with a hard, wild stare. 'Tomorrow lunchtime. We'll get everything sorted then.'

'Great,' said Sep, catching Arkle's eye.

'You all right, September?' said Tench, once again giraffe-like and calm.

'Yes, sir. Thank you, sir.'

'Good, good. Take no notice of these idiots – playing the hard man, that's all. I know you'd never start anything so unpleasant.'

'Yes, sir,' said Sep.

Maguire cuffed Daniels on the back of the head, and Tench raised his eyebrows.

'You'll have to forgive Mrs Maguire if she seems a little . . . even more . . .'

'On edge?' said Sep tentatively.

'On edge,' nodded Tench. He leaned down slightly. 'She got some bad news this morning, I understand – an old friend of hers in New York passed away during the night. Accident on the subway. Very unexpected.'

'Oh. I'm sorry.'

Tench clapped Sep on the shoulder.

'Good lad,' he said. 'I'll see you tomorrow. On time, I hope, Hope.'

'Yes, sir,' said Sep, and he forced a smile.

When he turned back the others had already gone, and the crowd had vanished.

Sep was sure Mack had tried to stop Daniels from punching him, but that didn't make sense. He shook his head, pressed play on Morrissey's warbling voice, then unclipped his skateboard and left, taking the stairs three at a time, emerging into a throng of tar-smell and chatter and juddering engines, all broiling under the blue-white marble of a summer sky.

7

Roots

In the distant forest, shadows moved, the ground twisting with unseen things. The split skins of mice and birds pulsed with bacterial growth, and the dirt was studded by the prints of midnight beasts.

A wind blew, and weeds gathered in the dappled sunlight. Narrow roots writhed in the shade, searching the ground like blind fingers.

At the centre of the clearing, the stone box lay open.

A crow flew to a branch, and was joined by another, then another, which settled on the ground. Presently a worm broke the earth's surface and twisted for a moment, a twinkling bud of pink in the gloom. It found feathers, and burrowed slowly through the third crow's skin.

Minutes passed.

The worm reappeared, dropping through the bird's belly, then wriggling into the earth. Above its vanishing tail, the crows stared at the sacrifice box with eyes like beads of oil, and the roots crept into the stone.

8

Mario

Music-filled cars puttered along the streets, limbs like wilted leaves spewing from their windows. Bikers and roller skaters cluttered the pavements, while spit puddles formed below panting dogs and sweating hands held freezing sodas to hot skin. Even the children moved slowly, no hurry to be anywhere except in the sunlight that bleached the world like an old photograph. Summertime Hill Ford smelled of sea spray and seaweed, of grass and the green tang that spilled from the forest. But it smelled mostly of heat – of baking asphalt and dry earth – and Sep lifted his shirt to catch the breeze as he rolled down the hill, the last few songs of his Smiths' side wobbling as the batteries began to die and the wheels' grind swamped the music.

The tide was in again. The dog-sized crabs, driven underwater by the heat, were gathered on the shoreline. Their submersion was summer's big plus as far as Sep was concerned – he hated their terrible, reaching legs, their shining eyes, flickering mouthparts and shells the colour of old blood. When he was younger his mum had called them 'stone spiders'. It hadn't helped.

He flipped up his board as he approached the little row of shops and carried it through packs of sticky children, clicking off his tape and opening the door as Morrissey was finishing his third plaintive 'please'.

It was cool in the silence behind the blinds and his eyes took a moment to adjust to the reception's gloom. A small, fair-haired girl was standing at the counter, damp-eyed and trembling. She had a kitten badge pinned to her pinafore, and was clutching her bag like a lifebelt.

'Hi,' said Sep. 'Caroline, right?'

She flashed him a look, eyes wide and staring.

'You brought Wobie a message about me today. Are you all right?'

She shook her head.

'Are you on work experience?'

She nodded.

'Did something happen?'

She nodded.

'You don't need to wait for him, don't worry,' said Sep, sighing. 'I'll tell him I let you go, OK?'

She tried to speak, but only inhaled in a series of quick, mucal gasps.

'I-I-I –' she managed.

'It's OK,' said Sep, strapping up his board. 'I know.'

'He ki– he k-killed – that dog –'

'It's tough, I know. Off you go.'

Sep held the door for her as she ran, tearful and wheezing, into the heat. An interior door opened and a broad, moustachioed face leaned out.

'Hello? Cathy? Katie? Are you still – oh, September, is you! Come inside, you are early.'

'Hi, Mario,' said Sep. 'Was she all right?'

Mario waved his hands.

'Fainted, you know: *bleugh*,' he said, rolling his eyes up and lolling his tongue. 'Is always a dead dog, and I kill dog so, you know, she upset.'

'You didn't – you need to stop saying that. You put the dog *down* – there's a difference.'

'Dog is dead,' said Mario, spreading his palms. He was washing the rubber table, arms sheathed to the elbow in rubber gloves. A fat, knot-furred dog lay on a trolley under a plastic sheet, stinking of disinfectant and its last, terrified shit.

'I know, but the wording is kind of important,' said Sep. 'People won't bring their animals to a vet who kills them.'

Mario frowned.

'But sometimes this is *exactly* what they bring dog for,' he said patiently. 'For death.'

'To be put – oh, never mind,' said Sep as Mario scraped the suds into a bucket and stripped off his gloves.

'Always like this with little volunteer from school. They want brush ponies and make happy time with animals. But I *hurt* the animals. I kill them; every day I kill them and see eyes in their heads looking at me, so sad, you know? But I kill them because it's my job – sometimes death is great kindness, and you must be brave. I am vet – this mean I kill all the animals.'

Sep closed his eyes.

54

'Maybe I should write down some phrases you could use to talk about this stuff.'

Mario laughed and clapped him on the shoulder with a massive hand.

'My customers, they love how I am speaking. Is business.'

He reached through a doorway at the back of the room, and as strip lights buzzed into life the chip shop's Formica and chrome flickered into view.

It was true. Mario – born Christos Papadopoulos in Heraklion – had won friends with directness that bordered on insulting, cheerfully telling people their haircuts were a mistake, that their pets were ugly and that, when the time came, the ugly pet would 'die by my Greek hand'. And people loved him for it. He'd opened The Ford Fry years ago, but when Nintendo got big in '85 he'd picked up the nickname and renamed the shop in his new image. He'd even painted an Italian flag on the door.

'What about your business, clever-shoes?' he said, tying on an apron. 'The school on mainland?'

Sep shrugged.

'I haven't finished my application form yet – I'm kind of stuck on the last bit. But the school recommended me, so it should be fine. I can't wait.'

'Then I am sad,' said Mario. He shook his head. '*This* is your place; is beautiful place where you were born a beautiful boy. You *belong* here – so stay, become vet, train with me. Is right job for you. Also money.'

'I don't think so,' said Sep. 'I'm not really an animal person. Besides –'

'But that is perfect!' said Mario, clapping his hands together. 'Vet who hates animals is *perfect*.' He drew his finger across his throat. 'Remember what I have told you. There is no more beautiful thing than looking into the eyes of tiny puppy who is squeaking his first little barks and knowing that, one day, you will kill him.'

Sep laughed.

'I remember.'

Mario nodded.

'Being vet is . . . is OK. I mean, is too many dogs, too many cats. I would *love* the big beasts, all the deers and the cattles, but the people from the big estate tell me go away, chip-shop man. And that is another thing to be staying for,' said Mario, lifting the baskets over to the fryer and turning on the heat under the oil. 'Make chips. I run two jobs so I can buy big, big house back home – and there is money in chips. Lot of fat people here. A *lot* of them. And fat people love chips.'

'I know,' said Sep, looking at Mario's chins.

'Is why they are fat in first place,' said Mario, with the air of one confiding a great secret. 'Because of chips.'

'Thanks,' Sep laughed, 'but I'll stick to the engineering thing. I've got a maths head. I want to build stuff. What's the code for the cold store?'

'Always you are forgetting,' said Mario, reaching across him and punching in the steel buttons. 'Two-five-zero-three. Greek Independence Day! *And* my birthday numbers, forgetty Seppy.'

He turned and waved his arm towards the giant windows and the view of the bay.

'If you must build things, build things here! Oh, my brilliant friend, do not go to the faraway school. I will miss you too much. Who will watch the comets with me if you go?'

'Halley's Comet won't be there,' said Sep, heaving a bag of crab claws from inside the big fridge. 'It only appears, like, once a century.'

'But is here now,' said Mario. 'We were going to climb on to the roof with telescope. It was going to be a special thing for me to do with my best friend.'

'We will. It'll be closest in a couple of days.'

Sep pushed his bad tooth with his tongue and wondered if the comet's proximity would make it worse.

'Am I making you embarrass?' said Mario.

'No, it's just –'

Mario laughed, hugged Sep into a headlock and pulled a Dictaphone from his trouser pocket. He clicked the button as Sep tried to wriggle free and spoke clearly into the microphone: 'You are my great friend, September. Mario loves you. And he knows you will do brilliant things, because you are clever and brave. The bravest person I know.'

He grinned at Sep.

'Now you must hear it repeated,' he said, rewinding the tape with a squeal. He pressed play, and his far-off voice hissed through the little speaker.

. . . dead tortoise, is been maimed by cat, eyeball torn out and is missing . . . most likely eaten by cat who also is dead . . . the intestines of the tortoise have been . . .

'Wrong part of tape. Too much rewind.'

He pushed more buttons.

. . . great friend, September. Mario loves you. And he knows you will do brilliant things, because you are clever and brave. The bravest person I know.

Sep relaxed himself out of the headlock and stepped back, tried to breathe away the stone in his throat.

'I don't have any friends here.'

'I am your friend.'

'I know, but at school I mean . . . friends my own age. And you work all the time, and –'

Mario held up a hand to stop him.

'I understand, of course.'

'I need to get away, Mario. I have to, or –'

'I say I *understand*.'

Mario watched Sep fuss with his Walkman and tilted his head.

'Something happened today?'

'No. Nothing. Just . . . It doesn't matter.'

'Oh, my Sep,' said Mario, propping his big head on his hand. 'Is difficult for you. You are skinny, messy hair, are bad at sports; sometimes your skin is not so good, also –'

'You can stop any time you like,' Sep cut in.

'I only mean –'

'No, I get it: they hate me. It's fine – I hate them too.'

Mario frowned.

'Do not hate, Sep. The only thing there is in the world, at the end, is love. When I was at school I was a target because I liked the boys, you know?'

'I know, you told me.'

'Sexually.'

'I know, Mario.'

Mario nodded.

'So everyone has stuff to be dealing with. Just know, no matter the happenings, that love will win in the end: "Always goodness and light win out," my father say. He say many other things, like: "Sometimes life lands in the stool of an animal."'

'So, like, "shit happens"?'

Mario beamed.

'Exactly! Is international.'

Sep looked around the shop, at the neon price tags, the cracks on the fridge doors, the sticky bottles of sauce shaped like tomatoes.

'I'll still come back sometimes.'

'For shift in chip shop?' said Mario.

'Well, I don't know. Maybe if –'

Mario laughed.

'Joke only! Big things are heading at you, no problem. But fat people love chips. Remember that. Always money. Now I must try to fix broken bloody fridge. Working yesterday but today – *bleugh*. You, forgetty Seppy, can wash my windows.'

Sep filled a white bucket with soapy water and heaved it over to the glass front of the shop. He snapped his headphones on again, slid new batteries into his Walkman and chose a different cassette – a Cure double side – then turned up the volume to drown out Mario singing Demis Roussos in the back of the shop.

As he scrubbed he watched the town passing by, already full in summer voice: music, laughter and the gurgle of boats. A gang of kids flew past on bikes, and Sep watched them until they were out of sight.

The mainland was just visible through the heat, but the sun was too bright on the water, bouncing on to the ceiling in shimmering ribbons. When the glass was dry he began lowering the blind, and it was only then he noticed that the forest looked different. The mossy lump of trees seemed bigger somehow. Swollen.

He pressed his face to the glass.

A fist smashed into his eyes, followed by the gawping face of Daniels – tongue out, Mohawk spikes touching the pane.

9

Broken

A few miles away, someone was running. The face was hidden in shadow, the hands streaked with earth and algae and filled with old, forgotten things: toys and tapes and secret objects.

Soft shoes skidded on moss, torn denim soaked in the mud, and a mixtape slipped. Another cassette fell in the grab for the first and was gripped in desperate fingers.

Finally the path came into view, and sweat-stung eyes blinked at the clearing.

The box was open. It sat, dark and staring, the black centre of an iris bloodshot with roots and the threads of dying grass.

Forcing reluctant feet, the runner tried to ignore how the littered creatures had burst apart; how the crows' feathers rasped like chalk on stone; and how the box's hunger and rage *pulled* at them like a rope being wound in with slow, terrible efficiency.

Fighting tears, they prepared to throw new sacrifices into the pit – when tree roots coiled like tentacles round their ankles.

The runner's mouth opened in a silent scream and the sacrifices fell on the rotten ground, just short of the box.

Leaping free of the roots' grip, they heaved on the box's lid – trapping their skin as it fell. Blood spilled from the wound, and the forest's whisper swelled to a roar of splitting wood and screaming leaves.

They fled, scattering the crows and plunging into the bright bloom of the forest.

The roots curled round the dropped and scattered things, and pulled them towards the box.

10

Claws

'What you staring at, Septic?' shouted Daniels. 'Your mum?'

He made a circle with his thumb and forefinger and prodded it rhythmically.

'Oh, Mr Tench,' he said. '*Oh*, Mr *Tench*, that's it, uh-huh, reel me in, baby –'

Sep stepped back from the window, saw Sonya and Chantelle wrapped round Manbat and Stephen. And, behind them, a sandwich in his mouth, Mack.

Daniels swaggered in. He was wearing his trench coat with the sleeves rolled up, and his veins looked like worms.

'Maguire and Tench aren't here to save you now, are they, you little pussy?' he said, mad laughter in his eyes. 'Give us some chips, Septic. And a burger.'

'We're closed, Daniels. Come back in half an hour.'

Daniels waved his gang in behind him.

'And what if I want it now, eh? What are you going to do, deaf-boy?'

Sep ground his teeth. He thought of Arkle leaning against the wall, hands shaking, and anger flared stupidly in his chest.

'Nothing, I guess,' he said. 'But I won't serve you until it hits five. I could do with a hand here actually. Maybe you could lick the floor clean –'

The gang oohed. Daniels clamped his hand on the back of Sep's neck.

'Maybe you want me to lick *you*, eh? Are you queer for me, Septic? Is that it?'

'Let me go,' said Sep, grabbing Daniels' wrist and staring into his face. His heart took an extra beat – a little quickening in his chest.

'Hey, Daniels –' said Mack.

Daniels ignored him, squeezed tighter, raised his voice. 'Is this your shit ear? Can you hear me?'

He punched Sep quickly in the gut, taking his wind.

'Daniels!' shouted Mack, but Daniels shoved him back.

'Let me remind you what you're dealing with, queerdo –'

'. . . *forever and ever you'll* – hey, greasy boy! What are you doing?' shouted Mario, emerging from the back shop and bustling round the counter.

Daniels threw Sep away.

'Just having a quiet word with my friend,' he said, straightening the chain round his neck. 'Nothing to do with you.'

'I know you, greasy boy, I *know* you,' said Mario, shoving him towards the door. 'You are always trouble. Get out, you are barred from here, get out!'

'Who are you calling greasy?' shouted Daniels, turning and puffing out his chest.

'You!' said Mario, flicking Daniels' forehead. 'Red spots with little yellow heads, is very greasy face!'

The gang stifled their sniggers as Daniels exploded.

'Oh, yeah?' he yelled, kicking over the ice-cream board in the doorway. 'Well . . . check the nick of you, fat boy! And I don't care if you bar me from this shithole! You sell cat burgers!'

'No cat burgers here!' said Mario. 'All clean, all inspected. But no more usual order for you: double fish with crab claw and chips, three pickled eggs. Always same, three times a week, is why you have boy titties – but no more because you are bag of scum, thank you, goodbye.'

He closed the door in Daniels' face and turned the key.

Daniels shook with fury. He pointed directly at Sep, then launched a couple of kicks at the glass door, shaking it in its frame. 'The next time it'll be just you and me, queerdo – and I'll beat the shit out you, you hear me? I'll beat the *shit* out you!'

Mario reached behind the counter and took out the heavy wooden pizza paddle. The gang scrambled away, hurling insults over their shoulders. But Sep noticed that Mack, before he joined the stampede, tried to catch his eye.

He waited for the sick feeling in his stomach to subside, and took slow, painful breaths.

'Don't worry, September,' said Mario, straightening his apron and fixing his hair. 'The greasy boy is mad mostly at me. Last year, you know – I kill his dog.'

Sep watched for Daniels the rest of the night, but the gang stayed away. Maybe they'd found another victim. Or maybe

Mack had diverted them, he found himself thinking, remembering the look they'd shared before he ran off.

Which was strange, because Mack had once held Sep down while Daniels hung a string of thick spit over his face, had chased him with the others through the fields behind the school, had thrown Sep's clothes into the showers while he fought back tears of shame. He was as bad as the rest of them.

And while they all called him 'Septic', Mack never called him anything at all.

Sep plunged his mind into the balm of a hectic service, his mind free to wander as his hands moved by themselves, salting chips and fishing for pickles; spinning mix-ups in paper bags and stacking sodas.

At first he read the headlines on the newspapers they used to wrap the suppers – Chernobyl's nuclear winds, Reagan's latest gaffes and the start of the World Cup – but after hours in the oily heat he was thought-blind and smudged with ink and no longer saw the words or the customers, just reacted and smiled like a trained seal. So he almost jumped when, instead of ordering food, a voice said:

'September! My man!'

He blinked, focused on the speaker. Arkle, a riot of mullet and teeth, grinned at him.

'What do you want?' said Sep. 'I told you, I'm working.'

'I know, man, I know. I'm getting my crab fix – can't get enough of that claw meat. How's tricks?'

'Darren, I'm *working*.'

Arkle held his hands up, then lifted his hair out of his collar.

'I *am* your work, Sepster. Give me a claw supper – don't hold back on the vinegar. And a can of Spike Sting.'

'The fridge is broken.'

'That's cool, man – I don't mind it warm.'

Sep slid the can over the counter. Arkle popped it and took a long pull.

'Oh my God,' he gasped. 'It's so sour. It's amazing. They're geniuses.'

Sep looked into the fryer.

'Another couple of minutes for the claws,' he said.

'Ideal,' said Arkle. 'All right, Mario? Where's Luigi?'

Mario looked up from the freezer.

'This joke is not funny. Every time, it is not funny,' he said, pushing through the bead curtain into the back of the shop.

Arkle watched him go. 'You know, that man thinks of me as a son. It's sweet really.'

'Look, there's a queue now,' said Sep, nodding behind Arkle.

Arkle turned to the old lady known locally as Christine the Psychic.

'Go right ahead, mystic one,' he said. 'I recommend the crab. It's tip-top, and young September here is a master of the fry – but you probably knew that already.'

Christine chuckled, then ordered a smoked sausage supper. As Sep was shovelling the chips on to the newspaper Arkle leaned over the counter.

'How was school?'

'What?'

'I'm asking about your day, you know – was it good? Mine wasn't. I ended up getting a detention off Sax Solo.'

'Who's that?'

'Curran, in music. I'm trying to get a nickname going, and since he looks like Harrison Ford –'

Sep frowned.

'Mr Curran looks nothing *like* Harrison Ford.'

'Well, he wore a waistcoat once,' said Arkle. 'Have you been thinking about what I said earlier?'

Sep glanced at him.

'Pardon?' he said, feeling colour in his cheeks as he angled his good ear.

'I'm saying, have you been thinking about what I said earlier?' said Arkle patiently.

'Oh. No. You didn't really say anything.'

'I know. I was going to, but Woodbank came over. Listen, something's happening.'

'Salt and vinegar?' Sep asked.

Christine nodded.

'Extra salt, son,' she said. 'And two pickled onions.'

'Excellent choice, madam,' said Arkle. 'I like to put a long chip between them and pretend –'

'What do you mean, "something's happening"?' said Sep quickly, unscrewing the pickle jar.

Arkle widened his eyes, but jerked his head and said nothing. When Christine had shuffled out, clutching her steaming bundle, he leaned over the counter again.

'You seem jumpy,' he said. 'How come?'

Sep lifted Arkle's glistening claws from the vat of oil and tipped them on to the newspaper. They fizzled and spat, curled to perfect arcs and skinned with bubbles of gold.

'Daniels came in earlier and kicked off,' he said. 'I'm expecting him back.'

Arkle made a face.

'He's a dick.'

'Yeah,' said Sep, wrapping the supper and handing it over. 'Thanks for, you know –'

'It's cool, don't sweat it. But you shouldn't be so scared of him: all he can do is hurt you, and if you're not fussed about getting hurt –' Arkle tapped his much-broken nose, but Sep remembered how his hands had shaken in the corridor. 'He's just angry at life. He needs a reality wedgie now and then.'

'Yeah, well,' said Sep, 'now he's angry at me. It's one pound seventy.'

Arkle counted two coins from a Kodak film case and slid them to Sep like they were state secrets. But when Sep tried to lift the money Arkle held it tight, their fingers almost touching.

'*They were in my house,*' he hissed.

'What were?'

'*Wings,*' whispered Arkle. Then he nodded at Sep and opened his supper.

'What do you mean, "wings"?' said Sep.

'Insect wings, like – right in my ear when I was trying to sleep.'

A shiver flicked over Sep's skin.

'Did you leave the window open?' he said.

69

'No! They were in the *room*, man. I'm knackered – whenever I was about to drop off, there they were. I had to take emergency action to tire myself out. My wrist's killing me.'

'So why are you telling *me*? You want me to, what –' Sep glanced at Arkle's crotch – 'sing you to sleep?'

Arkle shook his head, and fixed Sep with a serious stare.

'Because something might happen to you too, and if it does you need to promise to tell us.' He ate a chip. 'Can I get some more vinegar?'

Sep squirted vinegar on the claws. 'You're not making any sense. What do you mean – wait . . . "*us*"?'

'Yeah, us. I mean – the *others*,' said Arkle, waggling his eyebrows and blowing on a too-hot chip.

'Oh, you mean the other three people who've ignored me completely for the last four years?'

'Ah, don't be like that! You know, you were one of us, when we made . . . you *know*. One of them's yours.'

'So? Darren, I have no idea what you're –'

Arkle scribbled on his receipt and handed it to Sep.

'Here's my phone number. Ring me if something happens. If I don't answer just . . . keep calling till I do, all right?'

Sep took the paper, read Arkle's loopy writing.

'OK,' he said. 'Fine. Now you need to go.'

The door opened and Lamb, Mack and Hadley trooped in.

11

The Others

They were sweating through their T-shirts, all in high-tops and denim shorts. Lamb's dark hair was tied back in a scrunchied ponytail, while Mack had one eye covered with a dangling fringe. Hadley, hair down as always, wore one white studded glove on her left hand, her Gizmo T-shirt hanging loose on one side and showing a sunned, freckly shoulder. Her eyes were shadowed a bright blue, and she looked quickly at Sep through her fringe.

Lamb looked different from when he'd seen her in English, Sep thought as she strode up to the counter. Much older – almost an adult.

'Lambert,' said Arkle. 'What a thrill it is to see you again.'

'Shut up,' said Lamb, nudging him out the way. Her nose was peeling from the sun.

'S'up, Sep,' said Mack.

'"S'up"?' said Sep, his heart thumping. 'The first time you've spoken to me in four years and I get "S'up"? What are you all doing here?'

'I told you,' said Arkle, 'we wanted to see you cos –'

'We want to know why you opened the goddamn box,' growled Lamb, so aggressively that Sep took a step back.

'What the hell are you talking about?'

'You mean you haven't −' said Hadley, looking worried. 'The *box*.' She jerked her gloved hand at the window, towards the mossy blanket of forest that clung to the hills.

'The *sacrifice* box, from when we were kids? Is that what this is about? Why would −'

Lamb grabbed his collar.

'Don't bullshit me, you little dweeb,' she hissed. 'We *know* it was you.'

'Hey!' shouted Sep. 'You can't just − I'm working!'

Lamb let him go. Her mother's headscarf was tied to her wrist.

'I know,' she said, 'but we couldn't wait for you to close up − shit is happening, now.'

'Well, you can't stay here if you're not eating,' said Sep, smoothing his T-shirt.

'Don't you try to −' Lamb started.

'I could eat some pizza,' said Mack. 'I mean, we're here anyway, and Darren's already eating.'

'Jesus Christ −' said Lamb, rolling her eyes. She took a deep breath.

'I'd have a small Mario Special,' said Hadley, 'but no pepperoni on mine. I just want mushroom and pineapple.'

Mack was looking at the menu.

'Do you do extra-large?' he asked Sep.

'Yeah,' said Sep, 'the family-size. It's meant to feed, like, four people.'

'One of those then, with extra cheese. And three cans of Spike Light. Plus whatever they want to drink. Cokes probably.'

'The fridge is broken,' said Sep, lifting the folded note Mack left on the counter.

'All our fridges are broken too,' said Lamb, narrowing her eyes. 'Isn't that weird?'

'I don't know,' said Sep, trying to keep his face expressionless. 'Is it?'

She scowled at him.

'You'd better have a good reason for opening the box, Genius Boy,' she said through her teeth, 'because I am *pissed* off.'

'I swear to God, I have no idea what –' said Sep, but she'd already turned away, heading to join the others at their table.

Sep started to build the pizzas. He felt weirdly under pressure, like he was going to make a presentation in class, and as he sprinkled the mozzarella he saw his hands were trembling.

The sacrifice box? he thought, blowing a layer of dust from his memory of the day. *Why would I want to have anything to do with –*

He looked up.

Hadley was standing at the counter. She looked exhausted.

'Hi, Sep,' she said. 'Could I get a water instead of a Coke?'

'Sure, of course. I mean, of course. Water's cool. Yeah.'

She smiled, then went back to the table, climbing cross-legged on to the chair and pulling at her glove.

Sep spun the pizzas in the oven, squinting through the heat.

' "*Water's cool*"?' he said under his breath.

73

When the cheese started to bubble he loaded the pizzas into boxes and turned to find Mario beaming in the doorway. He winked. 'You have visitors?'

'I'm sorry. I'll serve them and then I can –'

'No, no, is wonderful! I can handle customers – you sit with friends. Is very good! Even if idiot boy is one of them.'

Arkle gave him a little wave.

'OK,' said Sep. 'Are you sure –'

'Go, my beautiful Sep, go. Have a break, is rare treat,' said Mario, then he frowned at the enormous box. 'For who is the big pizza?'

'Mack,' said Sep, gesturing with his forehead.

Mario leaned round him to get a proper look.

'My God,' he said.

Sep slid the boxes across the table, then started playing with his Walkman.

'All right,' said Lamb while the others started eating. 'So why'd you do it, Sep?'

'Holy shit! I didn't *do* anything.'

'Don't bullshit me –'

'I'm not! I hadn't even thought about the box for years. And why are you even asking – who cares if it's open?'

'We do, because mad shit's happening,' said Arkle, pointing round the table with a crab claw. 'I told you, man – insect wings. I sacrificed the dragonflies and now they're back.'

'The mirrors in my house smashed,' said Lamb, tearing a slice from Hadley's pizza. 'All of them – at once. My dad went mental. I sacrificed a mirror, remember? So it *must* be the box. And if we didn't open it then *you* did.'

'It wasn't me,' said Sep. He laughed and shook his head. 'Jesus Christ, nothing weird has happened to me, and even if it had it wouldn't be from the *sacrifice box*. How would that work exactly?'

'You're the genius,' said Mack. 'You tell us.'

'All right, I will: it doesn't. You're wrong. Finish your food and leave.'

Arkle looked down.

'Why don't you wear socks?' he said.

'What?' said Sep. 'I just – I just don't. It's comfier.'

'What are you, a hippy?'

'Shut up, Darren,' said Lamb. 'I don't believe you, Sep. This is just the kind of bullshit you'd pull.'

'Really?' said Sep. 'You know most of the abuse I get at school is because I *don't* pull any bullshit? Like, I follow the rules and do my homework, and now I'm some mage who can smash your mirrors?'

'The sacrifice was your idea!' Lamb snapped.

'What the hell,' said Arkle slowly, 'is a mage?'

'Like a magician,' said Hadley.

Arkle pulled a face.

'All right, geek.'

Hadley picked the mushrooms from her pizza, making a little pile in the centre of the box.

'They're not making this up, Sep,' she whispered, gloved hand in her lap.

'Oh, yeah,' said Arkle. 'Tell him about your dream, Milky Bar Kid.'

Hadley glared at him through her white fringe.

'Don't call me that.'

Sep saw how reduced and tired she was.

'Go on,' said Lamb.

Hadley sighed.

'I've dreamed about it the last couple of nights,' she said, eyes on the table. 'My sacrifice, I mean. There was a voice saying secret things that nobody else knows. Things I wrote when I was little.'

Sep remembered standing in the clearing that day, the five of them gathered round the stone box, remembered tossing Barnaby after Hadley's little red book.

'Your diary?' he said.

She nodded.

'It's the exact words. Words I thought I'd forgotten, but they're all there. I'm scared to go to sleep.'

Sep held his breath, fighting the urge to reach out and touch her.

'Your subconscious is a powerful thing,' he said after a moment. 'We don't ever really forget stuff like that – it just gets buried. We're all stressed from the exams, you know – the mind does funny things.'

'Well, I'm probably not suffering from exam stress,' said Arkle. 'I mean, I fell asleep in maths. And I nap *all* the time.'

'And the mirrors in my house?' Lamb asked Sep. 'Is that exam stress?'

'It is if you smashed them.'

'They smashed on their own, in the middle of the night!' shouted Lamb, slamming her fist on the table.

Mario looked over, and she settled back in her chair.

'They smashed on their own,' she muttered.

'And what about you?' Sep asked Mack.

'Nothing yet.' Mack pointed a droopy pizza slice at Lamb, 'But she made me come anyway.'

'That accent,' said Arkle, 'you're like the Terminator, Macejewski. Say, "I'll be back", I'm begging you.'

'Are you eating those chips?' said Mack.

Arkle tipped the last of his supper on to Mack's plate and gave the big athlete a pat on the head.

'Look at the way he *eats*. You inspire me, Golden Boy. I mean, look at you – pink and smooth and smelling of apricots.'

'Look, we all made sacrifices, right?' said Sep. 'So if the box is causing all this, why hasn't anything happened to Mack and me?'

Hadley pressed the soles of her feet together.

'It's happening in order,' she said.

'What do you mean?' said Sep.

'I was first, then Lamb, then Darren –'

'– Arkle! Jesus, call me *Arkle* –'

'– so today is the fourth day.' She looked up at him, and the sun made gold coins of her glasses. 'You were the fourth sacrifice. It's your turn. *Tonight*.'

The four of them looked at Sep.

'Listen,' said Sep, taking a step back, 'there's no way it's the box. But . . . I do have another idea –'

'Oh, we're all ears,' said Lamb, lip curling in a snarl.

'Well, I've been getting a toothache the last few days – ever since I started looking for the comet.'

Hadley looked up.

'You're watching Halley's comet too?'

'Oh my God, you guys are such total dorks,' said Arkle.

'Yeah,' said Sep, ignoring him. 'I haven't had a good sighting yet, but I did wonder if it was kind of . . . affecting my head. It hurts suddenly, when I'm outside. Or it could be Chernobyl – I mean, a nuclear reactor exploded. You don't think that might be affecting our heads? Or our fridges?'

'Who's Chernobyl?' said Arkle.

'Seriously?' said Sep.

Arkle shrugged.

'Chernobyl – it's a town in Russia. It's been all over the news, Darren.'

'I'm a cartoon watcher, Sep – think about it.'

'God, Darren . . .' said Hadley. 'A nuclear reactor there leaked and poisoned the air.'

'The Soviets are *poisoning* us? Oh, shit –' Arkle took a box of dental floss from his pocket – 'I knew it! I knew it!'

He pulled a string through his massive front incisors with a loud *ptwing!*

'That's dis-*gus*-ting,' said Lamb.

'I f'oss when I'm 'ervous.'

Sep's mouth curled with distaste as he watched Arkle work.

'I'm just saying, there's a logical explanation for everything, and I don't want to know about this.' He shook his head and stepped further away from the table. 'You can't just come in here after four years and carry on like you've not been ignoring me the whole time.'

Ptwing!

'It's got nothing to do with –' started Lamb.

'You really don't believe me?' said Hadley. 'Or any of us?'

'It's not that I don't believe you,' he said gently. 'I'm sure . . . I'm sure you *think* weird things have happened, and maybe they have – I'm just saying they *can't* be because of the sacrifice box.'

'Why not?'

'Because it can't be. It's not logical. Things can't happen for no reason.'

Ptwing!

Lamb's eyes narrowed. She took out her ponytail and shook her hair forward, before whipping it back and retying it.

'I told you the reason. You – or *someone* – has broken the rules. You remember the words, Sep? The ones *you* gave us?'

Sep tried to keep his face from betraying his thoughts, shocked by how easily the chant leaped into his head.

'Never come to the box alone,' she said, the others nodding along, mouthing the words with her. 'Never open it after dark. Never take back your sacrifice. It's so obvious you remember.'

'So?'

'Look, think what you want,' said Lamb, scowling as another anxious speck *ptwinged* across the table. 'I'm telling you, *we're* telling you, that this is what's happening. And it's your turn – tonight.'

'No, it's not,' said Sep, shaking his head and looking over his shoulder. Mario was pretending not to listen, polishing a steel jug that was already shiny. Sep felt his chest twist with embarrassment.

'You're only here because you need me to do something for you. Well, ask your *real* friends.'

'Ah, come on, Sepster,' said Arkle, floss hanging from his mouth. 'We can get the old gang back together.'

'Nobody said that,' said Lamb. 'We only hung out one summer. I don't need any more friends. I just want to find out what happened to my damn mirrors.'

'I want to stop my nightmares,' whispered Hadley, staring at her cold pizza.

'Well, I'm sorry I can't help you,' said Sep.

'Come on,' Arkle said again. 'It doesn't have to be like this, does it?'

But nobody spoke. The electrical hum of the lights filled the room, and they stared at the dew on their sodas. Mario cleared his throat and tried to look busy.

'You should go,' said Sep eventually, his throat tight.

'Fine,' said Lamb. 'But you're going to find out the hard way. And, if it turns out this *was* you, you'll pay for the mirrors.'

Hadley fixed Sep with another long look, then hopped from her seat. They started to file out, and Sep returned behind the counter.

Mack sidled towards him.

'A stick of rock, please.'

'Twenty pence,' said Sep.

Mack broke the rock in half, then handed the wrapped part back to Sep.

'You can't write this off,' he said. 'I didn't believe it was true at first, but they're so scared. And what you . . . what you think about me, it's not true. I'm not that guy.'

'All right,' said Sep, shrugging. He looked at the rock, the words 'Hill Ford' running all the way through its centre, then put it in his apron pocket.

Mack nodded, gave him a shy smile, then left.

He turned once, silhouetted by the blood-red sun, but Sep couldn't see his face. Behind him, Arkle mimed a phone call with his lit cigarette, and Hadley gave him a tiny, sad wave before she disappeared.

Lamb was already gone.

Sep put on his headphones, felt his heart rate settle into the perfect, urgent, downbeat optimism of 'Love Will Tear Us Apart'. Then he gathered their pizza boxes and cans, stacking them neatly in his arms.

12

Patience

The pellet smelled of lead, and left a circular dent on Daniels' thumb as he pressed it into the barrel, holding his balance against the whip of the forest wind.

Anger curled like a snake in his stomach as he pushed through the trees, cutting his skin on briars and thorns, thinking about Sep and the look on his face as he'd taken the piss in front of the gang, then hidden behind the fat Greek.

You're still mine, Hope, Daniels thought, grinding his teeth. *You'll get what's coming to you – and so will your toothy friend.*

He squeezed under a decayed warning sign at the entrance to the Windercross estate, its message rotted to a paint-flaking mess – and as he stood a coil of rusting wire tore a chunk from his ear.

Daniels fell to his knees, gripping his ear tight as though he could squeeze away the pain, and howled into the darkness.

The blood was shiny with moonlight as he lifted his hand away, and he wiped it across his chest, tensing his muscles as the night air hit the wound and it began to throb. Then he smashed the sign to bits with the butt of his air rifle.

When he reached the meadow he lay flat and still, his ear throbbing, feeling himself vanish into the trees. He watched an oblivious rabbit bump along, its tail flashing white in the gloom.

He let it go.

They all thought he was angry, that he lashed out. They thought he couldn't control himself. But he could be patient.

They didn't know how patient he could be.

A fox passed on the far edge of the paddock. A squirrel twirled up a tree trunk. More rabbits passed, their twitching noses empty of his scent. Minutes fell away, measured only by the pulse in his wound.

Still he waited for the target his anger craved – the hardest shot, the biggest prize.

A bird in flight.

And then he saw it: a crow dropping from the trees, its wings spreading as it banked to turn. He dropped his head to the sights, pictured Sep – and fired.

The crow carried on, silent and untroubled, wings fluttering as it landed on a distant treetop.

He climbed to his knees.

'Daniels doesn't miss,' he spat, looking again along the rifle's sights.

Just to prove it, he lined up a branch that hung from a nearby tree and squeezed the trigger. The pellet left a perfect circular hole in the centre of a dangling leaf.

Daniels looked at the crow. It had turned to face him.

'Bull*shit*,' he whispered.

A swallow dived from the treetop above him, swooping low over the meadow and banking sharply in a bow-winged arc.

Daniels raised the rifle, followed the little bird until it lined up with the horizon – and fired.

The swallow fell in an exclamation of feathers.

Daniels looked at the crow again. Its eyes were fixed on the swallow's twisted body.

'Daniels doesn't miss,' he said again, and loaded another pellet into his rifle.

Sacrifice: 1982

'*Raiders of the Lost Ark* is your favourite film?' said Arkle, leaning over his handlebars. 'That's just ... I mean ... I actually feel sorry for you. Have you even seen *The Empire Strikes Back*?'

'Obviously,' said Lamb, trying to scratch under her cast with a blade of grass.

It was the hottest day of the summer, and clouds drifted, high and thin, across the bleached-white sky. Sep lifted his T-shirt from the pink sunburn on his neck.

'*Friday the 13th: Part III* is the best film ever,' lisped Hadley.

'I've never seen that,' said Sep. 'Is it scary?'

'Oh, God, yeah,' said Hadley, giving him a little smile. 'The scariest. *And* it was in 3D.'

'I farted in 3D once,' said Arkle. 'It was a few years ago – I got a fright on the carousel. Then when I went home to change, my mum told me my dog had gone to live on a farm. Literally the shittiest day ever.'

'My gran went to live on a farm when I was six,' said Hadley.

Arkle's eyes flashed with mischief.

'I wonder if it was the same one as my dog?'

'Why are you smiling like that?' said Hadley.

'What are we going to do today?' said Sep quickly.

They sat watching the sea lash over the rocks, rainbows shining in its spray.

Mack finished his hot dog and took out a pack of gum.

'We could swim again.'

'Maybe,' said Hadley. 'It was so peaceful, floating together.'

'I don't think so,' said Sep, thinking of the crabs lurking under the surface.

Lamb rubbed his head.

'It'll be all right, Seppy. We didn't see any crabs last time, did we?'

'How'd you know I was thinking about that?'

Lamb grinned at him, and settled back with her cast behind her head.

'Swimming in the sea was ace,' she said. 'That was my favourite thing.'

'I'm up for skinny-dipping,' said Arkle.

Lamb threw a daisy head at him.

'No one said anything about skinny-dipping, dude,' said Mack, shaking his head.

'I loved it when we toasted marshmallows on the beach and listened to my new mixtape,' said Hadley. 'That's been my favourite.'

'I liked our movie day,' said Arkle. 'Pirate Betamax of *Alien* and *The Thing*, with plenty of Spike.'

'And a ton of popcorn,' said Mack.

'You really can eat, Golden Boy.'

'Touch it,' said Mack, flexing his arm at Arkle. 'I dare you.'

Arkle flexed his own noodle arm and they laughed, watching the clouds and smelling the air.

'We could go back to the woods today,' said Sep.

'Would we be sure of a big surprise?' said Arkle, rocking on his back tyre. 'Had we better go in disguise? Is today the day the teddy bears –' His bike slipped from under him. 'Ow! Oh, guyth, guyth – I bid my thung!'

'You might have deserved that,' said Lamb. She was facing away from them all, looking out to the mainland, where her *real* friends were at sports camp.

As Sep followed her gaze he felt the looming threat of separation, of school being the same lonely space he'd known before this summer of unlikely friendship ever happened. He remembered that loneliness, that slow passing of lunchtimes and weekends, and felt that without action, without doing *something*, this perfect bubble would burst – and he'd have to watch the sandcastle he'd built crumble as the others went back to their usual groups, to their *real* friends, while he went back to being alone.

And so he dipped his toe into the idea – the one he'd dreamed, that had stuck in his mind and blocked his other thoughts.

'We found that box the other day,' he said. 'We could go there.'

'And do what?' said Hadley.

'I thought we could . . . put something in it. It's got a lid and – it just kind of makes sense, don't you think?'

'To put things in the ground?' said Arkle. 'Like a time capsule?'

'Yeah,' said Sep carefully. 'Or a sacrifice.'

'Could I set it on fire?'

'What?' said Sep, turning his head.

'You've already burned everything. Even your *report card*,' said Hadley.

'I'd do yours too, if you'd let me. I bet it would even burn better than mine.'

'What do you mean, a sacrifice?' said Mack.

'Well,' said Sep, remembering the way the idea had arrived – sudden and hot – in his head. 'It's nearly the end of the holidays. It would be something for us all to do together, so we stay, like, friends. We each give the box something that's important to us, and it keeps us together.'

Mack blew a bubble, then ran a hand through his hair. Sunlight gleamed on his arms.

'I'm up for that,' he said.

'Definitely,' said Lamb.

A carload of New Romantics rumbled past, their sleeves and music wafting on the hot breeze.

'So we're doing it?' said Sep tentatively, as though he was creeping up on a wild animal.

'*Yeah*,' said Hadley. 'I know what I'm sacrificing too.'

'And me,' said Mack.

They all stood. Sep straightened his bike and joined the others in formation on their BMXs and Choppers.

'That's . . . brilliant,' he said, fighting a tremble in his voice as his throat tightened.

'Cool idea, Sep,' said Lamb. 'Cool thing to do.' She winked at him.

'Do you know what you're going to sacrifice?' asked Hadley.

'Yeah,' said Sep. 'Definitely.'

He cycled up the hill towards his house, quickly so they wouldn't see the happy tears in his eyes – turning his good ear so their voices stayed with him for as long as possible.

13

The Old Way

The route was familiar to the point of instinct. Thom Roxburgh moved along it with subconscious ease, staring only into his own mind.

The path was unmarked but clear: a flat furrow of ancient soil that ran from the big house to the hunting grounds. Every once in a while he found Roman pottery under his feet, made smooth as old soap by earth and time.

The estate was old, and so the way was old – and so the gamekeeper liked it.

Roxburgh was grubby and sinew-thin, sweating in a ragged suit and a layer of waxed cotton. Old tattoos spilled like bruises from his collar and cuffs: wave lines on his jugular, crosses on his knuckles and swallows behind his thumbs, their wings following the arch of his palm.

He strode past the bracken, thwacking its new limbs with his stick. His terriers, Lundy and Biscay, were chasing vermin somewhere in its thick tangle, silent as they focused on the scent. He'd always kept Patterdales, but he'd never known two as brave as these. A week ago Biscay had been cornered by a badger and Lundy had gone right in after her. They'd have torn it to pieces, Roxburgh thought, if he'd not intervened with a quick shovel.

He looked for the dogs, running his tongue through the spaces of his missing teeth. After a moment he spotted Biscay through a gap in the foliage, something gripped in her jaws. He narrowed his eyes against the needles of sunset that pierced the canopy, but couldn't see what it was.

He packed some more tobacco into his lip, sucked out its thick syrup, then spat. Later on he'd pick the bloody mess from their teeth while they listened to the shipping forecast.

Looking down, he saw the ground under his feet had been churned by deer hooves, and shifted the shotgun to his other arm.

He hoped not to fire it, but knew it was a fool's hope: the air had a raw, animal smell that raised his hackles – the way hot blood smelled in frosty air.

The old gamekeeper carried on – breathing with the forest's rhythm while his dogs hunted in the darkening shadows – towards the hunting grounds, and the secret thing he'd protected all these years.

14

Crow

Mario let him leave early. The last hour had been quiet and most of the cleaning was done.

'Of course,' the big man said, holding the shutters in the air for Sep to duck under. 'All the fridges have stopped working, is very strange – but I can finish here myself. You go. And remember, my Sep: is difficult to have friends; sometimes your pride is needing a spoonful of sugar maybe.'

Sep stood in silence, so Mario rubbed his head and laughed.

'You'll come in tomorrow afternoon, to help clean the cold store?'

'I don't know. I've got that application to finish –'

'Is no problem,' said Mario, shaking his head. 'I will manage.'

'No, I'll come in, I'm sorry,' said Sep. 'I can do the form after.'

Mario beamed.

'Thank you, my Sep. You are good boy. You remember the cold-store locking code?'

'It's . . . I do, it's –'

'– the special day of Mario *and* Greece.' Mario laughed. '*Everything* else you remember! Now be quick, there is a storm coming – and be careful of the greasy boy on your way,' he added, before the shutters rattled down. 'If he comes for you, hit first. My father always say: "Big men do not have wooden balls." Kick him there and he will sink like lead balloon, yes?'

Sep rolled his eyes, but left his headphones in his bag and walked, leaving his board strapped up. The music and the grind of wheels would fill his head with sound, blinding his good ear, and he wanted to be ready if Daniels was waiting for him.

And now he was outside, his tooth was *really* hurting.

He looked at the sky. The clouds were too thick to see stars, never mind the comet. But Sep wondered if it was out there, filling his head with cosmic agony.

Across the water, the mainland's street lights glowed like scattered jewels. The idea of the college and its freedoms glittered incorruptibly inside him, and this stupid distraction, this . . . *bullshit*, would not get in his way. He turned on to the thin strip of beach, avoiding the main street and Daniels' usual haunts, each step taking him deeper into his own mind.

His guts boiled.

The others were so casual, sitting in *his* chip shop and blaming him for – what? Some ridiculous paranoia? Well, he would find Arkle tomorrow, tell him to back off – they could chase their own wild geese.

He marched over the little worm towers that sat like knots of spaghetti among the ribs of the old tide. Slow clouds of salt hissed from the rocks and the bay sang with the tinkle of swinging masts, the sand shining silver as the earth lurched away from the sun.

As the island turned beneath his feet he thought of his mother sleeping in her chair, grey-skinned and off her food. Memories of the last time she'd looked that way – the treatments in the mainland hospital and the waxy tack of her skin – struck his mind like hailstones on tin and he shook his head, turning the pad on his headphones.

He thought of the sacrifice box – and the guilt he'd put inside it. After years of forgetting he'd been surprised by how bright and clear the memories had felt when Lamb mentioned it – how immediate the emotions had been.

'No,' he said aloud. 'She can't be getting sick again. Not *again*.'

His tooth throbbed suddenly, the pain running through the tubes of his head and into his deaf ear, while a smell of dampness and soil stirred his memory like footprints in dust. He sniffed.

The rock beside his foot leaped up.

Sep fell into a stream, his jeans soaking as he splashed backwards. The crab, a sharp-limbed boulder in jagged skin, unfurled slowly, mouthparts whirring as it balanced on the awls of its enormous legs, pincers held in warning.

Sep froze.

The crabs did not do this. It was too hot for them. In winter they filled the beach like rats, but in summer they stayed below the water. Even at night.

The creature poised on the tide's edge, white surf bubbling through its needle feet.

They hurt someone every year. Badly. Island kids were warned about them as soon as they could walk – *Don't let them grab you, because they won't let go* – but tourists always got too close, hunting for photographs, or trying to impress their friends. The year before Sep was born, the crabs had killed a little boy who fell off the pier.

As the animal finally eased into the water, step by agonizing step, Sep ran – heart flapping in his chest, headphones loose around his neck – all the way up the hill and along the silent streets until he reached his house and clattered through the front door, muscles seized up in terror.

He breathed out, clicked the buttons on his Walkman and let the soft scent of his house gather around him, making the world normal, making everything secure.

The TV was hissing on standby, and his mum was asleep on the sofa – still in her uniform, a plate of untouched chicken beside her on the floor. Sep tucked a pillow under her head and cleared away the dinner things. He filled a glass with water and sat it next to the chair, covered her with a blanket, then grabbed the remote and tried changing channel.

Every station was the same: snowy static filling the darkness with ghostly light. He pulled the plug out at the wall.

In his bedroom, he picked his way across the messy floor and swung the telescope to the window. But the clouds were as thick as wool, and he found nothing.

He lay awake long after his mum's snoring had subsided, watching the shadows grow in the blue of his bedroom. The house was silent but for the familiar click and ping of pipes as the building settled. A gap in the curtains spilled milky light across his feet. He shifted his legs. Flipped the pillow. Turned on to his other side.

Arkle's toothy face, all deep-lined concern, kept flashing in his mind. He wondered if the others had remembered that was their favourite table at Mario's – if they'd sat there tonight by instinct or choice. He thought of what it had felt like to be with them again – sitting in the chip shop just as they'd done that summer, eating Mario Specials while bike sweat cooled on their skin.

They were genuinely worried. He knew that. And it *was* strange, his mum asking about Arkle and Lamb for the first time in years – the same day they showed up in the shop.

He shook his head, thought of his application and the college – of his longed-for escape from Hill Ford. But an image came, unbidden, of the hospital gown gathered round the lumps of his mum's knees as she was wheeled into theatre. He closed his eyes against it, but it burned there anyway.

Sep lay for an unknown age, clicking his Walkman on and off as his waking thoughts muddled on sleep's gummy edge – when a moment settled on the house that lasted much longer than a moment. The world slowed, the blood swelled in his good ear, and when he opened his eyes the shadows had deepened. A car passed, the blades of its headlights slicing through the room.

The tingle of old, forgotten fears lit his veins, and he sat up sharply. He felt the skin of his younger self crawl inside him, alert to the darkness with a child's precision, and he searched the corners of his house with his mind like a tongue probing teeth. There was a sound, invisible on the edge of silence, like the drumbeat of his own heart.

He was not alone.

Something was on the other side of the window, watching him with cold patience, the way a lizard watches a fly.

A shadow moved on the curtains.

'There's no way it's the box,' he said aloud, pulse closing his throat, then sat up and threw the curtains wide.

Three pairs of dark, gleaming eyes stared back at him.

Sep looked at the crows. Their terrible beaks were touching the glass and their wings bristled, light playing through the blacks and blues and purples of their moonlit feathers – and as he met their stare a wave of cold gripped his body. He grit his teeth, snapped up the latch and opened the window, hard, sending the birds flapping silently into the night.

15

Bones

Roxburgh had known something was wrong as soon as he entered the paddock. It wasn't the absence of deer. It was the absence of everything.

After decades in the forest the little chirps and cracks of the world's shifting skin were as familiar as his own voice. But today all had been silent: unturned soil and still trees, cold air empty of birdsong. So he'd sat unmoving as night came, watching the sun leach from the sky – waiting.

Now his eyes flashed in the darkness. There was something in the clearing. The feeling was bright on his skin, as though he'd been caught in a flashlight's beam. He dragged some thick, tobacco-flecked spit from the gaps in his teeth, and tasted his own fear.

When he was young he'd fought a war he hadn't understood. As a scout, he'd crawled through the insects and the spiders of the Malayan jungle while the canopy dripped on his helmet and the Liberation Army slithered like cats in his cracked binoculars. One day he'd hunkered down to watch, cool and invisible in the green shade. Then a bullet had split the heel of his boot and he'd scrambled into a shell-hole before he'd drawn breath, a body moving independently of thought.

The sniper had toyed with him for the rest of the day, cracking the bark above his head or bursting the stream at his feet, and he had lain like an ant under a magnifying glass, guts baking in the sun, lips splitting as he burned. He'd waited until the sun set massive and orange through the trees, then crawled away on his belly, hiding from the moonlight in mud pits that spun with venomous snakes.

At his barracks the CO had given him new boots, a fresh canteen of water and sent him straight back – along the same path, into the same ditch. And as he'd marched there Roxburgh had understood what fear meant – not the jolt of a sudden noise, but *real*, primal fear – the chewing of reason between instinct's yellow teeth.

Even forty years on, there were nights when he lunged from bed having walked that path in his dreams, moments in his waking life where he felt those young bones quake in his old skin.

Now that primal terror was upon him once again. Something was watching him with the sniper's measured threat, the same patience – and the same deadly intent. And Roxburgh recognized something he'd not felt in decades, something from before even the jungle – something from his childhood. He'd almost forgotten what it felt like – the charge there'd been in the air that summer.

The old gamekeeper whistled for his dogs, but the silence took his brisk, efficient note and made it desperate and small, like a cry from a well.

Lundy and Biscay came reluctantly from the brush, close to his heels. They were whimpering deep in their bellies, and Roxburgh saw a gash in Lundy's side – pink and thin, like wet, pursed lips. He crouched and parted the fur. The little dog flinched.

'What's you done to yourself, girl?' he said quietly.

He reached into his pocket and withdrew a string of soft red meat, pressed it gently into the dog's mouth. She mashed it quickly, then licked the dirt from his hand, covering his wrist in glistening spit as he examined the wound. It wasn't from a tooth or a claw – it was deeper, longer. It could only have been made by Lundy dragging herself against something, like a wire snagged in her skin.

She had done this to herself. Even with her prey drive, she'd never have pushed through so much pain to chase something down.

So she'd been running from something. Running for her life.

Roxburgh lifted a feather from her lip, held it in the moonlight.

Black. A crow's feather.

He checked the little brass eyes of the shotgun shells, then snapped the gun shut and tucked it into the crook of his arm. He took a step towards the clearing, stopped – then, to his horror, inched back to the path, swallowing away the pebble that blocked his throat.

'These is my lands,' he called, fighting to control the tightness in his voice. 'An' you's best leavin' 'em now if you doesn't want your backside studded wi' shot.'

There was no answer. He'd known there wouldn't be. The sea-salt wind blew hard at his back, but the trees around him were silent and still.

The dogs drew closer to him.

And, in that moment, Roxburgh knew with the ancient certainty of the hunted that there was no friend near him, nobody within even the reach of his loudest screams. He was alone in the woods with his little dogs, surrounded by an anger that he felt with his blood but could not see.

He took a step back, felt bones crunch under his boot and turned, heart thudding, to find a pile of black feathers and the blue-black gleam of a razor beak.

The dogs growled, licking their lips with nervous whines.

Roxburgh nudged the feathers apart with the barrel of his gun, exposing the soft tangle of ribs. He bent to lift the thing into the bushes.

But the mess of feather and bone fluttered at his touch, torn wings flapping as it vanished into the darkness.

Roxburgh stood bolt upright.

The bird's chest had been ripped open – and the little pouches of the lungs had been completely still. The bird was dead.

And yet it had flown.

The gamekeeper turned and ran back to his little shack on the edge of the woods, thinking only of getting to Aileen.

The wind roared behind him, and the trees shook in the clearing.

Someone had broken the rules again.

16

Mack

Mack moved until the sliver of street light fell on his page: a picture of Darryl Strawberry's long, looping swing. He had never swung a baseball bat in his life, but read the statistics for the hundredth time, letting details he didn't understand – at bats, strikeouts, on-base percentages – wash over him in a comforting wave.

There was shouting downstairs: his dad raging at the broken TV, and the clatter of what sounded like the aerial hitting the wall. He heard his mum's muttered protest, then the fridge door slamming.

He reread the profile of the '85 Cardinals, moving the page like a sheet in a typewriter, snapping it back to the beginning each time he reached the end of the street light's glow.

Glass shattered downstairs, and he heard the raised note of his mum's dismay.

He wondered if they'd noticed anything different about him, his mum and dad – how his eyes were brighter, his shoulders straighter.

He shifted again, this time to relieve the ache in his bladder. If he went to pee then his dad might hear the footsteps and start up on him. But there was nothing for it – he had to go.

Mack dropped on to the bare boards of his room. He knew the pattern of silence and creaks off by heart – a kind of hopscotch roulette he played in the small hours when he'd guzzled water at training.

Easing open his bedroom door, he ghosted across the landing and into the bathroom without snapping closed the lock, aiming for the porcelain rather than the water. As he peed he looked up at himself in the mirrored cabinet – tired, red around the eyes from the strain of the last few nights, but happy. Definitely happy.

Mack washed his hands first, so he could flush on his way back to his room, making sure his door was closed before the sound roused the beast downstairs. He left the almanac open on his chest as he lay in the dark, listening to time's steady tick through his pillow.

And then – just before it had lulled him to sleep – someone outside whispered his name.

17

Visit

Sep gripped his pillow as the oily shadows gathered round him. Model aircraft twirled over die-cast figures, posters flapped in the breeze, and everywhere – on the floor and the desk and on top of the wardrobe – paperbacks leaned in soft yellow towers.

He closed his eyes, wishing for the release of a dreamless night, and for the darkness behind his lids to be empty and safe.

But the crows followed him into sleep – and he dreamed of *them*.

Cool moss was between his bare toes. Sep could almost hear the grass growing around him, almost feel the starlight on his skin.

He turned to the sea. The mainland was close, its windows glimmering like fragments of scattered diamond.

Sep reached out – but something moved in the darkness.

He peered through the bobbing leaves and saw a little patch of night flutter on to a branch. The crow shuffled its legs and rasped its bright tongue.

'Get!' said Sep. 'Go on, get!'

He looked about for a stone to throw. But the crow was joined by another, then another and another, their moonlit feathers a boil of blacks and blues and purples that obscured the mainland completely. Blade-sharp beaks snapped until the air was solid with cries that did not come from living throats, overlapping and echoing until they came from everywhere and nowhere.

Sep realized that their shining eyes, countless as stars, were watching him.

'Go away!' he said.

He took a step away from them and stumbled as he felt something loose and warm beneath his bare feet. And although it moved like a piece of clothing, his guts knew it for what it was. He looked down.

A human skin, a woman's skin — topped by mousy, lank hair — was splayed on the grass, empty and soft, like a blanket.

'Oh,' said Sep. He put out a hand.

And the crows screamed.

They came in a noisy cloud, wings beating his face, filling his lungs with their warm air and sour scent. He felt their claws on his scalp and their terrible beaks at his hands and face.

One bird landed on the empty skin and wriggled its head, then its wings, then its body between the lips and into the mouth.

'No!' screamed Sep, kicking, pushing, his forehead running with blood. 'Stop! You can't do this!'

Another crow pushed its way into the skin, then another and another and another until the skin began to tighten and rise from the ground.

Then the skin's eyes opened: wide and shiny and black.

And, just as he felt himself yield, a voice called wordlessly from across the grass, from inside the darkness, and he felt the warmth of a human connection flood through his veins.

★

He woke with a shrug of limbs and a thump in his chest, his head stuck to the pillow.

His bedroom was still. Cold sweat covered his chest and face.

A soft noise moved through him. At first he thought there was a tap dripping somewhere in the house . . . but it sounded strange, as though it wasn't moving through the air — just arriving in his head, heavy and thick, like wet cloth swelling around his sore tooth.

Then pain — hot, searing pain — lanced into his skull like a blade. He turned his eyeballs to the window.

There was a shadow on the curtain — a silhouette in the street-bulb orange. It was on the other side of the glass, not a crow this time, but something small and round — one circle atop another, flanked by rigid limbs.

And little round ears.

Barnaby.

The head turned. Eyes like burning green coals stared through the fabric.

Barnaby. The teddy he'd sacrificed, returned from the box — and *walking* on his stubby, cotton legs.

It's my turn, thought Sep.

His breath stopped, and he shook his head, trying to dislodge the insistent, tap-dripping sound . . . then he realized two things.

It wasn't a dripping noise. It was a whispering, breathy click, like phlegm catching in a wet throat.

And worse, so much worse . . .

He was hearing it with his deaf ear. It crackled strangely, like a dusty radio coaxed into life.

The blood turned cold and thick in his veins.

Barnaby took a small step, *searching*, flat paw smearing the glass with earth as he found the gap in the curtains – and Sep saw him, his unmistakable laced-up belly leaning on the window. His fur was muddy and wet; and thick with something, like a layer of snakeskin. He almost gleamed, unalive but . . . living.

A familiar smell came into Sep's room: a smell of grass gone flat and white beneath untouched pots; of trapped water gone sour in the heat; of wet, wriggling soil.

Of hospital corridors.

The teddy walked a few more steps and, as Sep watched him move towards the open window, a gut-knot of animal instinct screamed the reason the bear had come.

Barnaby was here to kill him.

Sep's heart stuck in his neck – and a stone ticked off the glass, inches from where Barnaby stood.

The teddy froze, the burning green light of his eyes flickering for an instant.

He blinked, thought Sep. *He* blinked.

Another stone, bigger and heavier, thudded against the wall and Barnaby dropped out of sight, leaving nothing but the tension in Sep's belly and a light rain that kissed the window with such gentle normalcy it took all his strength of mind to trust that the bear *had* been there, *had* visited him from beneath the ground, had not been some wakeful night terror.

Because he was awake: cold with sweat and seized with fear. Crumbs of mud clung to the glass, and that smell – that cold, dead stench – lingered in the air.

Another stone hit the window and, with all the courage he had, Sep threw open the curtains.

They were in his garden.

PART 2

Morning: 1941

'You're late,' said Thom, watching Aileen roll her bicycle into the bushes.

'Sorry,' she said without looking up. 'My mother again.'

She tucked the doll under her arm and pulled up her socks. Lizzie was propped on her elbows, her round cheeks tight in a frown.

'It's boring, isn't it?' she said.

Thom sighed.

'What is?'

'The countryside.'

'I like it,' said Thom. He stared past her, through the shimmering heat to the destroyers' lurking shadows.

'But you live on a farm — you always get real milk.'

'Don't you?' said Morgan, furrowing his dented forehead.

'Not when the ships don't sail,' said Lizzie, climbing to her feet as they set off. 'Then it's only powdered stuff. Do you get extra bacon?'

'Just the ration,' said Thom, shifting the knapsack to his other shoulder. 'But we snares rabbits when we can. My mam showed me how to skin 'em the other day — you don't even need a knife, you just tear —'

Lizzie pulled a face.

'That's what I mean. It's full of disgusting things — and there's nothing to actually do; everyone's a fuddy-duddy. I don't know why I had to be evacuated. If we were in the city we'd be able to go dancing, or to the picture house or a cafe, but here —'

'If you were in the city you'd have been blown to bits by one of Hitler's bombs,' said Aileen.

Lizzie stuck out her tongue.

'Lizzie's right,' said Shelley, who'd started wearing lipstick. 'I bet we'd be having all kinds of fun in the city. There's parties and money and . . . boys.'

'There's boys right here,' said Morgan, giving her a gap-toothed grin.

She frowned at him.

'I mean real boys. Men. The wireless said the Americans are there now.'

'You're a fast one, Shelley Webster,' said Thom.

'And you're too young,' added Aileen.

Shelley primped her tightly curled hair.

'But I look older. I'm going to bag me a GI the first chance I get, then I'll be living in Chicago, or Miami or . . . New York.'

'I don't reckon you will, though,' said Thom, pulling the moss from one of the standing stones and straightening his cap. 'I reckon you'll end up tumbling a dock worker an' get stuck here like the rest of us.'

Morgan whistled, then punched him on the arm.

'Jesus, Thom! That's the funniest damn thing I ever heard!' he said as Lizzie chewed a knuckle to hide her smirk.

Shelley scowled at them.

'I will not!' she said. 'Mother says I'm not to go to the docks, so there!'

The boys erupted, and Morgan rolled his tobacco pouch in fingers smeared with engine oil.

'I take it back,' he said, wiping his eyes. '*That's* the funniest thing I ever heard.'

Shelley flushed.

'I'll get away from all of you anyway,' she muttered, 'to America. You'll see.'

Aileen wiped a drip of sweat from her nose. The others were all a head taller or more, and she was struggling to keep up.

They picked their way carefully, the forest humming around them as they stepped over the thin prints of animals and brushed the bright growths on the trees.

'This is awful,' said Lizzie, her nose in the air. 'It's sticky and it smells. The city never smells as bad as this, even on bin day.'

'You an' that bloody city,' said Thom, holding aside a curtain of thorns for the others to pass. 'I bet our bins're cleaner than theirs.'

'Is that where you get your clothes?' said Shelley.

Thom shifted to hide the patches on his trousers.

'It's where you got your morals anyway,' he said.

Morgan laughed again, scattering the tobacco as he ran his tongue along the cigarette paper.

'So where's this box?' said Lizzie. 'I have to get back. My aunt wants me to muck out the chickens and gather the cabbages this afternoon.'

'Dig for victory,' said Thom, nodding. 'Bet there's rabbits where there's cabbages.'

'I don't mind digging for victory, but I'm to scrub the steps once I'm done. The outside steps. She's such a cow.'

'Scrub for victory,' said Morgan.

'You don't half nurse grudges, Lizzie,' said Aileen. 'The box is in the clearing — the one at the top of the paddock.'

'How did you find it all the way up there?'

'I sketch the deer sometimes, and last week, after all that rain, this box was just . . . there.'

'I got caught walking home in that rain,' said Morgan, handing Thom the cigarette.

'Wash your brains out, did it?' said Shelley.

'Nope. Got my hat wet, though. What we doing here again?'

'We're making an offering,' said Aileen. 'A secret thing, for just us to know about.'

'Like a sacrifice?'

Aileen thought of her father as the submarine vanished around him, leaving him twisting in the water, tearing at his uniform as he sank into the darkness.

'It's a silly thing to do,' said Shelley curtly. 'We're too grown-up.'

Aileen flushed.

'Well, I'm older than you,' she said after a moment, 'and I don't think it's silly. The war isn't easy, for anyone, and it's — it's important for us to stay together. We don't see each other as much now.'

'It's silly,' said Shelley again.

'Don't —' Aileen began, but Lizzie interrupted.

'It's not,' she said. 'It's a bit like magic. I've been reading about witches — they're real, you know. They curse people. I'm going to curse my aunt.'

'You don't half complain,' said Thom, taking a final drag before handing the cigarette back to Morgan.

They climbed towards the clearing. Off in the distance, over the canopy's green sea, thin blue smoke twirled from the gamekeeper's hut and was whipped back towards the town.

'This isn't about cursing anyone,' said Aileen, pulling up her socks again. 'It's to be a good thing. We've had such a nice summer, and recently we've — we just need to remember why we're friends. It was only us who got along at school. We used to be close.'

'I wasn't at your school,' said Lizzie.

'Don't tell me,' said Thom, 'your school was in . . . the city?'

'With central heating,' said Lizzie.

'We'd have been friends if you'd been at our school, and now we're going to make an offering,' said Aileen. 'It's nice to do something together when things are difficult and people in our families are away — and —'

Thom looked over sharply.

'It's — it's a nice thing to do,' she finished.

'You hear that, Lizzie?' said Morgan. 'A nice thing. Nice means nice.'

'You'd never have survived in my school,' said Lizzie, scowling. 'The city boys would have given you such a time about your weird-shaped head, and you'd —'

'What did you all bring? For the offering?' Aileen cut in.

'We had to bring something?' said Morgan.

'Yes!' said Aileen, turning at the edge of the clearing and throwing up her hands. 'That was the whole point of coming here. What did you think we were going to do?'

'Something nice. Like a picnic.'

The sky began to rumble in the distance and they looked up to see the specks of aircraft, tiny as flies against the white smear of cloud.

'They're ours,' said Thom.

Aileen kept on at Morgan. 'Do you see any picnic things? And didn't you wonder why I was carrying an old doll?'

'Sure. But, you know, you've been a bit odd lately, and —'

Thom dug him in the ribs.

Aileen was relieved to find the stone box where she'd left it, as though it might have retreated into the ground, like one of the crabs down by the shore.

She knelt beside it. A smell came from inside, of things that were old and dry — the way she imagined a desert might smell.

'Just give it something you've got with you,' she said. 'It'll keep whatever we give it, and that way we'll always know we're friends, even if we move away.'

'This is a lot of old rot, Leen,' said Shelley, raising her voice above the drone of the engines. The planes were visible now, the sun glinting on their turrets' glass.

Aileen turned her head so they wouldn't see the water in her eyes.

'You don't think it's silly, do you, Thom?' she said after a moment.

Thom shook his head.

'I reckon we're the first folk in a long time to find this thing,' he said, moving to stand beside her. 'An' it never hurts to do somethin' for your friends, does it?'

He glared at the others.

Shelley flicked her head.

'I suppose,' she said. 'Don't flip your wig.'

Aileen squeezed Thom's hand.

'Put in your offerings then,' she said, raising her voice as the bombers drew close, 'one at a time.'

Shelley leaned over the box and dropped in something small and dark.

'A lock of my hair,' she said with a sarcastic curtsey. 'Prettiest thing on my pretty head.'

'That's not –' said Aileen.

'My tobacco, I guess,' said Morgan, throwing the leather pouch into the box's dark space. 'Only thing I've got on me that's not part of my body.'

'No! You're not taking –'

'Aunt Louise's ration book,' said Lizzie, dropping in the little yellow book with a terrible smile. 'I curse you, you old witch – I curse you!'

'That's not what we're supposed to do!' said Aileen. 'We're supposed to give something good, to bring us together – a commitment to each other!'

Thom squeezed her shoulder, and kept his hand there while he laid a little white body in the stone.

'Here'n'now,' he said, 'the puppet I made with my grandad, given in the spirit of friendship.'

'Here'n'now?' mocked Shelley, and Lizzie rolled her eyes.

Aileen put her hand over Thom's, let go a sob and placed her doll in the box.

'My old doll, Sadie,' she said. 'Given to me by – by my father, when I was small.' She looked around them. 'Now we say the words. Here – I wrote them down.'

Shelley peered at the scrap of paper.

'Your handwriting's frightful,' she said.

'It does make it look like a spell,' Lizzie conceded.

'Just say them!' said Aileen, her voice wobbling. 'What harm can it do?'

The girls shared a look and Morgan puffed out his cheeks, but they stood in a circle and joined hands.

'Now?' shouted Lizzie as the planes roared overhead, shaking the teeth in their heads and throwing shadows over the clearing.

'Now!' shouted Thom.

'Never come to the box alone.'

Shelley sneered at the ground, while Lizzie grinned wickedly.

'Never open it after dark.'

Morgan shifted his feet awkwardly, brow furrowed in concentration, his voice a half-beat behind the others.

'Never take back your sacrifice.'

They stood back as the planes veered away, and the sound of the trees washed around them once more.

'Is that it?' said Lizzie, reaching past her elbow into the box. She lifted the ration book and tucked it in her skirt. 'Only I need to get this back before she sees it's gone – she'd kill me if she knew!'

'Oh, do we get them back?' said Morgan brightly. 'That's good – I've got half an ounce of golden in there.'

'No!' said Aileen. 'The rules! You said the rules!'

'I might as well take this then,' said Shelley, daintily tucking the lock of hair into the belt on her skirt and turning away. 'Never hurts to have a lock handy for an admirer. See you tonight – maybe!'

'But you can't –' Aileen said, dropping to her knees in a cloud of dust.

She watched them leave through hot, angry tears.

Thom knelt beside her.

'Somethin' happened to your dad?' he said quietly.

Aileen looked at the box, so deep and dark it might be empty.

'We haven't heard anything,' she said, 'only that the sub was lost. He might still be – I just wanted today to – I wanted us to be like we were before.'

Thom let her head fall on his shoulder and held her as she wept. The forest breathed around them in hot, floral bloom, and the air was livid with the zip of insects.

'My mum said that when the world's tearing itself apart, love is the only thing that can fix everything,' said Aileen once her tears had subsided. 'That if we just loved each other a little more, all the darkness would go away. I thought putting something in there — and leaving it — would remind us of why we're friends, and keep us that way.'

'Well, ours are still in there,' said Thom. He lifted her to her feet, and together they walked back down the hill.

18

Footprints

Cold rain speckled Sep's feet as he pulled open the back door. He went into the garden, stooping like that might keep him dry.

'What are you doing here?' he whispered.

'You shat it,' said Arkle, his face split by a grin, a flap of hair stuck to his forehead.

'I didn't.'

'Sure, sure.'

Sep looked around. There were no crows, no Barnaby, just the telltale rush of shadow as the fox darted along the treeline.

'Well, your faces were all dark,' he said, 'and you're outside my house in the middle of the night.'

'Hey, I'm not judging,' said Arkle, 'but let's face it — if you weren't shitting yourself you wouldn't be out here in He-Man pyjamas, freezing your sweets off in the rain, would you?'

Sep looked at his pyjama bottoms and swore inwardly.

'They're old,' he said, looking involuntarily at Hadley.

'They sure are,' said Arkle. 'It was nearly a full moon when you turned round to close the door.'

Lamb pushed Arkle out of the way.

'What was that at your window?' she said.

Her hair was heavy and wet, and Sep saw again how much older she looked than the others. He stared at them all, dark and serious in the rain, the moonlight making skulls of their faces.

'I had the dream again, Sep,' said Hadley. 'I only fell asleep for a second and the voice was there, whispering things. Tell us, please. It was your turn – that's why we're here.'

Lamb's eyes flashed.

'It was Barnaby,' said Sep, and as the words passed his lips they became things of iron and stone, heavy and permanent and true, and he felt the terror pour back into his chest. 'It was *Barnaby*! Walking around!'

'We told you it was the box!' hissed Lamb, spitting the words at his face. 'You still think it's the damn comet?'

'No!' said Sep. His heart was still pounding in his chest. 'Jesus Christ, what's going on?'

'It's the box,' said Hadley quietly.

'There were rules,' said Lamb, 'and they've been broken. It's the only explanation.'

'Who's Barnaby?' said Arkle.

'Holy shit!' said Mack. 'Don't you remember? That's the teddy he put in the box!'

'I *should* remember that – why don't I remember that?' said Arkle, looking worried.

'And apparently he's come to life,' said Sep.

'What was he doing?' asked Lamb.

Sep took a deep breath. For the first time in his life he'd been aware of his blood, hot and rushing round a fragile skeleton wrapped in thin, soft skin. He remembered the predatory intent, and the way he'd felt himself respond like an animal.

Like prey.

'I think he was trying to kill me.'

'Really?' said Lamb.

'Definitely. I heard this . . . noise, when he was close. It made my toothache worse. And it wasn't a normal noise. I was hearing it with –'

'Anyone want a Monster Munch?' said Mack.

'So have you, like, named your tapeworm?' said Arkle.

'It's you next, Mack,' said Hadley. 'You were last.'

'What did you sacrifice?' said Arkle.

Mack pulled a face, then frowned.

'My old watch.'

'Yeah,' said Lamb. 'You stopped the hands, then put it in.'

They all thought for a moment, remembering their sacrifice.

'Anyone want to admit breaking the rules?' said Lamb.

Nobody spoke. She shook her head.

'Pussies.'

'How do *we* know it wasn't you?' said Hadley.

Lamb glared at her.

'Because I'm telling you, that's how!'

'But we're saying it wasn't us! Maybe it wasn't any of us?'

'Think about it,' said Lamb, 'you *know* I'm right. It's like . . . knowing it's about to rain. So stop giving me your chicken-shit answers and just own up to it!'

The rain fell in gossamer rods, and Sep looked over his shoulder, wondering if he'd see Barnaby's eyes glowing in the shadows.

They listened to the rain in silence.

'Fine,' said Lamb, glaring at them. 'But we need to sort this shit out.'

'How?' said Hadley.

Mack finished his crisps and crushed the bag into his pocket.

'When did you hurt yourself?' said Hadley, frowning at him.

Mack waved his tightly strapped hand and forearm.

'Football,' he said.

Lamb leaned forward and pressed her finger in Sep's chest. The headscarf hung wetly from her wrist.

'What do you think, Genius Boy?'

Sep met her stare.

'It's obvious, isn't it?'

'Is it?' said Arkle, eyes darting between them. 'Oh, you mean the space thing? And the Soviets?'

'No,' said Sep. 'I've already said – I was wrong about that. You were right. We're each being targeted with the exact thing we put in the box, and that's nothing to do with the comet *or* nuclear fallout.' He took a deep breath. 'It's the sacrifice box. Once you eliminate the impossible, whatever remains, no matter how improbable –'

'– must be the truth,' finished Hadley.

'God, you guys would have clever babies,' said Arkle.

'So?' Lamb hissed. 'What do we do? Don't just *quote* shit – what do we *do*?'

Sep's mind raced. The rules had come to him suddenly, unbidden. There had been no guide for what to do if things didn't go to plan.

'We reverse whatever's gone wrong,' he said. 'So if the rules *have* been broken, we fix them. The rules say not to go there alone, not to go after dark – so we go together, in daylight.'

'And then?' said Mack.

'We make sure the sacrifices are where we left them – in the box.'

'And what if they're not?' said Hadley. 'I mean, your teddy obviously isn't.'

Sep thought. 'Then we'll make new sacrifices.'

'What about the Soviets?' said Arkle.

'It's nothing to *do* with them –' Hadley began.

'Reversing the broken rules is the only thing I can think of,' said Sep. 'Does it make sense?'

'I think so,' said Mack.

'All right,' said Lamb. 'Fine. Meet in the trees beside the hockey pitch before registration. Then we go to the box. Bring a new sacrifice, in case our old ones aren't there.'

'Wait, we're going to skip class?' said Sep. The water broke through the last warm parts of his slippers and his feet began to freeze in the mud.

Lamb smirked.

'Check your priorities, asshole – you want to waste time in English, or stop your teddy from murdering you?'

Sep held her eye.

'Probably the teddy,' he said.

'See you tomorrow,' said Lamb, pulling up her hood and walking into the darkness.

'And so will I,' said Arkle. 'Oh, isn't it wonderful? We're a gang again! We can go on hikes and have picnics, and lashings and lashings of ginger beer, and –'

'Shut up!' Lamb shouted from beyond the hedge.

'Night, Sep,' whispered Hadley, then slipped away, Mack at her heels.

Sep stood in the rain and watched them go, their figures melting away from the pale glow of the kitchen light, footsteps quickly beyond his ear's reach.

'Goodnight,' he said.

He was alone again, standing in the silence of the blue garden.

They might not have been there at all, he realized, as the night wrapped its cold tongue around his skin. Maybe all of it – everything they'd said, the moonlight on their faces – maybe it had all been some sleepwalked dream. He looked down.

Dented in the mud, four sets of footprints gathered round him, the toes pointing towards his – the space between them the size and shape of the sacrifice box.

He went back inside, past his mum's snoring doorway, and found his Walkman before he climbed, shivering, into bed. He lay for a long time in the dark, grinding his aching teeth and watching shadows move on the curtains.

-1
Choices: 1982

'Is that you, Sep?'

His mum leaned round the living-room door. Her hair hadn't grown back completely, but it was getting fluffier every day. Sep liked to run his hand through it. It was shining like gold around her head now, and she smiled at him as she cinched the robe tighter round her waist.

'Yeah,' he said. 'Did I wake you up?'

She waved her hand to dismiss the idea, but then yawned.

'I'm sorry, Mum.'

'It's fine. Chemo is *exhausting*. I'll get back to sleep in no time. Where were you today? In the woods again?'

'We were at the beach earlier, but we're going to the woods now.'

'It's nearly dinner time,' she said, raising a thin eyebrow.

'I know, I won't be long. I just told the others I'd –'

'"The others",' she repeated. 'You're enjoying these friends, aren't you? Darren seems a nice boy, even if he is a bit . . .' she searched for the right word, 'smoky.'

'He likes to burn things,' said Sep. 'I don't,' he added quickly.

'Well, I'll be back at work at some point – if I ever see him doing that aerosol thing, I'll cuff him – and you can tell him that from me.'

Sep paused halfway up the stairs. A sunshower started outside and a whip of rain hissed on the window.

'You're going back to work?' he said.

'Not until I've finished my treatment,' she said, tilting her head. 'Sep, we talked about this – the mortgage needs to be paid. And I'm looking forward to going back; it's been a while since I handcuffed a rowdy drunk. I miss it.'

'But I've got a job.'

She laughed and leaned against the bannister.

'And I appreciate it. But wrapping chips on a Saturday doesn't bring in enough, my brave boy.'

She gripped her side, and blinked slowly.

'I'm going to lie down again,' she said carefully. 'If I'm sleeping when you come back, can you –'

'I'll make myself something.'

'All right.' She smiled at him. 'What are you back for, if you're going to the woods?'

'I've got to find something. Something that . . . means something to me, like an important object. It's a kind of friendship thing.'

She smiled again as she turned back into the living room, her footsteps fading into her TV movie.

As Sep reached under his bed for the thing he'd always known he would sacrifice – the thing he'd taken to his mum before she came home from the hospital, that had sat beside her as sickly breaths rattled in her chest – the others rifled through their own childhood clutter, throwing open their closets and pulling out drawers.

Time coiled slowly round them as they chose.

Hadley flicked through the pages of a book she wanted never to see again – a book filled with regretful secrets. She turned the little key that bound the solid leather covers, and watched as it swirled in the toilet's flush, closing her eyes and wishing it eaten by the crabs.

Arkle's breath hissed through his clenched teeth as he gripped the charred dragonflies, thinking of the report card he'd burned just before he found them floating on the river. He writhed in a pincer of shame, remembering how the flames had forced the card open, exposing his stupidity – and how the others had looked away to spare his embarrassment. He took his lighter from its secret place in his bottom drawer and tucked a cigarette behind his ear.

Lamb brushed her hair and imagined the way her mother had looked in the dresser mirror. The bedroom still smelled of her: her perfume, her clothes, the sweet leather of her shoes and handbags in the too-small wardrobe. Lamb looked at herself, ran her hand along her jawline, then went to the dresser's bottom drawer and – snagging the headscarf she'd tied round her cast – took out the compact tortoiseshell mirror her mother had promised to pass on to her when she'd admired it as a little girl.

Mack sat on the edge of his bed, watching the second hand of his watch as it ticked a slow circle and wishing it might stop: wishing that the end of the summer would stay forever distant, that they'd always stay as they were now.

Sep's hand closed on something soft and fluffy, shoelace stitching on its round middle.

He pulled Barnaby from the dust swirls behind his comics and board games, looked at his ever-smiling face, and squeezed him until his fingers hurt.

19

Truth

Daniels – Mohawk long since wilted with sweat – sat trapped on the edge of his bed, fear burning inside him like a stoked brazier. He was cleaning his rifle with melodic swipes of an oiled rag, trying to draw his mind from the piss-ache in his belly with the song of fabric on steel.

His torn ear thrummed painfully, its swollen heat creeping inside his head and blocking out sound, and his brain felt hot and itchy. He thought of ice melting on his boiling skin and imagined drilling into his skull – releasing the pressure in a great hissing burst.

Sep's face danced in his mind.

Daniels scratched his ear and carried on cleaning the gun, trying to ignore the crow at his window. But it tapped the glass with the pellet lodged in its eye socket, and he heard a cruel voice in his mind whisper that most poisonous of things.

The truth about himself. About the person he was.

Daniels wept. Reluctantly at first, then uncontrollably, smothering his face in the pillow as shame filled him like dirty oil.

The bird shuffled its gleaming feathers as he pissed into the mattress.

'Daniels doesn't miss,' he whispered, tears leaking from tight-shut eyes. 'Daniels doesn't miss.'

20

Maguire

Aileen Maguire listened to the radio without focus, its words a shapeless blanket around her. Though it was past midnight she had not yet gone to bed. Instead she sat stiffly in the lounge, her husband's chair beside her – empty but for the pale shade that lived on the edge of her sight.

The small room was neat and warm, decorated in consumptive florals that had browned with age, like old blood. Maguire's empty glass had warmed in her hand. She rolled it, following the syrupy wisps of alcohol on its sides and wondering if she could stop herself refilling it before sleep eventually came.

If it came.

Rain lashed the window. Maguire took a deeper breath and felt – as she often did, sitting in the little room – tight and sore, like her skin had dried and shrunk on her bones. She thought of the school and the flash of violence in the corridor – thought of Sep, and the likeness he bore to a headstrong, clever girl who'd attended Hill Ford High more than forty years ago, and never left.

She thought of Shelley Webster – dead now, like Lizzie and Morgan. Shelley's daughter hadn't said much on the phone, just that her mother liked to stay out late and that she'd always kept her hair long. It was awful, she'd said again, before the phone fell on to the cradle.

Maguire allowed her thoughts to mellow.

Shelley's hair.

She gripped her glass tighter.

Of the five who had been to the box, three were dead: Morgan, lung cancer in '68; Lizzie, a heart attack in '76 – events that had blown mortality's cold breath down the back of her neck. And, with each death, a new crow had come. The old pair were there last night – watching with sharp, unmistakable eyes.

That morning, a third had appeared – right before the phone call from Brooklyn.

Shelley had always wanted to go to America. Now she was dead – killed on the New York subway.

Maguire set her lips, flattened her thin hair, stood.

And froze.

There was a noise at the other end of the hall. It was coming from the old study – the scratch and wriggle of tiny movements against stone.

She peered into the gloom beyond the lamp.

Another scratch came from the study.

'There's a bird in the chimney again,' she said quietly.

'You should take a pot,' said her husband's shade. 'I used to catch them in a pot.'

The scratching stopped for a moment, and she found herself leaning away from the door. Then it came again, quicker and more frantic.

Maguire's skin squeaked on her glass.

'It might die. Remember the seagull that got stuck up there.'

'I remember,' said the shade. 'Take care, love.'

'Bloody birds,' she muttered.

She went to the kitchen, took a small pot from the stand and walked along the corridor, each step massive in the silence.

The noise stopped when she touched the study door. She paused, listening to the sounds of the building: stone groaning in the wind, the gurgle of guttering and spat of rain. She leaned on the handle.

The study had been her husband's room. It might have been years since she'd been in, and the door was swollen tight in the frame.

The lock gave way.

Maguire tumbled into the room and stood still, listening through the dark. Then she raised the pot and clicked on the dazzling bulb.

Nothing. Just the calm of a room lying undisturbed beneath time and dust – but she felt fear, animal and sharp, raise its snout in her belly.

The bulb snapped out in a shower of breaking glass, and she yelped.

Steadying herself against the wall, she waited for her eyes to adjust to the sudden dark and for her breathing to slow.

Some noiseless thing moved in the black. Its paper whisper was *almost* smothered by the roaring silence, a flutter she felt more than heard, like the rattle of a train below the ground.

Then the scratching came again – small and trapped, like a hatching lizard – and her heart beat into her mouth.

Inch by inch, she forced herself to kneel beside the hearth, touch the flagstone base and listen, every sinew tensed for flight. She crouched until her knees hurt, listening to the wind snag on the chimney and her heart thump on her bones.

She hoped it was a bird up there – but some buried instinct howled that it was not.

'I'll get the pole,' Maguire said, startled by her voice in the silence. She tried not to think of the thing in the chimney, only of the hooked pole she'd used to fish out the seagull's maggoty corpse.

She stood, fists clenched.

The grate exploded with soot and she fell back, knocking her head against the bookcase and smashing a vase. She spluttered to her knees and peered through the cloud towards the settling pile of coal dust.

There were no wings, no spread feathers, no sharp little feet. The soot had fallen in a lump, gathered round something. But it was not a bird.

She ground the grit between her teeth, then gripped the pot's handle and blew on the dark powder.

A dark, furry lump, no more than a foot long, lay on the stone, little arms and legs spread at odd angles.

'What in God's name?' whispered Maguire.

She lifted it free, knocking the dust into the grate.

A soiled, wet doll stared out from under the grime. Its face was twisted by fire, its hair burned away. She brushed off more dust, found the puckered, broken smile, and the half-shut, gleaming green eyes.

Sadie. Her childhood doll.

Her sacrifice.

A thin, translucent skin covered Sadie's soot-black body, stretched tight and threaded by dark, spider-leg veins.

'What the hell is –'

Sadie's eyes fluttered as her head – the lashes burned away, the scalp scorched bare and black – rolled towards Maguire.

She dropped the doll and tried to cry out, but her breath would not come and her voice would not work.

Sadie righted herself, wobbled on her little legs – then came at her.

Maguire *screamed*.

The crows settled on the windowsill as she kicked and fought, tasting the salt of Sadie's skin as the little hands – sharpened by fire and tasting of rot – forced themselves between her teeth.

Maguire's vision blurred. Her head filled with a sluggish heat through which the crows' glass-tapping beaks fell like rain, and she closed her eyes, the muscles loosening on her bones . . .

And, just as her life ebbed away, the doll was ripped from her face in an explosion of light, oxygen filled her chest like liquid fire – and darkness took her.

21

Cats

It had been dark when the cats came to the box. Now, in the darkness before dawn, they prowled around it with tail-flicks and swivelling ears, pawing at the dropped toys, the green pearls of their eyes lit by speckles of moonlight. Every one of their little bodies whined with tension, like a scream held on the edge of release, and the hungry sound of their throats hummed like an engine buried in the dirt.

Above them, three crows watched.

When the first cat darted forward the others leaped yowling in pursuit. A hundred tongues found the rot on the box's stone, and they greened their lips and chins in a busyness of slicking spit.

When the first cat found the runner's blood it gave a strangled cry that drew the others' claws and teeth – and a few fell into the box.

Blood speckling their eager faces, they leaped and wailed as the roots curled in, closing the lid, the sliver of sunlight vanishing with a thud, trapping them inside with the trickle of crimson that had drawn them there.

The cats outside licked the stone, and the crows' bright eyes watched from the trees.

22

Morning

Sep woke before his alarm, had a scalding shower and burst a spot on his chin. Which was all totally normal. Except that it wasn't.

Yesterday he'd woken up with his world in order: his mum was well, his exams were over, his boarding school application was nearly complete. No obstacles. Everything he'd worked for.

And now what?

His mum was getting sick again.

He was bunking off school with the others.

And his teddy bear was trying to kill him.

He dressed slowly, sniffing his Vader T-shirt as he pulled it on, clipping his Walkman on to his belt and dropping the headphones around his neck.

The house was blinking sleepily, tidy and still in dawn's soft glow. His mum was in bed, and had yet to wake up. Sep looked at the windows and imagined Barnaby at the glass, his eyes glowing like green coals.

He felt, unexpectedly, alone. After *years* of living with only his thoughts yesterday had shaken something inside him, and he found himself fishing Arkle's phone number from his jeans.

He dialled it in, waited for the clicks to finish – then dropped the phone in its cradle and went into the kitchen. It was too early: Arkle would be in bed, or stuffing himself with cereal in front of the TV, and it would be hard to explain an early-morning call to Mrs Hooper.

Through the window he saw long, furry ears peeking out from behind a shrub, and he threw the fox a piece of bread out of the window. Then he made himself breakfast – a bowl of Ghostbusters cereal and some juice – and hid another slice of bread in his school bag.

There was a hologram on the cereal box. He tilted it back and forth as he ate, catching the spindly ghost in loops of yellow, blue and red, his stomach churning as he thought about detention with Daniels. By the time his mum came downstairs he'd finished his juice, and the cereal's milk was syrupy and warm.

'Morning,' said his mum, peering as though her face was an ill-fitting mask. 'I didn't hear you getting up.'

'I was awake early.'

'Eating rubbish, I see.'

Sep pushed a cereal puff around with his spoon and watched it fall apart. 'Are you feeling OK?'

His mum flicked the kettle on, then turned and gave him a bleary smile.

'Yes,' she said deliberately, like she hadn't heard him properly and was guessing an answer.

'All right. I'm going to school.'

'So early? What's going on?'

'Nothing, I just can't be late again.'

His mum gulped from a glass of water.

'Maguire?' she said.

'Pardon?'

'I asked if it was Mrs Maguire again.'

Sep nodded.

'She was there when I was at school, and she was the same then,' said his mum.

Her police radio crackled. He tried to listen beyond the static, straining his deaf ear to find the dreadful noise that had come with Barnaby.

But there was nothing. His tooth didn't hurt either. 'You eating today?' he said, following the pattern of the tablecloth.

She held up a pack of biscuits.

'I'll have a few of these. It's just tummy trouble, I promise.'

Sep nodded, then pushed his bowl away. The morning sun had hit the cereal box at the perfect angle, and the ghost hologram on the side was screaming its rainbow at him.

'Where did Barnaby come from?' he said.

She looked up, a ginger snap gripped in her teeth.

'Your teddy? You got him when you were born.'

'From who?'

She bit off a chunk of biscuit and chewed it slowly, looking at his face. Sep kept his eyes on the ghost.

'I can't remember. Why are you asking?' she said eventually.

'I just . . . haven't seen him for a while. And I wondered.'

She took another bite of the biscuit and clicked off her walkie-talkie.

'Barnaby was your favourite toy. He went everywhere with you – until you gave him to me for company in the hospital. You put him away when I brought him home. Haven't seen him since.' She gave Sep a kind of frowny smile. 'I was always kind of grateful for that – he reminded me of being ill. Then I felt guilty.'

'Why?'

'It was your favourite toy. And I felt bad for you. It felt mean to be glad he was gone.'

'It's fine,' said Sep.

'I wonder where that teddy is,' his mum said, crossing to the sink to top up her water. 'Might be worth some money – practically an antique now.'

'He could be anywhere,' said Sep, looking outside and feeling a coil of tension in his guts.

'Do you want a lift today? I'm off this morning, I don't mind.'

'No, it's OK, I've got loads of time.'

She pulled up his chin, so they were face to face.

'You don't have to worry, really. I'm not . . . but there is something I wanted to talk to –'

But Sep was staring past her, at the big black birds scrabbling in the treetops of the garden.

He leaped to his feet.

'Mum, I need to go.'

'What's wrong?' she said, turning to follow his eyes, puzzled and afraid.

'Nothing! It's fine. I just need to get there early. I –'

'Sep, wait! Sit down a minute, we should talk. I'm sorry, just –'

But Sep was already at the door, swinging it behind him, the hinges' creak drowning her words.

Outside the morning was cloudless and cool: the sky a flat blue above the trees, the sun's glare behind the mountain. He closed his eyes and breathed out, letting his heart settle.

Then he opened his eyes and saw them.

Crows. Three of them – staring blindly at the house.

No, not at the house, he realized.

At *him*.

And now that he was outside he could hear the velvet rasp of feathers.

All with his deaf ear.

The noise made his bones grind together, as though his joints were packed with sand, and it swelled through his head into his rotten tooth. He bit down on the hot pain, clamped his headphones over his ears and clicked on the tape – Frankie, straight into the middle of 'Two Tribes' – cranked up the volume and turned his back on the birds.

The fox was sitting on the path, head cocked beneath its swivelling ears, its little face sharp and alert.

Sep went to his bag and held out the piece of bread.

The ears froze, and the fox shifted on its paws.

'Come on,' said Sep. 'You always take whatever I give you. Come *on*, I'm in a hurry.'

He crouched down, his skateboard under his knee, holding the slice further in front of him.

The fox stepped forward, its muscles bunched so that its paws hardly touched the ground, ready to flee.

'I am glad the others are back,' Sep told it, surprising himself. 'But I still have to leave. I *have* to. Living on the mainland's all I've ever wanted.'

The fox took another step and waited, front paw held aloft, leaning from him in readiness of flight.

'And this will work. Making new sacrifices – obeying the rules. That must be what the box wants. Maybe then Barnaby will leave me alone.'

The fox darted forward and took the bread from his hand – and for the second it was held between them, Sep felt the animal's strength and the pungent heat of its fur.

He shot out a hand and brushed its chest, feeling its warmth with the tips of his fingers.

The fox broke for the trees as though stung, bread swinging in its mouth.

'And maybe it'll fix my mum,' he said as its tail vanished.

He boarded all the way to school, his Walkman blaring unnoticed as his mind boiled. A steady, sea-smelling wind rattled the high leaves, filling the air with a rattlesnake hiss.

The tide was in, a tight seam against the grass, narrowing the island like a shrunken jumper.

He looked for the mainland, but could not see it.

23

Caught

The bell was still a few minutes away, and the playground was heaving with bare-armed kids. Sep wove through them, away from registration and towards the trees on the edge of the hockey pitch, squinting through the sun for the red spikes of Daniels' hair.

Instead he saw Arkle flicking a hacky-sack between his feet. Lamb stood beside him – hockey stick strapped to her back like a warrior's sword, headscarf tight on her wrist.

'I thought you'd chicken out,' she said, snapping a pink bubble at him. Her face was broader than yesterday, more angular. Even her eyes had changed – and there was something familiar about them. Sep tried not to stare.

'And good morning to you too,' he said. 'Did you sleep well, Darren?'

'Eventually,' said Arkle, balancing the sack on his toe, 'after one of my "special moments".'

Sep and Lamb screwed up their faces, then met each other's eyes.

'Why would I chicken out?' said Sep.

'Come on,' she said. 'Playing hooky? Running around the woods? It's not exactly your scene, is it?'

'It used to be.'

She made a face.

'Well, the running around the woods bit.'

Lamb cracked her knuckles.

'I'm looking forward to this.'

'You are?' said Arkle. 'Oh, me too. I mean, it'll be so cool to be –'

'Oh, yeah: once we sort this out I'll never have to speak to you dweebs again, and it can't come soon enough. And when I find out *who* it was that broke the rules, I'll hurt them.'

Arkle stuck out a petted lip at her.

'Don't mind Lambert. She's pissed off because her hair won't sit properly.'

'It's *backcombed*, asshole,' said Lamb, folding in another stick of gum.

'You manage to sleep?' Arkle asked, lighting a cigarette.

'Kind of,' said Sep, wiping sweat from his face. 'I mean, I stayed awake for a bit, and my mum was –'

He bit off the sentence.

'What's up with your mum?' said Lamb.

'Nothing, she's fine. She was just . . . working late.'

'She getting sick again?'

'No!' said Sep quickly. 'Here, have you noticed the crows?'

'Yes!' said Arkle. 'What *is* that?'

'There were three of them watching me last night – they were on my windowsill for hours. *And* they were outside my house this morning. They have to be connected, right?'

Lamb shrugged.

'I've seen them too. Who cares?'

' "Who *cares*?" ' said Arkle. 'Have you not seen *The Birds*?'

'Nope.'

'Well, neither have I . . . I mean, it's in black and white. But it's a horror film about birds! Birds are *mental*.'

'You worried about them?' said Lamb, nodding at Sep.

'Well, it's weird. I mean, how come there's always the same number? And how come we're *all* seeing them?' He paused for a moment, then added, 'I think they're what's hurting my tooth.'

'Your tooth?' said Lamb, wrinkling her nose. 'How does that work?'

'I don't know. I just know my toothache gets much worse when the birds are around.'

'Maybe eat less sugar, dude,' said Arkle.

'And listen,' Sep went on. 'Last night I was dreaming about crows climbing inside this empty skin –' he tried to say it was his mother's skin, that the black eyes were hers, wide and flat with painkillers, but couldn't find the words. 'And when I woke up Barnaby was there. And so were you.'

Lamb went pale, then turned away and blew another bubble.

'You're not going all Hadley on us, are you?' said Arkle, blowing a thin cloud of smoke above his head.

'What do you mean?'

'Spooky-dreamy-mumbo-jumbo. Wait, here she is! Let's ask her: Princess Leia, can you interpret September's freaky dream?'

'What?' said Hadley, lifting away enormous round headphones.

'Sep joined your dream gang,' said Arkle.

Hadley looked at Sep intently, and fanned her face in the heat. She was wearing another white glove, this one lacy and fingerless, on her left hand.

'What was it?' she said.

'Crows pushing into an empty skin, like a person's empty skin,' he said, his face colouring.

'Have you noticed the crows too?' asked Arkle.

Hadley nodded.

'This morning,' she said, 'there were three of them, outside my house.'

'Right,' said Sep. A shiver gripped his spine.

'Right what?' said Mack, joining the group.

'Crows,' said Hadley. 'Have you seen them?'

'Yeah, they're big black birds. Why?'

'We know what they *are*, numbnuts,' said Lamb. 'But there's three in particular. They're, like, following us.'

'Oh. Then no.'

'What're you eating?' said Arkle.

'Muffin,' Mack mumbled indistinctly.

Arkle shook his head.

'You might look like a steak in a T-shirt, Golden Boy, but I want to be there when your metabolism slows down. It'll happen in, like, a second – BAM! You'll burst out like Jabba the Hutt. You can keep Hadley on a chain.'

'Shut up!' said Hadley.

Sep clenched his jaw.

'Where's your keeper?' Arkle asked Mack, grinning.

'What?'

'Daniels.'

Mack's face darkened.

'He says he's sick.'

'Really?' said Sep. He felt immediately lighter.

'It's your turn today,' said Lamb, pointing at Mack. 'Are you worried?'

Mack flashed her a perfect square smile.

'Not so far. And we're all together now – we can handle it.'

Lamb rolled her eyes. 'OK – we're all here, so let's go. I've got a surprise for you dweebs.'

'Hang on,' said Sep.

'Why?' said Hadley. 'We need to *go* – the bell's gone; the teachers will start their late-coming rounds.'

'Exactly! What's the problem?' snapped Lamb.

'I forgot to bring a new sacrifice!' said Sep, his stomach sinking. 'I was so distracted this morning, I left the house without one. I'm going to have to go back home.'

Lamb dragged a hand over her face.

'Fine!' she growled. 'But you'll have to do it *right now*, because we need to get to –'

'Get to where?' said Tench, leaning out from behind a tree, the sunlight glowing redly through his ears.

'Class, sir,' said Arkle quickly.

Sep blinked. The cigarette had disappeared as if by magic.

'Wonderful. Strange place to find you all . . . together,' said Tench, frowning at Sep. 'Another detention, I think, Darren. I could see your puffs of smoke from my office. Come along then, the bell's gone for registration.'

'But, sir, we can't,' said Lamb, slapping Arkle's head as Tench turned away. 'We have to –'

'What do you mean?' said Tench, puzzled. 'School's started.'

'But –!'

'But what, Miss Lambert?'

Tench turned to them, his broad face impassive, his eyes wide. Sep's heart sank.

'Nothing,' said Lamb heavily. Then, as Tench strode off, she turned and hissed: 'First break, all of you head back to my farm.'

'What?' said Sep. 'Why?'

'Come on, you lot,' called Tench, hurrying them on with sweeps of his huge hands.

They shuffled forward to catch him, then headed five abreast towards the side entrance. Lamb went first, letting the door swing closed in Sep's face. Arkle and Mack followed her, and Sep found himself holding the door for Hadley.

Looking over her shoulder at the distant forest, he tried to breathe out the knot in his stomach.

'This is a disaster, isn't it?' he said. 'I mean, think about what the box could be doing. We need to get there, like, *now*.'

She nodded.

'We'll just have to leave at break, like Lamb said.'

As she moved past he tried desperately to think of something to say, and blurted: 'What were you listening to?'

'It's a mixtape,' she said, looking fondly at her Walkman as though the bands were waving through the little window. 'Fleetwood Mac, Wham!, Hall & Oates –'

'Yuck,' said Sep, before he could stop himself.

She raised an eyebrow. 'Snob much?'

'I didn't mean –' Sep said, blushing. 'I just don't –'

'I love Hall & Oates. They're like a mix of new wave and soul. They're fun, and . . . sincere.'

She looked at him with her deep, warm eyes. Sep felt his defensive coil being stripped away with a little squeeze in his stomach, and opened his mouth to speak.

To his surprise, what came out was: 'Have you seen the comet yet?'

'*Yeah*,' she said. 'It was amazing. It's actually changed the way I think. You realize how tiny we are, and it makes me feel –'

'Insignificant?'

She frowned at him, then smiled.

'No,' she said. 'Not at *all*. Think about it: you, September Hope, cleverest boy in school. You're standing there, with all your skin shedding and hair growing and the blood rushing around. You're, like, a miracle –'

Sep realized he was leaning in towards her and tried to straighten up without her noticing.

'– think about it,' she went on. 'Every ancestor you've ever had avoided car accidents and wars and disease and . . . sabre-tooth tigers! And they had the *exact* babies they needed to, so you could exist, because they were your grandparents and great-great-great-great grandparents. Imagine if a cave person relative of yours had slipped at the wrong time and fallen off a cliff – all their children and their children's children would never have existed.'

She flopped her head on one side and looked up at the sky behind him, imagining the comet tearing through space.

'We're all little miracles,' she said, 'everything about us: all our stupid habits and our jokes and our weird faces, on a spinning ball that's a perfect distance from the sun. And now here we are, you and me, sitting on top of a million years of history.'

She smiled again, then turned into the lobby.

Sep followed her, wondering if she could hear the thud of his heart, and trying to remember how to breathe.

24

Change

Dust hung in the sunbeams. They were sitting in their usual seats, and Sep was shocked to feel oddness in his solitude, in having found it strange to part with Hadley and the others at the door. He'd never gone to class with anyone, never made plans afterwards. There were only ever lessons, work and homework.

He shook his head, felt the invisible barrier settle around him as it always did, and let his mind shift into learning gear.

Mrs Woodbank was moving around the room.

'Anyone?' she said. 'I know it's still early, but come *on*. You're not little kids any more –' She snatched a scrap of paper from an outstretched hand. 'Passing notes *again*, Stephanie? What's so urgent it couldn't wait? "I defo want to winch him up ASAP." What does that even mean?'

'As soon as possible,' said Arkle.

'Not the *acronym*, you – Just focus, all right? *Think*, and stop behaving like children.'

Sep looked at the poem. It was the same one they'd been looking at the day before, but its little threads and connections were gone, like his head was an Etch-a-Sketch shaken to grey blankness by the terror of the previous night. He turned to his jotter, read the words he'd written:

Life. Growth. Change.

He wrote over *Change* until the letters were thick, shiny dents in the page.

Hadley was watching him again. This time he held her eyes, just for a moment, before looking away.

Long enough to see her smile.

'We did this *yester*day,' Mrs Woodbank was saying. She rubbed her yellowed fingers together, as though asking for money.

Don't ask me, thought Sep. *Ask someone else. Teach them something, for God's sake. I've already got too much to think about.*

'September?' said Mrs Woodbank.

'*Septic, Septic, Septic,*' chanted the boys.

Sep took a deep breath.

'It's about life, growth and change.'

'Yes!' she said brightly. 'See, class – now we have some themes to go on, and that's really going to help us unlock this poem . . .'

Sep eased back in his seat. He could see the puffs of green forest above the town, like mould in a forgotten mug. They would be there soon, the five of them, in the clearing with the box at its heart – cold stone from which Barnaby had climbed after years in the dark.

'There,' said Mrs Woodbank, writing Sep's words on the board and drawing a circle round each of them.

'Hey, Lamb,' said Manbat. 'What's with your face? You break your nose or something?'

Mack slapped his arm. Lamb faced forward, saying nothing.

'Hey, Big Bird, did you catch deafness from Septic? I said what's –'

'*Wayne Bruce*,' hissed Mrs Woodbank, 'I won't have talk like that in my classroom!'

'Yeah, shut up, asshole,' said Arkle.

Mrs Woodbank's face went pink.

'Darren!' she shouted. 'Go and stand outside! How *dare* you use language like that in here!'

'But Manbat was –'

'I don't care! *I* will deal with Wayne, not you. There's no excuse for that kind of behaviour!'

'He deserved it, miss,' said Lamb.

'Yeah,' said Mack.

Everyone turned to look at him. It was the first time he'd ever spoken in class.

'Macejewski?' said Mrs Woodbank. 'What's got *into* you all today?'

Arkle rose and squeezed along the back row, stepping carefully through the chair-swingers on his way to the door.

'What's your problem, teeth-boy?' whispered Manbat. 'You hot for Big Bird or something?'

Sep saw it coming, but by the time Woodbank had shouted his name Arkle had already burst Manbat's nose and raised his fist to strike again. Sep was knocked over in the rush to gather round, and by the time order was restored a grey-faced Mr Tench had arrived.

The room smelled of adrenaline, and Sep's heart was thumping. Hadley had come to stand next to him, and he moved closer to her.

'Are you OK?' he whispered.

She nodded, then backed away as Arkle made another attempt to break free.

'Nice going, dickhead,' said Manbat, his quiff broken and squint, nose bleeding over his lips. 'We'll get suspended for this!'

'Good,' said Arkle, his eyes wild.

But Tench had not so much as looked at them since entering the room. He spoke to Mrs Woodbank in a quick whisper before leaving with Arkle in tow, catching Sep's eye briefly on his way to the door.

Sep looked at Hadley, who was holding her head as though she might pass out – then at Lamb, who nodded.

Something was very wrong.

Back at his desk, Sep looked outside. The town was bright and normal, but the woodland that tumbled towards it seemed to have grown, like a muscle flexed in anger.

'Right,' said Mrs Woodbank, once they'd all returned to their seats and Manbat had been taken to the nurse. 'Let's move on to something else, shall we? Macejewski, could you please open the windows? It's got a little tense this morning, so let's try to clear the air.'

Sep could see she was worried by whatever Tench had said. Her eyes kept flicking towards the door.

'*Hamlet*,' she said, dropping a pile of yellow books on to

the front desk, their spines torn and broken, a few still covered in wallpaper and gift wrap. 'I think we might have had enough of poetry for now. So here we are – a procrastinating, self-involved youth with daddy issues. Would anyone like to volunteer to read a part? September?'

'Pardon, miss?' said Sep.

'Would you like to read a part?'

'No thank you, miss.'

She scowled at him.

'Yes, *thank you* – you can be our Hamlet, and perhaps . . .'

Sep switched off while she handed out the other parts, his book closed in front of him, and watched the waggle of Hadley's pen as she drew on the desk.

'We're starting with Miss Lambert and Mr Ashton as Bernardo and Francisco then,' said Woodbank, looking at the door again and fidgeting. 'Miss Lambert, if you could read the stage directions too, thank you, and try to *enunciate*, people – nothing spoils the bard more than a surly teenage monotone.'

Lamb sighed, then ran her finger down the page to the start of the text.

Sep watched her brows knot in concentration. The room had grown warmer since the fight, even with the windows open. His skin crept with the heat.

And the pain was swelling in his bad tooth.

He turned to Hadley. She was already looking at him, her eyes wide with terror.

There was something in the classroom.

Everyone felt it, Sep realized – the smush of chatter had pitched a key higher, and he looked in panic for a sign of Barnaby.

Lamb caught his eye. He nodded, and she bit her lips.

'Now, please, Miss Lambert,' said Mrs Woodbank.

Lamb sighed.

'*I saw him again today*,' she read in a surly monotone. '*He's so handsome. I watched him finish training, but he didn't see me –*'

Sep's head exploded – his ear and mouth alight with pain, his guts seizing tight as he realized what was happening, his jaw shut in agony.

'What *are* you reading?' said Mrs Woodbank, pulling her focus from the classroom door. 'Has someone graffitied that book? Read the actual *play*, come on.'

Lamb screwed up her face and turned the page to check what was there. The rest of the class did likewise, and Sep forced his head to turn towards Hadley. Her eyes were brimming with tears.

'*But he didn't see me*,' Lamb carried on. '*So I watched him gather in the little cones. I think his eyes –*'

'Stop,' Sep managed between his locked teeth.

'*– and when I got home I thought about him again and imagined his arms closing round me. I really think I love him, diary. I do. I love Mack! And –* Oh –'

'Hadley!' shouted Sep as she ran from the room. 'Hadley! Wait!'

'Oh, shit,' said Lamb.

'What the hell is going on?' said Mrs Woodbank, grabbing Lamb's copy. 'What are you reading?'

She flicked through the book, took in the spidery writing and the misspelled words.

'What the hell is going on?' she said again, as the door slammed behind Sep and the class erupted in cruel, braying laughter.

25

Tracked

The sun soaked into the leaves. They glowed, luminous and pale, unmoving in the breathless air. The clearing boiled with stuck heat, its floor a carpet of moist, dead things.

Roxburgh shifted his weight to his other boot. His knees were screaming their age, but he kept still, working the beads of his rosary through his fingers.

The flies had come in their thousands, and they flowed like water – blacking the red, spoiling flesh. Above them sat the three crows, watching with eyes like dark glass, white bone gleaming through torn, dog-bitten skin.

Three.

Roxburgh spat. First there was Morgan, then Lizzie, and now Shelley. Three.

He turned to the box and moved his hands on the gun.

Roots as thick as his wrist had curled round the sacrifice box. The stone was wet. The wetness was red and black and brown. At its edge rotted leaves were packed with the forest's mammalian dead: fleshy piles of peeled, sticky skin. Occasionally one of the birds wing-squeaked its way across the clearing, striping through columns of sunlight, its shadow moving on the stone like a tongue running over dry lips.

A wind blew. A root twisted in the air. A bloodied leg kicked, once, then was still.

Roxburgh's gamekeeper instincts, bright and alert, shrieked of danger. He dropped his rosary in his pocket, placed his hand on the shotgun's stock and waited.

The wind blew his hair across his face and moved the clearing's dead lumps with a damp, rancid sound – a sound of terrible, insistent rhythm. He thought there might be a voice there, if he knew how to listen. Above his head the crows shuffled their feathers.

There were movements inside the box now, and it clicked with fluid.

Roxburgh pressed more tobacco into his lip and thought about the night before. It had been Aileen's own doll, no doubt about that – he'd never forget its little fire-soft face, and it had the rotten stink of the ground.

The doll had been trying to kill her. It had been so strong Roxburgh had had to plant his boots on Aileen's shoulders to pull it free. And it was still out there, some-where.

So he'd risen at dawn and spent hours tracking it through the chilly light, only to end up here, where he'd always known he would.

A tiny hand came out of the box.

Even though he'd been expecting it, he breathed in too quickly and spluttered as spit entered his lungs.

The dogs began to growl, and Roxburgh quieted them with his palm.

Another hand followed, then a soot-black head, and Sadie lifted herself into the clearing. She was sticky with blood, and the flies fell quickly upon her.

An evil thing, thought Roxburgh, gripping his rosary. *Save me, Lord.*

Sadie screamed, a violent sound of tearing flesh. The flies rose from their feast in a great buzzing cloud, then settled and fed once more.

She's hunting, Roxburgh realized, biting through his tongue as the doll began to prowl, swinging her head from side to side like a hound after a scent.

Something else climbed from the box then, something white and thin: a puppet moving on wind-chime legs, and dragging strings darkened by corruption and rot.

Here'n'now.

Roxburgh's mouth filled with thin, coppery blood as he looked at his old sacrifice.

He grabbed the dogs by the collar and stood, ready to run, preparing in his mind the barricades he would build round his shack – when he lost his footing and stumbled towards the box, crying out over the patter of the doll's footsteps as she bore down on him, followed by the whisper of strings.

26

Hadley

'Wait!' shouted Sep as Hadley's bright hair vanished down the stairs, scattering a couple of first-year girls carrying pillars of books.

He jumped on to the landing, jarring his knees and swinging from the bannister.

'Hadley, wait!'

'Leave me alone!' she shouted, turning to look at him before she disappeared between the fire doors.

Sep squeezed through the gap and caught her. She dropped her head and breathed thickly, embarrassment and anger catching in her throat.

'I'm sorry,' he said.

She nodded, hands over her face. The sun, still low over the trees, was trapped behind her head.

'It was in my copy of the play too,' she said. 'I'd read it all before Lamb even started, and I wanted to stop her, but . . . it was even my *handwriting*.'

She turned to him, her face hidden in shadow. He smelled her smell as she moved, and felt his chest tighten.

Then he saw how stooped she was – how empty of strength.

'Are you all right?' he said.

She nodded.

'Just . . . since yesterday, I've been so *tired*. And just now, in class, I thought I was going to pass out.'

'We'll fix it, all of it – your diary and Barnaby and Lamb's face.'

Her eyes widened.

'You've noticed that too?'

'What?'

'Lamb. The way she looks.'

'Yeah. Obviously – she looks totally different. Her whole face has changed.'

'Has she said anything?'

Sep snorted.

'To me? No. She can barely look at me.'

'You know who she's starting to look like?' said Hadley, checking behind her.

'Who?'

'Her *mum*.'

With a chill Sep remembered Mrs Lambert's strong, handsome face, her deep eyes and her broad smile; then thought about how Lamb had changed in the last few days.

'*That's* who it is,' he said. 'She was always like her dad, and it's been so long since I've . . . seen her mum. Oh my God, *exactly* like her, right?'

Hadley nodded, then took a deep breath.

'I know, that's why she seems pissed off – she's upset. She keeps seeing her mum all the time.' She wiped her eyes with the heel of her hand, then looked at him. 'Why did you come after me?'

'I just didn't want you to be . . . Everything in the room felt sore, so I ran after you.'

'*You* ran out of class without asking permission? Weird shit really is happening.'

He laughed, folded his arms behind his back and looked at his shoes. They stood between the fire doors and the sports ground, raised classroom voices meeting the burp of sheep and the rattle of tractors: murmurs of island life that somehow continued while their world fell apart.

'Why have you been watching me lately?' he said.

She shrugged.

'I just like watching you in class, sometimes.'

'What?'

'I said I like watching you in class,' she said, louder, leaning towards his good ear.

'Oh,' he said, hot lead filling his veins. 'Why?'

She shrugged.

'It helps me think.'

'How?'

'Just . . . your face. It goes all clear when you're working, and it helps me concentrate.'

Sep couldn't think of anything to say. He just looked at her baseball boots, following the lines of the ink drawings she'd made on the canvas.

'I always have, you know,' she said after a moment. 'It's just you only noticed in the past few days.'

'Oh.'

She sighed and watched the gull-shadows spiral on the grass, letting her head drop to one side.

'Should we go back in?'

'Maybe not yet. Just another minute.'

She sat on the wall, and he hovered beside her.

'So everyone knows,' she said, crumbling stone as she pulled some moss free.

'About what?' said Sep.

'About my diary . . . and me liking Mack. I started keeping it when I was getting bullied, and it was *four* years ago. I was just a kid – and then I sacrificed it so it would disappear.'

Sep felt a jab of nausea and smothered it, clicking the Walkman's buttons.

But she shuffled closer to him – and he let them go.

'Well, it doesn't matter what people think,' he said. 'Who cares?'

'You care.'

'How'd you work that out?'

'Well, you obviously do,' she said, 'otherwise you wouldn't be leaving.'

Sep thought about it for a moment.

'They think I'm an asshole,' he said eventually.

'Everyone kind of . . . hates everyone. It's just school. Do you like *them*?'

'Well . . . no.'

'So who cares?'

'I said I don't –'

'But you *do*. And you shouldn't. Mostly they're just jealous because you're so brainy. But it doesn't matter. People think I'm weird because my mum's Korean and I dye my hair. People dump on you for whatever you do, but you don't need to run away from it. If you're strong,' she continued, closing her eyes as though convincing herself, 'they can't get at you, even if they try.'

Sep watched the way the sun glowed on her skin, then turned away as she opened her eyes. He ran his tongue over his bad tooth, scanning the treeline for any sign of Barnaby.

'This is getting to all of us though, isn't it?'

She nodded.

'But it doesn't matter, I know it doesn't – what's happening is so much more serious than my old diary. If the box can do this to us, what else can it do? We could *really* get hurt.'

She was twisting the glove on her left hand. Sep noticed another dark stain on the fabric. 'What's on –'

'I'm fine,' she said. 'My bike, this morning – some leaves got stuck under my tyre and I fell. It's OK, I always fall.'

Sep remembered: Hadley falling into a rock pool and getting seaweed stuck in her hair; Hadley missing the seat of a park bench and landing on the ground; Hadley tripping and landing in his arms one night when they were walking home – even though there'd been nothing to trip over.

'*Right*,' she said, standing quickly and shuffling the feeling back into her feet. 'Let's go back to class.'

'We don't have to,' said Sep quickly, 'if you don't want to . . . Did you really fancy Mack that summer?'

She blinked at the unexpected question.

'Well, yeah. I think most of the girls . . . I mean, you know –'

'Let's pretend I don't.'

She shrugged.

'Everyone did.'

'Do they still?' said Sep, gripping his voice to keep it steady. He looked down, focused on the pitch's white-painted grass.

She laughed.

'Pretty much. What was it Darren called him this morning? A steak in a T-shirt?'

She turned and headed for the door, her shoulders bobbing in a deep sigh.

'But you're a vegetarian,' said Sep.

She laughed, then turned serious.

'Do you have to leave?'

'Yeah,' he said after taking a breath. 'I mean, why would I stay? Are *you* going to stay here forever?'

She looked past him, down to the tiny shops and paint-peeling signposts; to the pool-spotted rocks and the thin arc of pale sand.

'Definitely,' she said.

'Really?' he said. 'I mean, there's nothing here. And I want to be an engineer – I want to build things. What do you want to be when you grow up?'

She shrugged, then gave him a squint smile that spun the ground under his feet.

'Happy,' she said, then vanished through the door.

The bell rang, signalling the start of history class. Sep waited a moment, then followed her inside.

27

Ward Seven

They had polished the floor sometime that morning, and now sunlight bounced into her face.

Maguire tried to turn her head, but her neck was trapped in a thick, foam collar. She shut her eyes instead, watching the veins pulse in her eyelids. Nurses darted around, and she followed their movements by the squeak of their shoes.

She had no memory of the ambulance, or arriving at hospital. She remembered her husband's study, something exploding in the grate and . . . nothing. Just a deep, rotten stench and a small, misshapen face.

And now here she was, propped in a stiff bed on ward seven, plugged into a machine. Fire lit her throat whenever she swallowed. They had given her a cardboard tub to spit into, but she'd handed it back. Her head ached. They said it was her blood pressure, but she felt like she'd no blood left, like she was empty.

And tired – so, so tired.

Eventually she dozed, dreaming of her husband and cooking pots filled with birds; of a faceless child who spoke with Sep's voice – and of a small, wooden puppet named

Here'n'now, who laughed at things that weren't funny and waved at her with tiny hands.

As the sun climbed towards noon its glow dimmed on the floor, the corridor filled with the sky's pale light and a thread of drool spilled from the corner of her mouth.

She opened her eyes.

It was visiting time. Only a few folk had made it on a weekday morning, but the ward was warmed by the soft murmur of conversation.

'Would you like anything, Mrs Maguire?' said a nurse, a tray held in front of her.

'No thank you, dear,' said Maguire. Her voice came as a dry, hissing thing, like dead leaves.

'Are you sure I can't make you more comfortable? Cup of tea?'

Maguire shook her head, then winced.

'Too hot. It'd be like lava,' she said, narrowing her eyes at the pain. 'Tap water?'

'Of course.'

Maguire watched her go.

She let her eyes close again, gritting her teeth at the pain in her throat and letting herself drift away from the hospital towards the empty memories of the previous night.

Something stirred.

Thom, she thought suddenly. *Thom was there, in my house.*

Shoes squeaked towards her bed.

'Thank you, dear,' she said. 'I'm so thirsty, I can't – oh!'

A little girl was standing at the foot of the bed, hands behind her back.

'Who are you talking to?' she said.

'I *thought* I was talking to the nurse,' said Maguire. 'Who are you with?'

'Visiting my granny,' said the girl, pointing theatrically with one hand. 'What's wrong with you?'

'I've lost my patience,' sighed Maguire.

'What?'

'I'm not well. Go and see your granny now, off you pop.'

'Do you want to see my special friend?'

Maguire gave the girl a long blink.

'*Then* will you go?'

The girl nodded.

'All right. Who's your friend?'

'Her name's Jessica.'

'And where is Jessica? Behind your back?'

The girl nodded again, then grinned and produced a ragged, patchwork dolly.

'She's my favourite –'

But Maguire was already screaming, screaming though it burned her flesh, screaming even as the nurses pumped a sedative into her veins, her eyes wild and red – remembering in that instant the anger that had come for her, and the smell of Sadie's burnt skin.

-4

Visiting: 1941

Aileen answered the door on the third knock. Shelley, head wrapped tightly in a shawl, stood back from the step, her hand still in the air.

'Can I come in?' she said.

'It's nearly lunch,' said Aileen through the narrow gap. She heard the clatter of plates behind her and closed the door a little, embarrassed by the watery cabbage smell from the kitchen.

'Please. I'm sorry about all that, last week. I was — I didn't know about your dad's —'

'Come in if you're going to stand gabbing!' said Aileen, hushing Shelley with a flash of her eyes.

They tiptoed into her bedroom. Aileen saw that the pencil marks on the back of Shelley's legs were wobbly, and the tan of her liquid nylons was uneven. But she fixed her eyes upwards as Shelley turned round, resuming her hardest expression.

'Well, what do you want?'

'I'm sorry,' said Shelley again. 'We — Lizzie and me, and Morgan — we didn't mean to be so rude. If we'd known about —'

'Don't you mention my pa again,' snapped Aileen. 'Just tell me what you've come to say and be on your way.'

Shelley pursed her lips and squeezed her hands.

'Your room's always so neat,' she said, looking at the sharply made bed and the tidy bookshelves.

'Now,' said Aileen.

Shelley flushed and bowed her head. Her eyes were raw from crying, and her hands shook as she unwrapped the shawl from her head.

Aileen gasped, and clasped her hand to her mouth.

'It was a couple of nights after we went there, into the woods,' said Shelley. 'I was just brushing it, after a bath, and —' She choked on a sob — 'there were clumps coming away on my brush, like I was a moulting collie! At first I thought the Germans, you know: maybe they put something in the water? But when I went to see Lizzie her hair was fine, only —'

'Only what?' said Aileen, staring at the pocked, tufty surface of Shelley's bare scalp.

'She was so thin! Ever since she cursed her aunt with that box, she says she can't keep anything down — only the eggs from her chickens. Everything else comes from the ration book, and she can't keep the rations down! She's wasting away!'

'And you think *I'm* making this happen, do you?'

Shelley looked horrified.

'No! Lizzie thinks she's cursed herself, and I —' She covered her face — 'I think so too. We didn't do right by you, or the offering. If we'd known about —'

'I don't want your pity,' said Aileen quickly, then as her eyes filled she reached up and lifted Shelley's hands away. 'I just want your friendship, the way it was before your head got filled with boys and cities. When we told each other secret things.'

Shelley fell forward, wrapping her arms round Aileen's narrow shoulders. Aileen felt the soft skin of her head against her cheek.

'How's Morgan?' she said eventually.

'He's coughing non-stop: you'd think he had black lung. He says every breath is like the first time he tried smoking, and when he coughs it gets worse. He's miserable — can't hardly leave the house. You need to help us, Leen.'

'Me? What can I do?'

'You knew about it! You knew how it worked. It was —'

'But I don't know anything, not really,' said Aileen quickly, her voice urgent. 'I told you, I found the box by chance. So when the news came about my pa, I wanted you all back . . . and I somehow knew how to do it. An offering, made for each other, together. The strength we have in loving each other . . . it's the most powerful thing we have, when the world is tearing itself apart. Love. Just love. A sacrifice made for each other — made with love. That's all I know.'

'But how? How did you know?'

'A voice . . . spoke to me, like a waking dream. Those rules we said — I didn't make those up! They were spun out of my mind, like candyfloss. Like they'd been given to me.'

Shelley's eyes widened.

'By who?'

Aileen looked away.

'I don't know,' she said, taking a key from around her neck and unlocking her cupboard door. 'But now . . . now I don't think it was anyone friendly.'

She opened the door and stepped aside.

Shelley gasped, smothering her cry with her shawl.

'Is that –'

'Sadie,' said Aileen, her chest tightening as the little green eyes paced the closet's darkness with unblinking intensity. 'My doll. My offering.'

'But how –'

'A few nights ago,' said Aileen. 'The night before Thom's puppet climbed in through his window, and I'll bet a few nights after your hair –' She squeezed Shelley's hand and spoke more rapidly, relief tumbling with the words. 'They're coming in order. I found her on the front step, dirty and wet, like she'd walked from the forest. I tried burning her, but all it did was melt her face and scorch her hair. She's been watching me ever since. I can see the light of her eyes under the cupboard door. And every once in a while it winks out – just for a second. Like she's blinking.'

'Why?' said Shelley, her hands trembling. 'Why is this happening?'

'Because it was done wrong: we broke the box's rules and now it's angry. Even with me and Thom – even though we left our offerings, like we were supposed to.'

Sadie's face turned towards them, and Shelley shrieked. 'Close it! Close it, please!'

175

Aileen slammed the door and turned the key as Sadie took an uneven step forward, and Shelley fell into her arms again.

'Aileen?' shouted her mother. 'What's all that banging? You're supposed to be setting the table!'

'I'm coming! I'm just finding some music,' shouted Aileen, clicking on the wireless and filling the room with Glenn Miller's soft brass.

She beckoned Shelley closer.

'We need to put them back,' she whispered. 'I've been thinking about it ever since she arrived. We were meant to leave the offerings behind – so it must want them back.'

'I think so too,' said Shelley, wide-eyed and teary. 'I just . . . the thought of going back there, I don't think –'

'You can do it! We'll all go, together! We'll do what we meant to do in the first place.'

'All right,' said Shelley, shivering as she was bundled out of the door. 'All right. Today?'

'Yes. Mother's got Land Army at four, so meet me round back, under the big elm. And never mind your lock of hair, bring something else – something that makes you think happily of us together.'

'What do you mean?'

Aileen pressed her face to the narrow gap. The sun was high and bright behind Shelley's head.

'I think . . . I think the box has real power,' she said, 'and we could have borrowed that power with our offerings. But it only works if we follow its rules, and when we broke them I think it started . . . feeding on the bad feeling we made that day. I think we let it see our upset and pain – and our worst fears,' she added, brushing her fingers lightly over Shelley's head.

Shelley closed her eyes and took a deep breath.

'We're going to set it right,' said Aileen. 'We'll show it that we're real friends by giving it all the love we have — and keeping our promise to each other by following its damn rules.'

'Yes,' said Shelley, nodding tearfully. 'Yes, you're right. I do love you, Leen.'

'And I you, Shelley Webster.'

They smiled at each other.

'Aileen!' came the voice from the kitchen. 'The table!'

'Go!' said Aileen. 'And it'll be all right,' she added, squeezing Shelley's hand quickly before the door closed. 'We'll show that bloody thing what we're made of.'

28

Wobie

Wobie had eaten a bacon sandwich for breakfast – the ketchup was still bright on his shirt, like new-spilled blood – and unwisely opted for the paler tweed; dark circles were already spreading from his armpits into the stains of earlier sweat. His next cigar was tucked between his lips, wobbling as he muttered to himself.

Sep watched him dab his tongue on his fingers, wetting them just enough to tease the newsprint apart.

He'd sat in this seat hundreds of times, and knew it with his soul: the brownness, the heat, the dusty, clammy air and the textbooks; the yellow walls, from which drooped Kitchener's moustache and a curling world map with the British Empire shaded pink. Everything was the same.

Except today Hadley had sat next to him, and everything was different.

People kept looking over and whispering behind their hands. He sat straight, self-conscious and alert. Hadley ignored them all – just drew intricate patterns on her folder and looked at him every so often.

Wobie's poached-egg eyes peered over the front page, then disappeared.

'Having trouble, Hope?' said Wobie.

The eyes of the class turned to Sep.

'No, sir.'

'Then is there another reason you are staring into space, an expression of the utmost vacuity on your unremarkable little face?'

'No, sir.'

'You retrieved your textbook from Miss Wright following your gallant loan, did you not?'

'Yes, sir.'

'And you have consequently availed yourself of the impact of the Corn Laws' repeal?'

'Yes, sir.'

'Woe betide you if you lie, Master Hope – the muse of examination is an unforgiving mistress, and she is not like to be sated by the undeserving.'

'No, sir.'

'*No, sir,*' said Stephen, turning in his seat and flicking his wrist at Sep.

'Shut up,' said Sep and Hadley together.

The class gasped. Stephen frowned. The newspaper lowered.

'Master Hope, Miss Anderson – it may be that the Face and Hair of Stephen Ashton is a despicable cretin . . .'

The class waited. Stephen shifted in his seat.

Wobie licked his fingers and raised the newspaper.

'But?' said Sep.

The dribbly eyes reappeared.

'But what?' said Wobie.

There was a knock on the door. Arkle came into the room. He shot Sep and Hadley a grin, then handed Wobie a note.

Wobie looked at him, eyebrows furrowed to a single caterpillar.

'What are you wearing, Master Hooper?'

'My T-shirt? It says: "Come with me if you want to live", sir. It's from *Terminator*.'

Wobie gave him a slow blink.

'Or did you mean my foil helmet, sir?'

'I did,' said Wobie, nodding at Arkle's pointy, tinfoil hat.

'They're very in,' said Arkle. 'You should get one.'

'Perhaps tomorrow,' said Wobie, opening the note.

The cigar fell from his lips.

Then he rose, placing a heavy, four-fingered hand on Arkle's shoulder, and stood in front of the class.

Hadley looked over in alarm. Sep craned his neck.

He had never seen Wobie's legs before – they were always hidden by the desk, or piles of unmarked assignments. The class leaned forward, expecting something bizarre – some dangling appendage or a tentacular sprawl, glistening under smears of mustard.

But there were just the short, stocky legs of an elderly man – the knees of which were visibly shaking.

'The school has just been informed,' he said, dabbing his lips with his tongue, 'that Mrs Maguire has suffered a dreadful accident –'

'Holy shit,' whispered Hadley. 'Is she dead?'

'"... she was attacked in her home late last night, and remains in a serious but stable condition at Hill Ford

General,"' read Wobie, his voice breaking. ' "Given that the nature of her assault remains unknown, the school will be closed until further notice. You are instructed to make your way straight home, immediately. Make sure you're not alone; go with friends – talk to no one you don't know and trust." '

He crushed the paper in his hand.

'Be safe. Pack up your things. Off you go now.'

He slumped in his chair, fumbled the cigar back between his lips and lit it with trembling hands. The class watched him, silent and unmoving.

'There's another note, sir,' said Arkle.

Wobie looked at his desk.

'Oh, yes,' he said. He unfolded the piece of card, scanned it quickly, then looked at Sep. 'Hope, you're to attend the headmaster. Go on now, the rest of you. And be careful.'

The class rose and packed up in a stupefied quiet, then shuffled away. Nobody ran, nobody tried to catch their friends – just moved with an eerie stillness.

'What does he want now?' said Hadley.

'I don't know,' said Sep, hoisting his bag on to his shoulder.

Wobie was letting the cigar burn, watching the smoke's thread unravel into the air.

'Are you all right, sir?' said Sep.

Wobie shook his head without looking up.

'She does so much for others,' he said. 'It's terrible.'

Sep went to pat him on the shoulder, but stopped his hand halfway and made an awkward fist instead. He turned to go.

'You've got out of detention anyway,' said Arkle once they were outside the room.

'Jesus, Darren,' said Hadley.

'Keep your hair on, Milky, I'm just kidding. It's grimbiscuits what's happened to old Magpie, it really is. And, by the way, nice secret diary – as if Mack didn't have a big enough head already.'

Hadley kicked his shin, and he grinned.

'I passed Lamb in the corridor just now,' he said. 'She told me to tell you to get your butts back to her farm, pronto.'

'Why her farm? Shouldn't we just head to the woods?' said Hadley.

'And I need to go home for a new sacrifice,' said Sep.

Arkle shrugged.

'I'm just passing on the message. She's definitely mad keen to get to the box. Like, she was running when I saw her.'

'Was that all she said?'

'Oh, no – she called me an asshole and gave me a dead arm.'

Hadley nodded.

'What's with the tinfoil?' said Sep as they turned down the main corridor. It was already empty, and their feet echoed along its length.

'Clever, right?' said Arkle. 'Tench gave me notes to give to all the teachers, so when I was in home ec I nicked some foil. And a thing of cookie dough.'

'Why?'

'I was hungry.'

'No, why did you steal tinfoil? And why are you *wearing* it?'

'Cosmic rays, Sepster. Like you said, the asteroid –'

'Comet –' said Hadley.

'– is poisoning us, right? But if we wear these, we're sorted!'

He tilted his head as though he'd reached the end of a catwalk, the corridor's strip lights bouncing off his head.

'Darren, the comet's got nothing to do with all this.'

'But you said it did! And you know about everything, like . . . photosynthesis! And maths!'

'I know, but –'

'And the Soviets too – I'm on to them.'

Sep shared a look with Hadley.

'What are you going to do, invade Russia?'

'What? No, obviously not, I'm only fifteen. I'm going to nick one of those counters from the science cupboard, so I know if they're trying to poison us with radiation. Smart, huh?'

'A Geiger counter?' said Hadley.

'Yes, that,' said Arkle, snapping his fingers at her. 'The Pube thinks I don't know the door code for the cupboard, but I do – it's the same as his briefcase.'

'Why would you need to know the code for the science cupboard?' said Sep.

Arkle looked at him blankly.

'Magnesium,' he said.

'Why is Mr Bailey called "The Pube"?' said Hadley.

'Don't you even know that?' said Arkle. 'He's only got one pube, right? But it's massive, like, six feet long – he has to roll it up to get it in his pants.'

'That is so not true,' said Hadley.

'It is!' said Arkle, indignant. 'McCall saw him in the swimming baths last summer. Ask him.'

'Ask Mr Bailey if he's got a six foot pube?'

'No, don't ask *him* – ask McCall!'

They reached the stairwell. A column of silent children spiralled down it, wobbling like penguins. A few people spoke, but they got no answers, everyone unsure of how to react; of how to hide their fear.

'Hey, look!' shouted a voice. 'It's the lil' sweetheart who's into Macejewski! *I love him! Oh, Mack – I love him!*'

They turned to see Manbat, wads of bloody cotton wool up his nose, Stephen looming behind him.

'Piss off, asshole,' said Arkle. 'I've already bust your nose – you want me to smash your mouth too?'

'You're Tench's little bitch now,' said Manbat, sweeping past them as Stephen knocked into Sep with his shoulder. 'You might still be in detention when . . . *if* . . . you graduate. Laters!'

Arkle gave their backs the finger.

'We need to go,' said Hadley. 'Lamb'll be waiting for us.'

'I need to see Tench first,' said Sep.

'I'll come with you, Sepster,' said Arkle. 'We'll be there, Milky, it's cool.'

'You'd better be. I wouldn't want to get on her bad side.'

Sep nodded. 'We'll be at the box soon, don't worry.'

Hadley's hand brushed Sep's as she turned to go and electricity lit his arm.

'I'm scared,' she said.

'We'll be fine,' said Arkle. 'Nothing bad ever happens during the day in a horror film, so we're good for ages yet.'

'What about *The Shining*?' said Hadley as she was swallowed by the crowd.

'I haven't seen it,' called Arkle.

Sep watched her move down the stairs.

'You're in there,' said Arkle, digging his ribs.

'What?' said Sep.

'I said you're in there,' said Arkle again, louder. 'With the Milky Bar Kid, I mean – she's got a geek-on for you.'

'She does not,' said Sep.

'She does too. You could talk about the periodic table of the elements.'

'Shut up.'

'You could hold hands and name all the bones in your fingers.'

'Shut up.'

'Then maybe she'll feel *your* bo–'

'*Darren*, seriously – shut *up*,' said Sep, holding open the swing doors. 'How much trouble did you get in?'

'Not much, considering I hit someone in class. Tench hardly even reacted. This Maguire thing's got him pretty distracted.'

They were outside Tench's office. The corridor was spookily quiet.

'What do you think he wants to see me for?' said Sep.

'God knows,' said Arkle. 'Maybe he's got new waders and he wants to give you a fashion show.'

'Maguire's properly hurt, you know. You don't think that's weird?'

'How?'

'That all this stuff is happening to us, then she gets hurt?'

Sep ran his tongue over his tooth and waited for a flash of pain.

'Nah,' Arkle shrugged. 'Right, in you go – I'll get the goggle –'

'Geiger –'

'– Geiger counter, then I'll wait for you out here.'

'Why?' said Sep, half turning from the doorway.

'Just cos . . . you know.'

'Do I?'

'Yeah. Like, friends,' said Arkle. He set to playing with his lighter.

'All right,' said Sep, and went inside.

29

Breathe

Hadley clipped in the Wham! cassette as she left the school building. The last bars of 'Come On!' led into 'Young Guns (Go For It!)', and she rolled the volume control under her thumb, bumping through the throng of bodies.

It would only be a matter of time until the others found out – she couldn't keep it secret for much longer, and they were going to the box now.

She suppressed a shiver as she pushed through the playground's broiling heat towards the gate, keeping her head down in case anyone from English saw her, or worse . . .

'Hoi, freak show!'

. . . Sonya.

Hadley turned to see her leering down from the top of the wall. Her face was framed by a tangle of badly permed hair and her eyes were so thickly lined they seemed almost closed. She gestured for Hadley to remove her headphones.

'Heard about your little *diary*,' she said, nudging Chantelle. 'Can I read it? I could use a laugh.'

'No,' said Hadley.

'No? You don't say no to me, you little bitch. I still *own* you. Gimme your diary.'

Hadley put her music back on and turned away. The familiar, forgotten panic, unfelt since the summer of sacrifice, began to squeeze her insides, and the world moved in a slow, hyper-real blur.

'Don't you walk away from me!' Sonya shouted, dropping from the wall and pushing after her.

Hadley reached the gate and ran, past the parents leaning on the bonnets of cars, through the buses and into the woodland at the back of the school. As she moved under the trees she felt her lungs squeeze and fumbled for her inhaler, slipping and plunging her foot into a puddle of sticky mud.

'You can't run, you wheezy bitch!' said Chantelle as they reached the edge of the trees. 'Or hide – we can *hear* you!'

Hadley felt her chest closing, and wished at that moment she might run into Mack or Lamb – or Sep. Sep, who would have given her one of those looks where she could tell exactly what he was thinking, and they'd have wandered off in their own little world, not speaking – and not needing to.

She found her inhaler, dropped it, leaned down to grab it in a head-swimming haze.

Sonya's frizz of hair loomed into view and Hadley ran again, throwing herself into a thicket of bushes and pulling her knees up to her chin.

The woods became very quiet, and she heard the distant rumble of engines from the car park. The sound of safety, of people going lightly about their day.

And here she was – a hundred feet away, trapped like a rat.

'Where are you, freak show?' whispered Sonya, alarmingly close.

Hadley opened one eye and saw the big flat feet almost within reach, and she knew that all Sonya had to do was lean down, and they'd have her.

Her chest constricted again and she felt her lungs slam shut.

She looked at her inhaler. If she used it, the burst of sound would give her away. If she didn't . . .

'Where *are* you?' Sonya roared, laughing and banging a stick against the trunk beside Hadley's head.

Hadley started to rock as her breathless chest began to pull on her consciousness.

She thought of Sep again. She imagined his gentle hand on her back as he reached for the inhaler, guiding it to her mouth and pressing it with a *hiss* that filled every vein and threw her lungs open with a desperate, painful rush.

Sonya's feet stopped moving.

Then her upside-down face loomed in the little gap through which Hadley had crawled, and she banged the stick on the trunk again.

30

Messenger

Mrs Siddiqui was crying at her desk, a handkerchief clasped to her mouth.

'Go in, September, he is waiting,' she said with a weak smile.

'Are you OK?' said Sep.

'Oh, yes, fine, fine. It has been a frightening morning. We are all very worried.'

The door to Tench's office jerked open and the headmaster appeared, enormous and gaunt, his normally pink face grey and slack.

'Come on in, Sep,' he said.

Mrs Siddiqui blew her nose, nodding as Sep passed.

Tench's office was sweating behind half-drawn curtains. The headmaster, his face blank, sat behind his desk and began to wind in a reel of fishing line with a loud *whirr*.

'Sit down. You've heard about Mrs Maguire?'

'Yes, sir. Wob . . . Mr Clarke told us.'

Tench nodded.

'A wonderful woman, and an excellent guidance counsellor. I know you're all scared of her, but she really . . .' He tailed off and shook his head. 'She thinks a lot of you, you know.'

Sep blinked.

'She does?'

'Absolutely.' Tench nodded. 'Did she never show you the recommendation she wrote for your scholarship? No wonder you were invited to apply, with prize bait like that.'

'Oh,' said Sep. He tried to connect Maguire's snarls to a glowing reference.

'Anyway,' said Tench, 'she's stable now and the police are investigating – your mother, in fact. And that's what I was wanting to talk to you about actually. Your mother wanted me to keep you here until –'

'What?' Sep shouted. 'Why?'

Tench blinked at the outburst, then looked at Sep's fist in the centre of the desk. Sep took his hand back sheepishly and sat down again, his back straight and his stomach hard.

'Well,' said Tench, 'since you've nobody to walk home with and it's not safe to be out on your own –'

'But I do have someone! Darren's waiting for me.'

'Hooper?'

Sep nodded.

Tench puffed out his cheeks and grimaced.

'I'm not sure Darren Hooper is really the best person for you to be spending time with.'

'And why not?' said Sep, his teeth clenched.

'Well, for one thing he's on a totally different . . . academic trajectory, and for another he's got a standing appointment in my detention. Not to mention the *world* of trouble he's in for that incident in Mrs Woodbank's class this morning –'

'But that was Manbat's fault. He deserved it!'

Tench frowned.

'Nothing Wayne could have done would justify –'

'And so what if Darren's not doing well in school?'

'Well . . . I . . . your mother said she'll come and collect you as soon as she's able. But since she's working at *least* a double shift, you might have to get your dinner at my house.'

Sep shook his head.

'You're not my dad.'

Tench dropped the reel on his desk.

'I'm not trying to be,' said the headmaster firmly. 'But while your mum's busy and . . . not feeling well –'

'I can take care of her,' said Sep shortly. 'I can keep the house clean and make her food. I'm older than last time; we don't need you. Sir.'

'Last time?' said Tench, looking puzzled. 'Look, you can't be on your own, so you just have to –'

Sep stood up.

'I'm not on my own. And I'm leaving.'

'Now listen here, young man,' said Tench, his voice dropping. 'The last thing Eleanor needs is –'

'The last thing she needs is you,' said Sep, trying to keep control. He gripped his headphones. 'I can look after her. I can. We don't need *you* to do anything.'

'September –' said Tench through his teeth, half turning away before looking back, his face calm and open. 'I'm not trying to be your father. Only to look after you. At some point you'll have to let people love you. You can't hide behind the books forever.'

Sep pulled a face.

'I don't –' he began.

Tench sat down, and began winding the reel once more.

'You're to stay here,' he said over its *whirr*. 'That's what your mum wants you to do. She doesn't need to be chasing you around in her condition, and when one of my closest friends has nearly been killed, you'd better believe I've got more pressing concerns than your teenage mood. All right?'

'No fish talk?' said Sep.

Tench stopped winding and spread his palms with a half-smile.

'Just straight talk,' he said. 'And here it is: your mother loves you. I love her – and she loves me. Understand?'

'Yes,' said Sep, swallowing hard. The guilt began to tear at him with its sharp, heavy claws as he thought of the care and love and attention his mum would need, how he was claiming *he* could provide these things – while he was making plans to leave her behind.

'Good. So, what's it going to be?'

They held each other's stare, then Sep went straight past Mrs Siddiqui into the cool, shiny corridor.

31

Swallow

Roxburgh stood over the swallow's twisted corpse. It lay beside a crude fire in a little circle of pale feathers, flies swirling above. Lifting the body on the point of his knife, he watched blood well from its solitary wound and spill over his tattooed hands.

Pellet gun, he thought. *Bloody kids*.

He breathed deeply, blinking through the pain in his leg. Lundy trembled at his feet, teeth bared, growling so deeply he heard it through the soles of his boots.

'It's all right, lass,' he said, still out of breath. 'It's all right.'

He switched his pipe across his mouth, then moved it back again. The doll's footsteps had vanished. But it was nearby – the trees were empty of birdsong.

It had bitten him – there was a dark, sticky hole in his calf muscle. It had borne down on him with impossible speed, leaping at him with its little mouth. And when Biscay had thrown herself in front of Roxburgh, the dead-smelling thing had bitten her neck.

He blinked, tried to focus, clutched the dog's limp body to his chest as the flies climbed over him.

'These is my woods,' he said aloud, spitting out a shred of tobacco and swiping as the flies covered Biscay's wounds in buzzing slabs, then swarmed over his face, landing in his eyes and mouth.

Roxburgh stumbled, and might have fallen but for a distant cry that came through the silence like a javelin.

He ran again, Biscay swinging loosely in his hands, Lundy tight to his heels. He heard the voice again and scrambled on through a muddy gorge, snapping two shells into the barrels of his gun.

He raised the weapon, ready for the old offerings, for the puppet and the doll: but found instead a boy – a huge, red-faced, Mohawked boy, his face shiny with tears – swinging a pellet gun like a bat, and screaming.

32

Arkle

'Hurry up!' said Arkle, hopping from foot to foot as Sep emerged into the corridor. 'You took –' he checked his watch, then rubbed the bruise on his arm – '*eight* minutes! Lamb's going to kill us!'

'We're fine,' said Sep.

'We're *not*! The farm is *miles* away, and we're already hours behind after this morning!'

'And whose fault was that?' said Sep, but he quickened his pace as they jumped down the last few steps and jogged through the car park. 'You got the Geiger counter then?'

Arkle held up the heavy yellow box. With the big handle and round dials, it looked like an old flashlight.

'Easy-peasy.'

'Didn't Mr Bailey see you?'

'Nah, he wasn't even there; must have stayed home to wash his pube. And here, check this out.' Arkle produced a blotchy photocopy from his pocket. 'I nicked this from his briefcase. He really shouldn't leave it lying around,' he added with a serious expression. 'You never know who might get their hands on it.'

'You really don't,' said Sep, side-eyeing Arkle as he took the crumpled sheet. 'A staff memo?'

'Yeah, top secret for teachers, like. Says Magpie's stable now. And guess who apparently found her and called the police? Creepy old weirdo Thom Roxburgh. Remember him?'

'The gamekeeper?' said Sep.

'Yeah – he was always chasing us with his little dogs . . . Monday and Biscuit, or something. Bet you *he's* the one who attacked her too. So it's fine; her accident's nothing to do with the box – it was just some maniac trying to kill her.'

'How fortunate,' said Sep.

'Yup. Productive trip to the science department, I must say – I also lit a small magnesium fire and freed the, um –'

'Snails?'

'No, green things. Frenchies eat them.'

'The dissection frogs?'

'Frogs!' said Arkle. 'Jesus, my head. I'm forgetting everything.'

Sep looked down towards the bay as they emerged on to the road. High white surf was hissing on to the rocks. It was too far away to see the crabs, but they'd be there, massed against the shore, climbing over each other and flexing their claws.

He shuddered, remembering the incident on the beach.

Arkle set off up the hill.

'I still need to go home, remember?' Sep called after him, crossing over towards his own house.

'*Nooooooo*, no, no, no,' said Arkle, pulling his sleeve. 'We're going to Lamb's farm. Then no one will get shouted at. Or punched.'

'Let go! I forgot to bring a new sacrifice – I have to get something!'

'Just get something from Lamb's house,' said Arkle, pleading. 'One of *her* teddies – she's probably got a mountain of them.'

Sep thought for a moment. He and his mum never argued, but a few times she'd been . . . *disappointed*. He imagined her coming back and finding him there, after the conversation he'd just had with Tench.

Then he imagined being there alone when Barnaby returned.

'All right,' he said. 'Let's go.'

'Thank God!' said Arkle, his shoulders visibly sagging with relief. He set off with quick, loping strides, flicking his hair out of his collar and lighting another cigarette.

They trotted a few steps in silence, and Sep tried to think of something to say.

'Why do you smoke?' he said eventually.

'I love it,' said Arkle, the little white tube flapping in his lips.

'Why? What's to love about it?'

Arkle exhaled a fat burst of smoke, looking thoughtful.

'Everything,' he said. 'I like the solid square of a new pack – how satisfying it is peeling away the plastic cover, then ripping off the foil. And then they're in there, all neat, lined up all perfectly – twenty little treats. And the smell . . .

and the taste and the feeling of smoke filling me up inside and then –' he made an exploding gesture with his hands – 'whoosh! A big cloud of smoke.'

'But it smells terrible, *and* it kills you.'

'There is that,' said Arkle, accepting the point with a little frown, 'but there's no one alive that could convince me to stop. Besides, I don't always inhale. I'm not daft,' he finished, the sunlight gleaming from his tinfoil helmet.

Sep scanned the streets for signs of Barnaby and ran his tongue over his teeth.

'Have you seen your dragonflies today?'

'Oh, no – they mostly come at night. I'll be fine until it gets dark. I mean, I don't think they're even real – I just hear them. It's when I'm lying in bed, they're in my ear – you know that noise when a fly goes right in there?'

Sep turned his head.

'Sometimes,' he said.

Arkle blushed.

'Ah, shit. I wasn't, I mean –'

'I'm kidding,' said Sep.

Arkle gave him a big, soft smile.

'What did Tench say anyway?' he said.

'Nothing.'

'Ah, come on.'

'He said you're in a world of trouble for hitting Manbat.'

'Pfft, I'll believe that when I see it. But seriously, you've not come out of there like a scalded cat cos you were talking about school stuff. What was it?'

Sep looked at him quickly.

'He wanted me to stay with him until my mum came to get me. And I had to eat at *his* house.'

Because I've got no friends, he added in his head.

Arkle spluttered on his cigarette.

'Holy shit,' he said, grinning. 'She's got him giving you messages now? He's your new daddy.'

Sep ground his teeth.

'I knew I shouldn't have told you.'

'I'm kidding!' said Arkle, jogging to catch up as they turned on to the farm track. 'But seriously, holy shit, right?'

'I know. I mean, if she's getting sick again – Tench is the last thing she needs. I mean, *Tench*.'

Arkle pulled a face, then blew out a thin column of smoke.

'Well, I don't fancy him, like, but I'm not your mum. Maybe those lips of his are just what forty-year-old women want.'

Sep recoiled.

'What the hell, man?'

Arkle laughed.

'Look, I'm just saying you're only looking at it from your point of view, you know? To your mum, he's a guy about her age who's got a good J.O.B. and isn't a total dick.'

Sep's mouth was still open.

'Tench?' he said again. '*Tench?*'

'You're being very short-sighted about all this,' said Arkle.

'Oh, really? How would you like it if he started going out with *your* mum? Would that –'

'Whoa there,' Arkle, scowled. 'Ain't no need to talk about my mammy. My mammy's a virgin – you're looking at an immaculate conception right here. Listen, Tench and your mum seem pretty serious, but you'll be away on the mainland and you won't have to worry about it, right?'

'I guess.'

Sep took the rock Mack had given him from his pocket.

'You want a bit of this?'

Arkle shook his head, then flashed his massive teeth at Sep.

'That's just tooth rot, like.'

'I know. My teeth are killing me; I'm having to suck on this.'

Arkle grinned.

'How come you eat rock if you hate it here so much?'

'What's that got to with anything?'

'It's just such a Hill Ford thing. I mean, it's got the name of the town running through the middle.'

Sep folded the jagged piece of rock into his pocket. 'It's just my favourite sweet,' he said.

He wondered what might be read in himself if he was torn in two. He felt the jumble of the last twenty-four hours boiling inside him: his mum, the box, Barnaby, the crows, Daniels, the noise in his deaf ear – each one fighting to the surface like a drowning rat.

'There it is, Castle Lambert,' said Arkle, stepping over the tree roots that split the track. The farmhouse was still far off, but already they could see its big red door and the curtains fluttering like ghosts from its open windows. The sweetness of summer flowers billowed around them in thick, heady waves.

'I love it here, like,' Arkle went on, looking around as they jogged towards the house. 'Why *do* you want to move away?'

Sep shrugged.

'My mum says I've always had itchy feet.'

'Me too! My mum puts a special powder in my socks. But why would anyone leave here? Hill Ford is class.'

'I want a good job.'

'Yeah,' said Arkle hesitantly. 'I used to think I might do something at the hospital, but I'm not going to be qualified for anything.'

'You could volunteer,' said Sep.

Arkle made a face.

'What's the point of that? I mean, apart from helping the sick. Nah, I'm not going to get anywhere. I wasn't kidding when I said I'd fallen asleep in my maths exam. Even I didn't think I was as thick as that. I'm getting worse.'

'How is that possible?' said Sep.

Arkle shot him a look.

'I didn't mean it like that,' said Sep quickly. 'I meant how could that happen?'

'I don't know, but I am. I mean, I couldn't remember what a frog was called just now. A frog! Sometimes when I'm in class I can actually feel the things they're trying to teach me like little strings in my head, and I try and grab them, I really do – but they just slip away, and the last few days it's happening more and more. You ever tried holding a fish? They're bastards to hold on to, fish, and so is . . . that guy. The triangle guy.'

'Pythagoras?'

'That's the bugger,' said Arkle, clicking his fingers.

'Pythagoras is a bastard?'

'A *slippery* bastard.'

Arkle began to climb the gate at the end of the long driveway. He checked his watch. 'We might actually get away with this. But you're taking the blame if she kicks off, all right? Say you got detention, but bailed. That sounds badass.'

'But it's not true.'

Arkle looked down from the gate and raised his eyebrows.

'You want to tell them that Tench was planning a candlelit dinner for the two of you?'

He dropped down and kept running.

'Fair point,' said Sep, and climbed after him.

33

Tarot

The old lady known locally as Christine the Psychic stirred her soup, pausing every once in a while to rattle a box of cat treats at the back door.

'Puss, puss, puss,' she called in her sing-song voice. 'Here, puss!'

In her distraction she spilled some of the bright liquid on the linoleum, and left it there as a further incentive for the cat.

But by the time her soup began to bubble, the animal still had not come, and she took her lunch into the sitting room, arranging the buttered bread and the tea things on her tray.

Her house was old and small, a post-war wooden three-room that smelled of nutmeg and cloves. Its walls were hung with dreamcatchers and feather wards, and the surfaces were piled with the occult bric-a-brac of a thousand yard sales. Everything in the room had some connection to the world that existed beyond human sight, except one: the stag's head her father had mounted before he died. It remained, glass-eyed and mighty, on the back wall above the settee – its antlers hung with the chiming silver of charms and totems.

Christine turned on the TV and sat below the stag, lifting the tray on to her lap.

'Oh, this again,' she said as static filled the screen.

She rose and crossed the room, clicking the off switch with a *thunk*. Then she sat on the settee once more and blew on her soup.

'What on earth –'

There was something on her seat. She cocked her leg, patting her buttocks and the fabric of the settee.

It felt damp – but so did everything. The whole town seemed to be sweating in the heat.

She took a spoonful of soup, slurping a little from the deep spoon. The silver above her head chimed as the breeze moved playfully through the room.

Christine reached to her side and lifted a Tarot card from the top of the deck on the table, flipped it over dramatically.

'The World Reversed,' she said. 'Feeling stuck. Nearly at the finishing line.'

She flipped the next card and looked at the skeletal figure.

'Death,' she said, sticking out her tongue. 'Sucks to you, boyo.'

She took some more soup, this time dipping her bread and letting it soak.

A petrol lawnmower started outside – the Brodys' boy, next door, earning his allowance. Christine rolled her eyes, set down her tray and crossed to the window.

'*I'll* pay you twice as much to shut up!' she shouted as she slid the glass closed, trapping the sound outside and the heat in the room.

She sat back down, lifted her tray. And felt the seat wet again below her legs.

She hopped up, feeling embarrassed although there was no one there.

'What on earth is –'

A drop fell into the hollow worn by her body, at the centre of a little damp patch that was forming there.

Christine looked up – and screamed.

Spit was running from the dead black mouth of the stag's head and pooling on the edge of its lips.

'No!' she cried, backing away as the antlers began to swing, filling the room with the clang of metal. 'No!'

As the head thrashed on the wall Christine shut the kitchen door, pulling a chair across to keep it closed – but as she turned to run she slipped on the spilled soup and cracked her skull on the kitchen worktop. Vision fading, she gripped the charms around her neck so hard the skin split on her palms.

Her body lay a while in the heat, the mower growling its way across the lawn outside. Presently came the sound of antlers smashing on to carpet, and the *swish* of a cat flap as it swung gradually closed.

34

Lamb

The big red door opened to reveal Mrs Boyle, the housekeeper.

'All right, Mrs B?' panted Arkle, his breathing not yet recovered from their run.

Mrs Boyle's big owl-glasses peered down at them. Her face was wide and lined, red from sun and creased by laughter. Sep remembered it well – it was the face that had run the house since Lamb's mum had died, and that had loomed over trays of sandwiches and lemonade during the summer of sacrifice.

'Hooper and Hope,' she said. 'The whole gang's here now.'

'Hi, Mrs Boyle,' said Sep. 'Are we last then?'

'Weren't you always?' said Mrs Boyle, shrugging her coat on. 'Haven't seen you in a while.'

'They've closed the school cos of what happened to Mrs Maguire,' said Arkle.

She nodded, then gathered her handbag.

'I heard about it this morning; it's a terrible business. Why are you wearing tinfoil, Hooper?'

'Science,' said Arkle.

'Uh-huh. How's your mother?'

'Fine, fine.'

'And how's school?'

'Good,' said Arkle warily.

'You've not been in trouble? Or set anything on fire?'

'Of course not!' said Arkle. 'Hahahaha.'

He gestured at Sep with his eyebrows.

'Hahahaha,' said Sep, frowning.

He glanced over Mrs Boyle's shoulder. The hallway looked exactly the same, and he breathed in its familiar smell: gravy, Mrs Boyle's light perfume and the rich tang of cigarettes. He felt he could close his eyes and reopen them as an eleven-year-old boy, waiting for Lamb to bounce down the stairs and hop on her bike.

'So what's that you've got?' Mrs Boyle said as she moved past them into the yard.

'A Geiger counter,' said Arkle.

'And where'd you get that?'

'School. It's for . . . homework.'

'D'you think my head buttons up the back?' said Mrs Boyle. 'Have you stolen that?'

'Of course not!' said Arkle. 'Hahahaha.'

He gestured again.

'Hahahaha,' said Sep.

'I don't see what's funny,' said Mrs Boyle. 'I wouldn't want to bring more bad news to your mother's door, Darren Hooper – not after that thing in October –'

'Mrs *B*,' said Arkle, wide-eyed with innocence, 'I told you at the time – it was on fire when I got there.'

Mrs Boyle gave him a hard look.

'Hmmm,' she said. 'I see your eyebrows have grown back at any rate. Did you see Jones on your way here?'

'Jones is still *alive*?' said Sep.

'Well, we hope so,' said Mrs Boyle as she walked down the path. 'He's been missing two days. The only certain things in life are the sun rising and that cat coming in for his dinner, so it doesn't bode well. Behave yourselves, now. There's snacks in the cupboard.'

'What happened in October?' said Sep as they watched her go.

'Oh, nothing. A minor fire, that's all.'

'Wait . . . the *timber yard*? That was *you*?'

'Sepster! I'm telling you – it was on fire when I got there.'

'Darren . . .'

'Hahahaha,' said Arkle, moving through the door.

The farmhouse *was* exactly the same. It was even the same carpet, Sep noticed: a head-aching swirl of brown and cream, threadbare on the edges of the stairs, like the bald spot on a monk's crown. There were voices coming from the kitchen.

'Are you scared?' said Sep.

'Of Lamb?'

'*No* – of the box.'

'Oh, God, yeah.' Arkle smiled weakly. 'I'm shitting myself. Maybe literally, I've gone kind of numb. Are you?'

'Obviously,' said Sep. He wondered what the box was doing at that second – and what it had done in the hours since they'd been caught outside the school, in the time they might have stopped it.

The kitchen door burst open and Lamb bore down on them, eyes flashing and hair wild.

'Where the hell have you been?'

'Tench wanted to make Sep dinner!' Arkle blurted out, ducking behind the sideboard.

'Hey!' said Sep, throwing up his hands.

'What?' Lamb shook her head. 'Never mind, we've had to sit and pretend we were doing *homework* because Mrs Boyle wouldn't leave – she made *sandwiches*! I haven't been able to look for them at all!'

'Look for what?' said Sep.

'The car keys! My dad hides them when he's away –'

'Oh my God!' said Arkle. 'Are we taking the tractor? Please say we're taking the tractor!'

'Yeah, we're all going in the single-seat tractor,' said Lamb, pausing long enough to punch his arm.

'Ow! Right on the same . . . Where are the sandwiches?'

'Right here,' said Mack, working his way through a tower of thick-sliced bread.

Lamb started rummaging below the kitchen units.

'We can't *drive* to the box!' Sep said to the back of her head. 'Won't your dad be back soon?'

'Nope,' replied Lamb, her voice muffled, 'he's at a live-stock auction – then he's going to see Run-DMC on the mainland.'

'God, my old man still listens to Prog Rock,' said Arkle. 'Your dad is so cool. I mean, his name's *Clint*. He's such a badass.'

'Sep's right, Lamb,' said Hadley. 'You've got no licence, and there's police everywhere.'

Sep leaned further into the kitchen, saw her sitting in her old spot at the corner of the big table. He smiled – then noticed the bruise on her cheek.

'What happened to your face?'

'She won't tell us,' said Mack, his mouth full.

Hadley moved her fringe.

'I'll find them in a minute, I always do,' Lamb grunted from behind the fridge.

'What if he took them with him?' said Hadley.

'He can't. One of the labourers might need the truck. The keys have to be on site AT – ALL – TIMES!'

The fridge took three jerky steps into the room.

'Any luck?' said Mack.

'No!'

'You got anything to drink, Lamb?'

'Darren . . .'

'I need to keep my strength up!'

Arkle opened the fridge door as Lamb wedged it back into place.

'You've got Spike Sting? Oh my God, that's amazing.' He cracked open the can, took a noisy gulp, then let go a huge burp. 'It kind of coats your teeth with sugar. It's the *best*, even when it's warm.'

'You'd better have brought your sacrifice,' said Lamb.

'Oh, I have,' said Arkle, patting his pocket. 'Toy soldier, burned with a magnifying glass – same as last time. Sep still needs something, though.'

Lamb rounded on Sep, her face thunderous.

'I told you that this morning!' Sep said.

'But –'

'Look, it was either go home and get a new sacrifice, or come straight here. What would you have done?'

'He can get something from here, right?' said Arkle. 'You must have a teddy the Sepster can use.'

'Do I *look* like I've got teddies here?'

Arkle studied Lamb's expression.

'No,' he conceded.

'Do you have *anything* I can use?' said Sep.

Lamb took a deep breath, then gripped her hair above her head.

'My dad hoards stuff in the cupboard in the living room. But be quick! As soon as I find these keys we're out of here.'

Sep looked round the kitchen as he followed Arkle into the hall. It was so strange to be back in the place of their old happiness, with the photos and the tiles and the fridge magnets all the same. Like Hadley, Mack was in his favourite seat – leaning on the big range cooker with his feet on the table.

'Holy shit!' Arkle called from the living room.

'What?'

'She's got a *Nintendo*!' Arkle dropped to his knees in front of the TV and blew into a plastic cartridge. 'Oh, this is amazing.'

'But we need to find –'

'Yeah, we will. Just give me two minutes to –'

'Darren . . .'

'Lamb's still looking for the car keys, Sepster. Be cool.'

'*Darren!*'

'Oh, all right!' snapped Arkle as the Nintendo logo flashed up on screen. 'Here –'

He flung open the cupboard doors.

'Jesus, big Clint has some pile of rubbish here . . . one ice skate . . . a box of trophies . . . some slides . . .'

'Just find something, quickly!' snapped Sep, rifling through a heap of old clothes.

'. . . a travel iron . . . oh! Here, perfect,' said Arkle, lifting something from the top shelf.

'What is it?'

'A Chewbacca teddy. And Jesus, it's an old one – from when the first film came out.'

'Still in the box?'

'Yeah. Why would he keep *this*?'

'I don't know. To sell it?'

'Ha!' said Arkle, tearing the cardboard apart. 'Who's going to buy this old tat?'

He tossed the Chewbacca to Sep, then hunkered down with the joypad in his hands.

'Now we can Nintendo, right? Until Lamb finds the keys?'

'I suppose,' said Sep reluctantly.

From the kitchen came the clatter of falling plates, followed by Lamb swearing.

'What game is this?'

'*Donkey Kong Jr*. I played it at my cousin's once. It's so freaking brilliant. He's trying to rescue his dad. From Super Mario, see?'

Sep looked at the little character at the top of the screen.

'I thought Mario was a hero?'

'Nah, only in *Super Mario Bros* – he's the bad guy in this. A dangerous dude.'

They watched Super Mario release bug-eyed, toothy critters from a bag. Arkle's thumbs flashed and Donkey Kong Jr climbed out of reach.

'I don't really get it,' said Sep, moving to the window.

'What's to get?' said Arkle, his mouth open in concentration. 'Mario goes bad, tries to kill the hero; the hero escapes by climbing. Done.'

Sep looked out into the farmyard.

A flurry of wind threw the bushes about, and he thought he saw something moving under the leaves. There were trees all around the farmhouse, and their waving limbs threw a kaleidoscope of light and shadow over the grass.

Something moved again, at the garden's edge – gone before he could see it.

Sep shook his head. The noise was there again, in his deaf ear – creeping up like the tide in a seashell, glowing through his jaw and into his tooth.

'What is that?' he said, closing his eyes.

'What?'

'That kind of . . . breathing . . .' Sep managed, 'like when you've got a cold and you need to spit. Can't you hear it?'

Arkle looked worried. He put down the controller and cocked his head.

'No,' he said, sipping his can of Sting. 'I can't hear anything.'

Sep ran his tongue over his bad tooth. It felt suddenly tight and hot, like a pustule ready to burst.

'It's in my bad ear,' he said, 'and it –'

A bright, sharp pain struck in towards the centre of his head. He cried out, grabbing his skull and dropping to his knees.

'This happened last time,' he hissed. 'When ... Barnaby ... came to my house.'

'Shit,' said Arkle, hovering over him and hopping from foot to foot. 'Shit shit shit shit.'

Sep shut his eyes and squeezed his head, waiting for the lights to stop flashing in his eyes. Eventually the pain eased and he lowered his hands. They stared at each other.

'We need to go,' said Sep. 'Now.'

'But Lamb hasn't –'

'Yes!' yelled Lamb. She leaned in the room, dangling some dripping wet keys. 'In the cistern. Should have looked there earlier, it's so – Jesus, what's wrong with you?'

'Sep's ear's doing the same weird thing it did when the teddy came to his house,' said Arkle, flapping his hands. 'He says we need to go. Right now!'

'Yeah, good, that's what I said. Come on then!'

Lamb helped lift Sep from the floor and he staggered to his feet.

'It's the box,' he said. 'Like ... its voice or something. I can hear it.'

'What's it saying?' said Arkle.

'I don't know. It's just like ... an animal noise. Like a growl.'

Lamb leaned into the kitchen, Sep's arm round her shoulders.

'All right, let's go!' she shouted.

'Sep!' shouted Hadley.

'He's fine, Milky,' said Arkle. 'He's just – *ack!*'

He lurched over the kitchen table and grabbed his throat.

'Darren! Aargh!' shouted Sep, his tooth bursting again. He grabbed Arkle round the chest. 'What is it?'

'*Ack–aaaaa–ack!*' said Arkle. He turned red, then purple, his eyes bugged out and watering. He grabbed Sep's arm and pulled him so close Sep could feel the panicked nostril-heat on his cheek.

'Jesus, what is it?' Sep shouted, thumping Arkle's back. 'Say something!'

Arkle opened his mouth and heaved. Sep tensed, preparing for the splash of vomit, when a little burnt leg, dry and black, stuck out from Arkle's lips – *tarsus and tibia*, thought Sep, his horrified mind flashing to the cool, calm pages of a musty textbook – and then the rest of the dragonfly followed on to the tabletop, a twiggy excretion of dead insect, thorax scorched to a sooty bronze, wings singed to brittle, sparkling bubbles.

'*Aauugh, aauugh*, oh, God,' said Arkle, spit dripping from his mouth in thick strings. 'It's cut my lips. Oh my God, Sep, it's cut my li– *ack!*'

He heaved again, and another insect came, then another and another, each as corrupted as the first and smelling of bonfires and charcoal and heat.

'Jesus, Darren,' said Lamb as Sep rubbed Arkle's back. 'I mean . . . Jesus Christ.'

Arkle was leaning over a wet puddle of spewed-up dragonflies, his wet lips speckled with flecks of black shell. He looked up through pink-rimmed eyes.

'Thank God I was wearing my foil helmet,' he said.

Sep's heart was thudding. He felt dizzy and hot.

'Do you want a drink?' he said.

Arkle nodded and drank deeply from his soda. Then he reached into his mouth with thumb and forefinger, and lifted out a little black arc about the size and shape of a clipped fingernail.

'The sting,' he said, then vomited for real.

'My *table*!' said Lamb.

Something flashed past the kitchen window.

'We need to go,' said Sep. 'I think Barnaby's outside.'

'– right in the middle of . . . this is an *antique* –'

'Lamb!'

'Right,' said Arkle, green-faced as he lifted the sodden dragonflies into a plastic bag. 'This can be my new sacrifice. The box can have these straight back.'

The four gathered in the hallway, close behind Lamb.

'Just follow me,' she said. 'The pickup is beside the barn. I'll open the doors as quickly as I can. Ready?'

'Yeah,' said Sep.

The others nodded.

'*Go!*' Lamb shouted, throwing the door open.

The second he was outside Sep fell on the path, the noise a scream in his deaf ear that sent a drill through the pulp of his bad tooth in spikes of bright agony. With a massive effort he lifted his head – and saw Barnaby standing on the garden wall; damp fur gleaming like slug-trail in the sun, eyes glowing green, the little mouth still locked in a smile.

'Shitting hell!' screamed Arkle, running back to gather Sep under the arms, almost carrying him to the truck.

Barnaby leaped from the wall, scrambling over the uneven ground, soft legs wobbling under his weight.

'Shiiiiiiiiit! Shiiiiiiiiit! Shiiiiiiiiit! Shiiiiiiiiit! Shiiiiiiiiit!' Arkle screamed, and Sep roared as Mack grabbed him by the other arm.

Lamb jumped into the cab, then reached over to pop open the other doors.

'Hurry up!' she screamed, starting the ignition.

Which stalled.

'Oh my God, oh my God, oh my God, oh my God, oh my God, oh my God, oh my God –' said Hadley, scrambling with Arkle into the back seat.

Sep turned to look at Barnaby.

He was only a couple of metres behind, the glow in his eyes getting brighter as he closed in.

Mack leaped into the passenger seat as Lamb frantically turned the key.

'Come on!' Arkle shouted, reaching out for Sep's hand.

As Sep jumped he felt Barnaby's soft paws grabbing at his ankle and thought he was lost – when Hadley reached past Arkle and the two of them pulled him into the truck.

The engine roared into life.

'Hold on!' said Lamb.

She sped off, the big tyres throwing up stones that hit Barnaby like gunshot, knocking him into the middle of the yard.

'You got him!' shouted Hadley.

Barnaby sat up, watching them go with undimmed eyes.

'Oh, bollocks,' said Arkle, gripping Sep's arm as the car bounced towards the forest.

PART 3

35

Barkley and Snuggles

Mario washed his hands, working the chemical soap between his fingers and under his fingernails. His surgery was warm, the air sluggish and thick beneath the open skylight. Sweat glistened on his forehead and dripped from his top lip.

'Another day, another dog,' he said to himself, wiping his face with his sleeve.

The morning had already been busy: a series of routine injections and ear-baths followed by the timely end of Barkley, Mrs Adamczyk's cheese-smelling Labrador. He looked at the heavy ball of fur lying on the trolley beneath a rubber sheet.

'No more chasing of sticks, my friend – you have licked the testicles of death,' he said, tucking Barkley's tongue back in his mouth.

The bell sounded. Mario dried his hands quickly and went out into the cool of the shaded reception. A bar of sunlight cut the room in half, framing a little figure in shadow.

'Hello? Oh, Mrs . . . Mrs . . .'

'Hutchison,' said an elderly lady.

'Of course, and how is little . . .'

'Mr Snuggles,' said Mrs Hutchison.

'Mr Snuggles,' said Mario, drawing the appointments book across the desk. 'Yes, of course, he is one of my favourite . . . cats?'

'Iguanas.'

'The cats of the reptile world,' said Mario smoothly. 'And how is Mr Snuggles on this hot and sunny day?'

'Dead,' wobbled Mrs Hutchison. She pressed a hanky to her mouth.

Mario looked into the crate, a thin green tail hanging limply from its bars. When he saw that the iguana was wearing a little pair of trousers and a stovepipe hat he remembered exactly who Mrs Hutchison was.

'Ah,' he said. 'I am sorry. He was a very fine lizard. Well, if you would like to –'

'No, you don't understand,' said Mrs Hutchison quickly, grabbing Mario's arm with surprisingly strong fingers. 'He died yesterday, but today he's . . . moving again.'

'Then is not dead!' said Mario brightly. 'Wonderful news! The consultation fee is –'

'But he *is* dead!' said Mrs Hutchison, and Mario noticed for the first time how raw she looked – how pale her lips were, and how pink the whites of her eyes. 'He died yesterday afternoon, and I *know* he was dead last night because I was taking some memorial photographs of him in his favourite costumes – then this morning he was moving. Not opening his eyes, but, well . . . *moving*. Is it just nerves?'

'Could be, could be,' said Mario, lifting the little tail. 'Have you tried drinking herbal tea?'

'Not *my* nerves! His! The nerves in his body, or –'

'Well,' said Mario, 'is not like headless chicken, you know. Lizard is dead – it looks dead. Maybe you could leave him here today. I keep very close eye on him.'

She nodded, lifted the crate on to the counter.

'It's so upsetting,' she said. 'I was just getting myself accustomed to . . . I mean he never even *wore* the Charlie Chaplin costume. It took so long to knit the little moustache, and –'

'Leave him with me,' said Mario, leading her out by the shoulder. 'I will see what is what and I will let you know. Perhaps he is in coma? I will check to see if big lizards can go into comas.'

'Do you think that's what it is?' said Mrs Hutchison, nodding tearfully.

'I have no idea,' said Mario, blinking in the sunshine as the bell chimed her exit. 'I will investigate. Goodbye for now.'

The wind from the closing door dislodged one of the notices and he bent to retrieve it. He had difficulty finding space for the pin: the noticeboard – normally a few tacked pamphlets for pet food – was covered in handwritten notes. And every scribbled message was about a different missing cat.

The door opened again.

'As soon as I can, Mrs Hutchie, I promise – oh –'

'It's my parakeet,' said a tear-stained man in an overall.

Mario looked over the man's shoulder and saw a queue of people clutching cages and crates.

'Ah,' he said. 'One moment, my people – I must examine this animal first. Please come into waiting area and I will be only a moment.'

The crowd gathered in the small space, and Mario took the iguana into the surgery.

'So many dead pets, Mr Snuggles,' he said, gently nudging the lizard's tail as he carried it through to the surgery. 'And you are one of them, I'm afraid. As dead as our friend Mr Barkley, and he is –'

He froze in the doorway.

The trolley was empty, the rubber sheet crumpled on the floor.

Barkley was gone.

Mario crouched to follow the trail of wet pawprints, and the crate began to swing in his hand.

36

Truck

'That was far too close,' said Arkle, gripping the headrest with trembling hands. 'Did you see him running? Did you see his *eyes*?'

'Yes,' said Hadley quietly. 'I feel like I can still see them. Like when you look at the sun.'

They thought about Barnaby's eyes, and shuddered.

'How do you know how to drive?' said Sep.

'My dad taught me,' said Lamb. 'I worked the combine when I was ten. You're expected to muck in on a farm. And it's lucky I *can* drive,' she added, glaring at Arkle in the rear-view mirror. 'Don't think I've forgotten it was *your* smoking that got us hauled in by Tench this morning.'

'Let it go, Lambert.'

'Doesn't everyone on the island know this is your dad's truck?' said Sep, before Lamb could respond.

'They just wave at the truck,' said Lamb. 'They don't really see inside.'

Sep saw how much of her mother's look she had now. From his angle it looked like Mrs Lambert herself was driving.

They were already on the forest's narrow road of chipped stone, tyre tracks gouged into their surface like the grooves on

227

an old chair. The road was an avenue of hanging branches filled with sounds: bird calls and rustling wind, the bleating of hidden goats and the chirps of squirrels that ran in liquid hops through the branches. The pickup smelled of mushrooms and farts.

'What have you all brought to sacrifice?' Sep asked.

'I've got the Troll Doll pen I wrote my diary with,' said Hadley. 'It's as close as I could get to the same thing.'

'I brought this alarm clock,' said Mack. 'It stopped working today anyway.'

Arkle held up the plastic bag. 'Vomit-bugs. You all saw it.'

'I got another teddy at Lamb's house,' said Sep.

'Lamb?' said Hadley.

'I've brought something,' Lamb growled, shifting the scarf on her wrist.

They drove in silence for a moment, watching the trees flashing by and thinking about what they were going to do.

'I'd love to drive a combine harvester,' Mack said wistfully, jaw muscles bulging like golf balls as he chewed his bubblegum. 'I used to have a tractor when I was little. You could sit on it and push yourself round the garden.'

'Jesus, Golden Boy, that's a fascinating story. I bet it would make a brilliant film. Please,' Arkle sat back and stroked his chin, 'tell me more about your favourite childhood toys.'

'Shut up.'

'No!' shouted Arkle, slapping his arm. 'I just spewed up giant insects! And we *all* saw Sep's teddy running about in *bloody daylight*! This shit is getting too real; stop talking about your damn tractor!'

'I thought we'd got Barnaby with the stones when we drove away,' said Hadley.

It seemed to Sep, but he knew it couldn't be, that she'd shifted closer to him than the back seat demanded.

They were nearly at the end of the track. The trees had emptied, and the world was quiet and still.

'But he sat straight back up – he's a zombie teddy,' said Arkle. 'We'd need to remove the head or destroy the brain. Actually –' he screwed up his face – 'he doesn't have a brain. Holy shit, how *do* we kill him?'

'Same way I'll kill whoever broke those damn rules and is too scared to admit it,' said Lamb. 'Rip. Him. Apart.'

'That'll probably do it,' said Arkle approvingly. 'Anyone feel like admitting to it now?'

'No!' said Sep. 'Why does it even have to be one of us? Couldn't someone *else* have found the box and taken the stuff out? Wouldn't that be just as bad for us?'

'Maybe,' said Lamb reluctantly. She jumped on the brakes, then started to back up, feeding the huge wheel through her hands.

'So we're all innocent,' said Arkle, looking relieved. 'Here, you need to put these on.'

He handed out squares of tinfoil.

'Seriously?' said Lamb. She screwed her foil into a ball and bounced it off Arkle's forehead. 'Piss off.'

'I'm probably not going to wear this, Darren,' said Hadley.

Sep handed the foil back to Arkle.

'Yeah, I don't think it's going to make any difference,' he said. 'I think we can rule the comet out now, don't you?'

'But –' Arkle began.

Mack took the pink blob of gum from his mouth and wrapped it in the foil.

'Are you all right?' said Sep.

Mack blinked.

'Yeah,' he said, 'why?'

'Just . . . I don't know why you're not freaking out. So much weird shit is happening, it seems like the box is trying to hurt us. And you're next. Why aren't you worried?'

Mack looked at him a moment without expression, then smiled.

'I am, I am. I guess I'm just hungry too.'

Lamb killed the ignition with a jerk of the keys, and the big truck shuddered to a halt.

Sep realized in the silence how companionable the engine had been, how safe a sound of civilization and home. Without it they were suddenly cut adrift, miles from anyone in the great ocean of the forest, all help beyond even their wildest cries.

And heading straight for the sacrifice box.

He wiped the grime from his window.

'Is this near the gamekeeper's hut?'

'Yup,' said Lamb, pointing. '*Roxburgh*. He lives up there, along the side of the ravine.'

'That thing freaks me out,' said Arkle. 'Remember that Scout troop who fell into it and ate each other?'

'That was a stupid rumour, numbnuts. But it is dangerous, and so's Roxburgh. We need to watch out for him – the box is on his land.'

Hadley leaned across Sep, pressing her weight on his arm.

'Oh, God,' she said. 'He's mean and weird. He's been in prison.'

'How d'you know that?'

'The birds. On his hands – they're swallow tattoos. That's what they mean.'

'Prison's not like a youth club,' said Arkle. 'They don't stamp your hand so you can get back in. You need to, like, steal some more bread. Or kill again. Here,' he added, fishing in his pocket, 'I forgot to tell you guys – The Pube had a memo in his briefcase that said Roxburgh was the one who found old Magpie after the attack.'

'Mrs Maguire knows Roxburgh?' said Lamb.

'Apparently. But I reckon it was *him* who attacked her in the first place.'

'Why d'you have to say *that*?' said Mack.

They stepped into the afternoon heat, the truck clinking as it cooled, the midday sun shrinking their shadows to discs at their feet. Arkle switched on the Geiger counter, which began to tick slowly.

'What's it doing?' said Mack, wiping his brow.

'I don't have a bloody clue,' said Arkle, scrunching his tinfoil hat into a ball. 'Ask Sep.'

'Why'd you even bring that thing?' said Lamb. 'It's not going to help us.'

Arkle tapped the dial with his knuckle.

'You never know,' he said.

They went into the forest, leaving the light behind.

'Was it this hot before?' said Sep after a few minutes, his jeans already green from the constant mildew. 'Everything feels tight. It hurts to move.'

Arkle took off his jacket, his bare arms impossibly pale. The Geiger counter's metronome tick was steady and slow, and he rapped his knuckle on the dial again.

'I don't think so,' he said.

'You're so unfit,' said Lamb, glowing with sweat.

'Yeah, this is what pre-season is for,' said Mack.

'Good advertising,' said Arkle. 'Football practice: hang out with assholes, go running, and get tired.'

'Are you calling me an asshole?' said Mack.

Arkle, leaning on a tree trunk freckled with lichen and moss, thought for a moment.

'I think I am, yeah,' he said, swapping the Geiger counter to his other hand. 'Jesus, would you look at my trainers?'

'Who cares about your stupid L.A. Gear —'

'Stupid *new* L.A. Gear,' said Arkle. 'And Mrs Arkle's mum will care. I should have worn my crappy old trainers, like the bold Sep.'

'These are my best shoes,' said Sep.

Arkle grinned.

'I know, dude. Here, what you make of that diary, Mack-stick? Another boost for the old ego, eh?'

'Shut up,' said Hadley, her eyes flicking to Sep as Mack blushed.

Sep, peering through the sprawl of mud and leaf, tried to keep his face still, listening to the rasp and snick of creatures in the scrub. The woods were lumped by stones and roots, puddles reeking with summer's hot stink, and the air zipped with insects. He scratched his deaf ear. Its swollen tubes — and the rotten tooth they led to — felt fine again, and he thought of how far away Barnaby must be after Lamb had driven so quickly for so long.

'We're nearly there,' said Hadley, waving her hands as she walked through a spider's web. 'Urgh, I don't — I don't feel well.'

'Do you need a rest?' said Sep.

She shook her head, then strode on, back purposefully straight.

'What's the Geiger counter doing?' said Sep.

'Hurting my damn shoulder,' said Arkle.

'But what's the reading?'

Arkle peered at the dial.

'I've got no idea,' he said.

Sep leaned over.

'0.15.'

'What does that mean?'

'It's normal.'

'But I thought we were being rained on by Soviet warheads?'

'I *told* you,' said Sep. He tapped the glass, watched the needle settle into the same spot. His tooth had begun to hurt again, and he bit down hard. 'It's the *box*. We don't need this.'

Arkle looked around.

'Let's catch up,' he said, and they jogged forward to join the others.

They were standing at the top of the paddock, looking down the alley of trees at the box. The body of a swallow hung from a branch like a uvula, and everywhere there were flies, numberless and loud and black.

'Oh, God,' said Hadley.

Arkle hugged his Geiger counter and carrier bag tightly, half turning back the way they'd come. Sep could feel the box pulling from the clearing's centre, like a whirlpool's spinning point.

'It really stinks,' said Lamb. Her voice was soft, and she tugged at her mum's headscarf.

'We should hold hands,' said Hadley. 'Just like before. We'll go in the same order, then join hands and say the rules.'

'I'm not holding Mack's hand,' said Arkle. 'It's in his pants most of the day.'

The clearing was a riot of flesh and rot. Small mammal bones were scattered between the lumps of grass, and the ground was sticky with their decay.

'Oh my God,' said Sep. He looked at a pile of skulls, grinning up at him through torn fur. Textbook images of sockets and jaws flashed in his mind, and he swallowed.

'These are *cats*,' he said.

'Cats?' said Lamb, her voice breaking. 'Oh, shit, you think Jones is one of them?'

'I don't know,' said Hadley, touching Lamb's hand for a second.

Sep saw Lamb's profile as she bit her lip: hawk-like and strong. Her mother's face, more so than ever in the clearing's sallow light.

'The lid's off,' she said, voice trembling. 'I told you someone had broken the rules!'

'Oh, God,' said Hadley, swallowing as though she might be sick. 'Oh, God.'

Sep saw something plastic on the ground and picked it up.

'Why's there a mixtape here?' he said.

'What?' hissed Lamb, looking over. 'Whose is that?'

Sep wiped the label with his thumb, but the handwriting was smudged with rain and mud. 'I don't know,' he said. 'It doesn't matter now. Let's just get this done.'

He stepped between a decaying gull and what might have been a mouse. A bone crunched beneath his feet – and he felt the attention of the place shift towards him.

There was a fluttering overhead and they all looked up.

'*Shiiiiiiiiiiiiiiiiiiiit* . . .' said Arkle.

Three crows shone like dark blossom, their feathers prisms of purple and blue. They were watching the box.

'Ready?' said Sep. He heard the sound, the deaf-ear sound, but it was smothered – like breath held in anticipation. He looked at the clearing's shadowy edge. 'Hurry up!'

Hadley and Mack stood beside him, Hadley's weary head almost rolling on her shoulders. They peered into the sacrifice box.

It was empty, the original sacrifices gone. Now only roots fell hungrily inside, their surfaces pink and sticky, like torn skin. The box's stone was thick with flies, and Sep felt the prey instinct tremble inside his heart.

'*Shiiiiiiiiiiiiiiiiiit* . . .' said Arkle.

Sep followed his stare and found a squirrel – its head split neatly in two, its brains bulging like a purple walnut – moving its skinless jaw. And with each flex of the rotten flesh came a matching spasm in his rotting tooth.

'How is that happening?' said Arkle. 'Sep? Is that photosynthesis?'

The squirrel's stomach was torn open, its guts trailing behind it in little bags of yellow and brown.

Sep bit down and turned away. The noise was growing louder.

'We need to do it now!' said Hadley. She threw in her Troll Doll pen and grabbed Sep's hand. 'Lamb!' she shouted.

Lamb stared into the box, her eyes burning with tears.

'There was a look my mum used to get, when she was annoyed. It used to wind me up, but now . . . I miss it so much. To see it just one more time –'

Hadley looked at Sep, who shook his head.

'What are you doing, Lamb?'

'Her eyes were closed when I got there, and she never opened them again. I just want her to see me, once. That's all! To see me . . . and know I'm with her.'

She tore the headscarf from her wrist and dropped it inside.

'Oh my God,' said Hadley. 'Lamb, your *scarf* –'

'I've given it everything I have!' Lamb shouted back, choking back a sob and grabbing her hand. 'Darren, go!'

Arkle looked between them.

'But –'

'Do it!'

He upended the plastic bag, dropping the dragonflies inside. Sep tossed Chewbacca into the darkness, then Mack threw in the alarm clock and stood back.

The wind rose, whipping round them and throwing their hair about as they looked into the dark pit of the box, their sacrifices swallowed by the shadows.

This isn't going to work, thought Sep.

'Now say the words!' said Hadley.

Sep looked at them and wondered how it had come to this, how they had come to this place – balanced together on the edge of chaos.

Lamb nodded, and they spoke together.

'*Never come to the box alone.*'

Sep felt Hadley's fingers in his.

'*Never open it after dark.*'

He squeezed her hand, and felt Arkle doing the same to his.

'*Never take back your sacrifice.*'

They let go.

The sun beat through the trees, their breathing settled and the box sat motionless at their feet.

The noise rose in Sep's ear, and its pain stabbed into his mouth.

'Did it work?' said Arkle.

The squirrel's jaw clicked behind him. They turned as leaves parted on the clearing's edge and a tiny, melted doll burst from the gloom, her mouth open, a green glow in her bobbing eyes.

The box's sound filled Sep's deaf ear like a siren, and as he opened his mouth to scream the crows burst from the trees.

'RUN!' shouted Lamb, slipping on a pile of dead fur.

The doll bore down with impossible speed. It pushed Lamb to the ground, then began to climb over her body.

Arkle screamed and heaved the Geiger counter at the doll's face, knocking it on to the ground before bringing the dial down on the plastic skull.

'I *knew* it was a good idea to bring this!' he said, helping Lamb to her feet.

'Don't get cocky,' she muttered, pushing him on as Sadie staggered upright.

They ran breathlessly through the trees, the sound of tiny footsteps only feet away as the doll cut through the forest behind them.

Sep had never run for so long without stopping – the breath hurt in his chest, and his heart beat painfully.

He saw Arkle turn his head and duck – saw Lamb follow his eyes and scream. Hadley, wheezing uncontrollably, tripping on a wet stone, Mack shouting as he reached down to grab her.

And then the forest exploded.

37

Miracle

Mario leaned over Mr Snuggles. He prodded the little belly with his scalpel, then lifted the tail and let it fall.

It flicked away, as though indignant at being handled.

He'd stored the other animals, and calmed their owners. Then he'd locked the door and switched off the lights.

'Is most unusual,' he said into the Dictaphone, running his hand over the scaly, slender corpse. 'Subject: Mr Snuggles, iguana dressed as Abraham Lincoln. Is clinically dead, but responding to stimulus.'

He swung the light over the table and passed his hand through the beam, watching as the shadow struck the nerves and twitched the legs.

'Parietal eye is active, although –' he checked the orange eyeballs, their pupils wide and still – 'ocular dilation is static.'

Mario stood back, hands on his hips.

'Is a miracle,' he said. 'A miracle. This is the Jesus of iguanas.'

He turned to Barkley, back on his trolley.

'And this is dog-Jesus.'

Barkley was bug-eyed and warm, his breathless mouth running with thick, warm drool. Mario angled the light over the dog's head.

'Subject: Barkley. Although also clinically dead, he propelled himself from table and into cupboard, displaying motor function in excess even of Mr Snuggles –'

The iguana's jaw moved, and the mouth closed like a pincer.

'– and his eyes are –'

A pinprick of green light in Barkley's eye swelled quickly to a bright glow that shone against Mario's scalpel.

'– they are –' said Mario, staring.

Barkley's head snapped up and, as the dog's teeth sunk into his hand, Mario heard the slither of scale on steel, and screamed.

38

Forgiveness

Plumes of cordite rose from Roxburgh's shotgun. Daniels lurked behind him, his face pasty and damp, one ear massive and purple. The little terrier growled deep in her chest, teeth bared.

Daniels? thought Sep.

He looked at the others, each of them frozen in terror, eyes fixed on the shotgun. He could see what they were all thinking, faced with this bleeding, tattooed wild man: that he'd tried to kill Maguire and now he was here, pointing a gun at their heads.

But Roxburgh hadn't shot them. He'd shot the doll.

And, more than that, Sep realized – he hadn't seemed surprised to see it.

'So it's you's been doin' this?' said the old gamekeeper. The skin on his face was red and thick, his eyes deep behind a broken, orange-peel nose. He was holding another terrier close to his chest. Its neck was limp, and Sep saw its fur was soaked with blood.

He stared at the little doll. Blown apart, it looked like any other broken toy, the terrible light gone from its eyes.

'Speak!' said Roxburgh, stabbing the gun at them.

'That's not ours,' blurted Lamb, her voice shaking.

Hadley sobbed, then took a quick burst of her inhaler.

'I know *that*,' said Roxburgh, 'but –'

'All right, Septic?' said Daniels.

'You shut it,' said Roxburgh. 'Now, for the last time, is it you's what's been at the clearin'?'

'Pardon, sir?' said Sep, the noise of the shotgun still ringing in his good ear.

Roxburgh angled his head, narrowing his eyes.

'You that deaf boy?'

'Yes, sir,' said Sep.

'Oh, I remember you lot,' said Roxburgh, spitting at his feet. 'You was the ones found it in '82 – always on your bikes, an' settin' things on fire. Wasn't there a stupid kid with big teeth?'

'You tried to kill Mrs Maguire!' said Arkle, his eyes wide. 'You're a killer! You're a *killer*!'

'There you are,' said Roxburgh, pointing the gun at Arkle.

'Holy *shiiiiiiiiiiiiiiiiiiiiiiiiiiiiii*–' said Arkle.

'I asked if it's you been skulkin' these past nights, but I reckon I've got my answer.'

'That wasn't – we've not been here before today, sir,' said Sep.

The terrier's growl rose in its throat and Roxburgh shook his head.

'One of you has.'

'I knew it,' said Lamb, her voice shaking as her eyes flicked accusingly at the others. 'I *knew* it!'

'Sir, what *was* that?' Sep pointed at the shards of wet plastic.

'A doll. Been huntin' it since sunrise, an' I found it climbin' out the stone this mornin', dangerous little bastard. Took a chunk out my leg –' he gestured to the bloodstained patch of torn fabric on his trousers – 'an' it's your meddlin' what's brought it out.'

The five looked at each other.

'Don't play dumb wi' me! You broke the rules!' Roxburgh snapped. 'You said the words, an' you've gone back on 'em.'

'Wait, you know about the rules?' said Lamb, lowering her hands. 'What the hell?'

'What rules?' said Daniels.

'Shut it,' said Roxburgh again. 'You think you were the first ones to find it? *Never come to the box alone. Never open it after dark. Never take back your sacrifice.*'

'They're the same as ours,' said Lamb. 'They're the same rules we made.'

'Of course they are,' said Roxburgh slowly.

'You tried to kill Mrs Maguire,' Arkle burst out, panic driving his mouth. 'You've got prison tattoos and everything!'

Roxburgh spat again, sending a black blob into one of his giant bootprints.

'That ain't so, son – it was me saved 'er. This bloody doll was 'er sacrifice. Meant to choke 'er to death, but I got there in time.'

Sep's head spun.

'Maguire made a *sacrifice*?' he said. '*Mrs Maguire?*'

'Wasn't her name then,' said Roxburgh, shifting the terrier's dead weight on to his other arm. 'She was Aileen

Gordon, brightest girl in the school. It was her idea to make the offerin'. So we did. Five of us,' he added, looking around at them each in turn.

'And it tried to choke her?' said Sep, remembering Barnaby's shadow on his window. 'The *doll* tried to kill her?'

Roxburgh nodded.

'Sadie,' he said, tasting the name. 'She came back when you messed it all up again – and mine's out there too, somewhere. We were the only ones left, me an' Aileen, after Shelley moved away.'

Sep's memory flickered.

'Did she move to New York?'

Now Roxburgh looked surprised.

'How'd you know a thing like that?' he said quietly.

'She died. Mr Tench told me Mrs Maguire's friend in New York died suddenly. Yesterday.'

'That's right,' murmured Roxburgh, almost to himself. He looked at them and smiled without humour, his teeth stained like an old teapot. 'Means I'm next then, doesn't it?'

'So it *does* go in order?' said Hadley.

Daniels looked from her to the gamekeeper, his brow furrowed in confusion.

'Aren't you clever?' said the old man, packing more tobacco into his mouth. 'Not clever enough, though – you don't know what you're dealin' with. The box gives you the rules, an' takes everythin' you give it – much more than your sacrifice, though you don't know it at the time. All the secret things. An' so long as you keep your promises you'll be safe . . . but it can't stand the rules bein' broken. It gets *angry*.

Look, you all know me, an' how I keep these woods. Well, I've been keepin' an eye on that box. I buried it good and deep, an' nobody'd found it until that damn storm spat it out an' you little bastards started messin' around. But this –' he kicked the doll's broken skull – 'this never happened back in my time.'

'What did happen?' said Hadley, her voice no more than a breath.

'Well . . . we did it wrong – broke one of the rules,' said Roxburgh, his eyes far off as he settled into the confession. 'They came back, tried to scare us, but they never tried to *kill* us. Then we did it a second time, properly.' He refocused, glared round at them all. 'I don't know what you've done, but this is worse. Even the forest knows it. Nothin's growin' except the mushrooms.'

'We don't know what we've done. We don't even know what rule we've broken. But we've tried to fix it,' said Sep. 'Just now, we tried to put the rules right – reverse whatever went wrong. We're here together, in daylight, and we mean to –'

'But you've not done it *properly*!' Roxburgh snapped, his voice like a thunderclap in the silent forest. 'Well,' he said, noting how they stood apart – seeing the distance between them. 'I'd say you're not capable of anythin' else, lookin' at you. You can't bring that kind of resentment here an' expect it to work for you. I can't do it for you. Even if I could, I'm old an' tired an' it's already killed one of my damn dogs.'

'The doll killed your dog?' said Hadley.

Sep saw how pale she was, how unsteady on her feet.

'Jus' get out of here an' don't come back,' said Roxburgh. 'An' take this lump with you.'

Daniels looked at him, snapping out of his trance.

'I'm not going with them,' he said, 'they're assholes.'

'Watch your goddamn language,' growled Roxburgh, snapping open his gun. 'An' you'll do as you're told. I was plannin' on holin' up when I found you skulkin' around.'

'I'd nearly caught it,' said Daniels.

'Caught what?' said Sep.

'The pellet-eyed crow.'

Sep looked at Daniels properly for the first time. His eyes were red and sore, and his Mohawk had flopped over his sunburnt scalp.

Daniels snapped his teeth, and grinned.

'I *told* you,' said Roxburgh, 'they's already *dead* – you can't hunt 'em any more'n you can scoop up the moon.'

'The crows are dead?' said Sep.

'You've seen 'em?'

'Yes. They've been outside our houses – and they were at the box just now. Three of them.'

Roxburgh nodded, and took his time answering.

'They's not usual crows,' he said eventually.

'So what are they?' shouted Arkle. 'Aren't you going to give us, like, guidance?'

The gamekeeper squinted at him, shook his head.

'Those really are some teeth, son.'

'Sir,' said Sep, taking a half-pace, 'how do we stop the sacrifice box from hurting us?'

Roxburgh pocketed his leather tobacco pouch, the tattooed swallow wings beating as his hands moved. He slotted in two new shells, holding Sep's eye.

'I told you, you've come to it all wrong,' he said, closing the gun. 'Too bitter, too resentful. I don't know if you *can* do anythin' now.'

'But . . . *you* did,' said Lamb, hand on her face. 'You did something! You managed to stop it! So why can't we?'

'I told you – what you've done must be worse than what we did. Now get out of here, an' don't come back. Stay safe. *Hide.*'

'You're meant to be *wise* – and *helpful*,' said Arkle, almost to himself.

Roxburgh lifted the gun back on to his shoulder.

'Are you scared, little children?'

'Yes,' said Sep. 'We are.'

He could feel the others holding their breath.

Roxburgh shook his head, and smiled.

'No, you're not. You don't know fear – not *real* fear. But you might, before this is over.'

'*I'm* not scared,' said Daniels.

Roxburgh shot him a look.

'You'd already pissed your trousers when I found you.'

'That's amazing,' said Arkle quickly.

Daniels' face darkened.

'I *fell* – in the river.'

'Ain't no rivers of piss around here, son,' Roxburgh snorted. 'Get goin' now. Fast as you can.'

'But –' said Lamb.

'Go! These is my woods – you've already done 'em enough harm!'

They edged past him, Daniels storming ahead, the others helping each other through the streams and over the rocks.

'What do we do?' Sep called back. 'Please?'

'Forgive each other,' said Roxburgh, without turning round.

'What?'

'You heard me. I can see it when I look at you – all that resentment's like storm clouds around your heads. Forgive each other, then you'll have a chance.'

'All right,' said Sep uncertainly. 'Thank you.'

Roxburgh listened as their footsteps faded into the trees, waited for the pickup to rumble into life and speed off. Then he shifted the dog's dead weight on to his shoulder, stamped the last shards of Sadie's body into the dirt, and headed home.

39

Escape

'We almost got shot!' screamed Arkle, grabbing Lamb's hair over the headrest.

'There was a *mixtape* on the ground, *and* the goddamn lid was off!' she screamed, stamping on the accelerator. 'Are you all going to keep pretending no one went back to the box? Someone has – let me go, you little freak!'

Mack reached over and prised Arkle's fingers away. He locked on to the seat instead.

'We didn't almost get shot,' said Sep. 'He saved us!'

'What did he say when you hung back?' said Lamb, eyeing Sep in the mirror.

'He said we . . . he said we had to forgive each other. That we resent each other too much to fix this.'

'Eh?' said Arkle. 'That's crazy, I don't resent you guys.'

'I do,' growled Lamb, gripping the wheel tighter.

'You shouldn't have stayed there on your own,' said Arkle, shaking Sep's shoulders. 'He had a gun, September! A *gun*!'

'But *he* didn't attack Mrs Maguire – her doll did! Isn't that crazy? She and Roxburgh sacrificed stuff when they were kids – and now the box is trying to kill everyone who's made a sacrifice!'

'They had the same rules as us,' said Hadley, shivering.

'And someone's broken them!' shouted Lamb, hammering the wheel with her fist. 'Who was it?'

The truck skidded on the gravel, righting itself too quickly and knocking them against the side. Sunlight was strobing through the canopy with a flickering light that hurt Sep's head.

'Well, it wasn't me,' said Arkle. 'First I knew about it was the damn wings in my ears.'

'And it wasn't me,' said Daniels, his bulk and Mack's almost filling the small cabin. 'What are you dickheads even –'

'Shut up, Daniels!' shouted Lamb. 'One of *you* has done this,' she hissed, her teeth locked tight.

'You know, Lamb, we've all got shit to deal with, OK?' said Arkle. 'I threw up bloody dragonflies, you know? And Hadley –'

'Look at my *face*!' Lamb screamed, tears in her eyes. 'What do you think it's doing to me? I gave it my mum's mirror, and now I look like her. Do you think I can't see it? I had the same dream as you, Sep, the same dream – only in mine the birds couldn't fill my mum's skin. She just stayed empty, then they flew away.'

'You're such –' Daniels began.

'Nobody gives a *shit* about you, Keith! You're *nothing* – don't you get it?' shouted Lamb as Daniels sat rigid with shock. 'Can't you lot see what's happening to us? Why did we choose those things when we were kids? Why *those* things?'

'I just like to burn stuff,' said Arkle. 'Sometimes, when school doesn't go well, I make little fires and watch them. I did the dragonflies just after I'd burned my report card, remember?'

'It was my favourite watch,' said Mack.

'My diary had all my secrets inside.'

'What about your teddy, Sep?' Lamb interrupted. 'Whose was he?'

'Mine. But my mum had him for a while, in the hospital –'

'And now she's ill again, isn't she?'

'How do you know that?' said Sep quietly. The others had frozen.

'Don't you see? It's not just trying to kill us – it's trying to destroy our lives!'

Sep thought of Lamb's changing face, of Hadley's bruise and Arkle's failing memory; of his mum, lying glassy-eyed and pale on a hospital bed – and he remembered at once the desire he'd felt, even then, to leave the island.

He thought of what Roxburgh had said: *everything you give it – all the secret things*.

He felt sick.

'Oh my God,' he said. 'Is that it? Is that what we sacrificed?'

'What?' said Arkle, looking scared. 'What are you guys talking about?'

'It makes sense when you think about it: the rules coming in a dream, and the *compulsion* to make a sacrifice. The box wanted *us*; it called *us*. And we didn't just give it *stuff* – we gave it all the messed-up shit in our heads.'

He pictured Barnaby tucked in beside his mum, lying in the box, and then standing at his window – smelling of hospital.

'And now that we've broken the rules,' he said, 'all that shit is coming back to us.'

Arkle started to whine, like he was coming to the boil.

'So this is why I'm getting picked on again?' said Hadley.

'Holy shit,' said Arkle. 'Holy shit, I am getting stupider, amn't I? Will I get stupider and stupider until it kills me?'

'Who was it?' Lamb's voice fell into tight, angry sobs as she rubbed the empty space on her wrist. 'Who? Admit it! Who?'

Sep kneaded the foam pads of his headphones in his fists. Then he blinked.

'We could play the tape,' he said.

'What tape?' said Hadley quickly.

'The one that was lying beside the box – if we can –'

'Give it to me,' said Lamb. She grabbed the cassette from Sep's hand, slammed it into the stereo and turned up the volume.

At first there was silence – just the hiss of tape winding through the heads. Daniels' eyes flicked over their faces.

'No!' shouted Lamb, jamming down the forward button.

'Maybe it got rained on,' said Arkle.

'This has to work,' said Lamb, forwarding and playing, forwarding and playing. 'Whoever did this to us left this behind, so if it plays we'll –'

The opening bars of 'You Make My Dreams' blared from the speakers.

'Hall & Oates?' said Lamb. '*HALL & OATES?*'

'Oh my God,' said Sep.

'What's going on?' said Arkle. 'What does that mean? Whose tape is it?'

A sob escaped Hadley's lips.

'Hadley?' said Sep.

She was pulling at her glove. It was freshly stained by the forest, bright streaks of green on the palm. Sep looked at the stain he'd thought was mud, but could now see was something else – something that had been brighter before it dried.

'Why are you wearing that?' he said, a sick feeling pooling in his stomach.

She sighed.

'The lid's so heavy,' she said, and pulled off the glove.

40

Confession

'Holy shit!' said Arkle.

'You did this?' said Lamb. '*You?*'

'No, I swear! I only went there *after* I had the dream!'

'I'm going to kill you,' said Lamb with icy calm. 'When we get back I'm going to drag you out this car, and –'

'You don't understand!' shouted Hadley. 'It wasn't – I tried to fix it!'

Sep took her hand in his. The edge of her palm was split by a raw-edged cut, livid with blushing pink and spotted with dark crusts of blood. It looked like a bite wound.

'What do you mean, fix it?' he said, swallowing a tight ball of anger.

'The box was already *open*,' said Hadley, looking round the car at them all. 'You have to believe me. I tried to make more sacrifices – some old stuff I found in the attic – but when I got there I couldn't do it, I – I got too scared and I dropped everything. Then I tried to close the lid, but –' she ran a finger gently over the cut – 'it's so heavy.'

A thin trickle of bright red ran down her arm and they watched it in silence, all the way to her elbow, until it snapped free and landed on the pickup's dusty floor.

'You put blood in it,' said Sep as the truck buzzed over a cattle grid. 'You put blood in the box. A human sacrifice!'

'Christ on a bike,' said Arkle.

'What does that mean?' asked Hadley, eyes wide and panicked.

'I don't know,' said Sep. 'But it's using the things we gave it to hurt us.'

Tears spilled from Hadley's eyes, and she dropped her face in her hands.

'I'm scared, Sep.'

Sep put his hand on her shoulder, feeling her warmth on his palm.

'It'll be OK,' he said.

'The hell it will,' said Lamb, guiding the truck round a sharp bend. 'You stupid –'

'It will!' Sep snapped. 'We can figure this out. Roxburgh and Maguire managed it.'

'You need to do the thinking, Sep,' said Arkle. 'You're the brainbox, so think of a plan – now. Go! Plan something!'

'Hang on,' said Lamb. 'Wait. Hadley, do you swear the box was already open when you got there?'

'Yes!' said Hadley, her face shiny with tears. 'I had the dream, with the voice saying those things, and I knew they were from my diary, so I thought –'

'So, if you didn't open it, who did?'

'Anyone want an M&M?' said Mack.

'Mack?' said Lamb.

Mack opened the M&Ms, tipped a few on to his bandaged hand and ate them one by one as the others watched.

Sep caught Lamb's eye in the mirror.

'How did *you* hurt your hand, Mack?' he said.

'I told you. Football.'

'It was,' said Daniels. 'He pussied out this tackle, and I –'

'Did you open the box, Mack?' said Lamb, her hands tight on the wheel.

'What box are you losers talking about?' Daniels snorted.

'Shut *up*, Daniels!' shouted Lamb and Sep together.

Mack ate a few more M&Ms, then crushed the packet and sighed, looking out of the window at the sun.

'I had to open it,' he said, almost to himself, his face expressionless. 'But I didn't mean for this to happen.'

'*You?* You *swore* to me you didn't know what was going on!' screamed Lamb, half turning in her seat and swinging the truck across the narrow road. 'I swear to *God*, I'll –'

'The road!' shouted Arkle.

Lamb swerved away from a log pile, crushing them all together. Sep pushed away from the meat of Mack's shoulder. 'But what did you do?' he asked. 'Which rule did you break?'

'Oh, all of them,' Mack sighed, sounding almost relieved to be saying it aloud. 'I went there on my own, at night, and I took the sacrifices out. The box is pretty deep. I thought it was empty – I was in up to my shoulder before I found anything. But I got them eventually – even the ones that weren't ours. Everything.'

'But *why* would you – don't you see what you've done?' said Sep, 'Look at what's –'

'I didn't want any of this! I just – I missed you guys. I've been so lonely without you, and –'

'Eh?' said Daniels, pointing his un-torn ear at Mack. 'Lonely? But we hang out, like, every night.'

'Shut up, Daniels,' said Mack. He turned to Sep, pleading. 'I had to do *something*. I was so happy that summer. You were . . . real friends, not like these *animals*. They hate me! And they hate each other. Everything is –'

'Wait,' said Daniels, 'who are you calling –'

'Where do you get off thinking *you're* lonely?' shouted Sep. 'I've been on my own since we started high school, and you were meant to be my friends! That's why we went to the box in the first place – we promised it would keep us together, but I've spent the past four years alone, and now *you're* complaining about being lonely?'

'I wanted to talk to you, but –'

'But what? You're scared of your stupid gang?'

'Yes!' Mack shouted, punching the back of Lamb's seat.

'Hey!' she shouted.

'Of course I'm scared of them! They start on you for anything and everything – they just pile in and there's nothing you can do!'

'Maybe if you didn't –' Daniels began.

'So your friends are assholes,' said Sep, leaning across him. 'What does that make you?'

'A coward,' said Hadley, staring at Mack, her eyes burning. Mack shot her a dark look.

'Maybe,' he said. 'But I've tried. It's –'

'I've been torturing myself about this, but it was you!' Hadley yelled, hitting Mack's shoulder as hard as she could. He didn't flinch, just kept staring at the floor. 'You were going to let me take the blame! Because everyone thinks I'm so weird, it must be the weirdo – it's never the *cool* kids!'

'When?' said Sep. 'When did you do it?'

'Four nights ago,' said Mack, puffing out his cheeks and looking at the cabin roof, his eyes shining as the car bumped off the end of the path and on to the main road.

'That was when I had my first dream,' said Hadley.

Mack nodded.

'I could see on your face something had happened, and I was happy, because I thought we might – but then Lamb told me about the mirrors, and when I saw her face I just –'

'Where did you put them?' said Lamb.

'In a sack, and I threw that in the river,' said Mack. 'Then things started to go wrong, and I panicked. I went looking for it, but all that was left was –'

He held up his watch, still smeared with mud.

'I started it again,' he said, looking at the scratched face. 'It still works.'

'Asshole,' said Lamb, screwing up her face in disgust. 'Coward.'

Mack squeezed his eyes tight, sending tears down his nose.

'I'm sorry,' he said. 'But you need to understand –'

'Shit, Mack!' said Sep. 'When I've nearly got out of here for good, and I – my mum! If she's ill again because of you I swear to God, I'll – and nothing's even *happened* to you! You've just inflicted this on the rest of us!'

'I didn't mean any of this. I just wanted to be with you again! I hate them, the team. I *hate* them; they just *do* things to each other all the time, and I *hate* it –' He began to cry in steady, hissing bursts. 'But I love football. It's all I can do. So until I can play in college I have to pretend to like these assholes, because there's five of them and one of me – and you guys weren't there any more.'

'You're such a pussy, Macejewski, seriously,' said Daniels with a sideways sneer.

'Shut up!' shouted Mack, turning and hammering his fist on Daniels' arm. 'Shut up! Shut up!'

Arkle grabbed Mack's arm and held it, both hands round the massive bicep.

'All right, Golden Boy,' he said, 'I can't believe I'm saying this, but that's probably enough.'

'What do we do now?' asked Hadley, her voice trembling.

'We're going back to mine,' said Lamb decisively. 'We need to hide out and figure out what the hell to do next. My dad's away –'

'Your house?' said Daniels and Sep together.

Daniels dug an elbow into Sep's ribs – but Sep gripped his arm and held it clear.

'*I'm* not going to your farm,' said Daniels. 'Drop me at home.'

'As if I'd let you anywhere *near* my house,' said Lamb, giving him a disgusted glance in the mirror. 'And I'm not taking you home either. I'm dropping you in town. You really don't get it, do you? You're *nothing* to us.'

'All right, Big Bird, why don't –'

'SHUT UP, DANIELS!' they all shouted together.

A fragile moment hung between the five of them, and Sep took a deep breath. Something had happened when

Lamb said 'us'. It felt like another layer of skin had grown around him.

Daniels blinked, stupefied and quiet.

'I'm meant to be in work. Mario's expecting me,' said Sep.

'You can't sell pizzas after fighting a zombie doll, can you?' said Arkle. 'Even, like, hygiene-wise.'

'I know I can't *go*! But if I don't show up, Mario might call the police or something. Or my mum.'

'Just tell him you're sick,' said Lamb.

'Lie to him?' said Sep. 'I've never –'

'Yes! Jesus Christ, Sep!'

'Drop me at the back of the shops then. You know, beside the graveyard?'

'I know the graveyard,' Lamb said, almost too quietly to hear.

She guided them down a side street and under a willow tree. She turned the keys, and the truck shuddered still.

The silence was immediate. The willow fronds made a little cocoon around the cabin, with chirps above them and sunshine on the ground. The raised voices of children playing on the beach came on the wind – and in that moment the forest and the doll seemed to belong to another world. Sep had to remind himself that it was real, all of it: all the dead things and Barnaby, the crows and the waiting, hungry sacrifice box.

Something landed on the roof.

'Well, you clowns talk some pile of shit,' said Daniels. 'I'm out of here.'

Another thump came from the roof, followed by the scritching of talons on paint.

'What was that?' said Daniels.

'On you go, tough guy,' said Sep, looking at the blood-crusts on Daniels' ear.

'Yeah,' said Lamb, 'now – or I'll hurt you in secret, *private* ways.'

'You don't scare me,' said Daniels. 'You can't –'

'She scares me,' said Arkle. 'But I kind of like it.'

There was another thump, this time from the bonnet. A crow hopped towards the windscreen. There was something in its eye, Sep thought, something dark and shiny.

Daniels' lips went tight.

'It followed me,' he said shrilly. 'It followed me!'

'Don't flatter yourself,' said Arkle. 'This is nothing to do with you.'

The pellet-eyed crow tapped on the windscreen, and the six occupants stared at the spectral blues of its gleaming feathers.

Sep held his lips close to Daniels' untorn ear.

'*Go,*' he whispered.

Daniels screamed as Mack opened the car door and tipped him into the sun. The pellet-eyed crow leaped from the bonnet as he ran, his bright, wet hair flapping on his neck.

'What an asshole,' said Arkle.

'Be quick,' said Lamb, looking at Sep in the mirror. 'I don't want to sit here any longer than I have to.'

'Right,' said Sep, wondering how he was going to lie to Mario without his face betraying him.

'Sep, I'm sorry,' said Mack, touching Sep's shoulder as he opened the door. Sep ignored him, reached for Hadley's hand. She smiled at him.

'I feel better now that we're back here,' she said.

'Me too,' he whispered, squeezing her fingers for a second. 'It'll be all right.'

'Check out the bold Sep,' said Arkle, grinning.

Sep tried to walk away normally, but his heart hadn't settled since his explosion of anger at Mack, and his head was spinning with everything they'd learned.

Mack had deliberately broken the rules to bring them back together. Mrs Maguire had sacrificed a doll in childhood — and it had returned to kill her. They had unwittingly sacrificed painful, secret things — and the box was using them as weapons.

And Hadley had given it blood.

He flexed his fingers. His skin still tingled with her touch.

But he felt fear, cold and hard, curling in his stomach.

Town was busy, real life somehow carrying on despite the madness in the woods: the air was full of tinny music and the putter of boats. Cars drove slowly, and as he moved down the row of shops people fanned themselves and complained about the heat. It was impossibly normal, and he thought with sharp envy of their small problems.

The blind was down on the vet's surgery door. He tried the handle, but it was locked, so he shook the door in its frame and tried again.

'What the hell?' he said under his breath.

He pressed his face to the glass, hands cupped to close out the sun.

There were no lights on inside.

Panic shook him, and he battered the glass with his knuckles.

'Mario? Mario?'

'Is closed!' came Mario's voice, far-off and muffled.

Sep gasped with relief.

'It's Sep!' he shouted. 'What's going on?'

'September?' said Mario.

Sep heard him stomp across the reception, the rattle of keys as the door swung open on its chain, then Mario's face – sweat dripping in his moustache, his skin pale – appeared in the gap.

'September? You are early.'

'No, I . . . you wanted me to come in and clean the cold store?'

'Oh!' said Mario, his eyes widening. 'This I had forgotten, forgive me. Yes. No. No, tonight I will not open chip shop, is OK, something has –'

'What do you mean? It's Friday, it's the busiest –'

'Something has happened,' said Mario urgently, glancing back over his shoulder. 'Something amazing. I – I may not need chip shop much longer. I must find out . . . incredible, my Sep, it is incredible.'

'Right,' said Sep, looking past Mario into the darkness of the surgery. 'I, um –'

'You want see what is in here?' said Mario.

'Isn't it always a dead dog?' said Sep, trying to smile.

Mario looked at him for a second or two.

'Yes,' he said.

'Mario, I was going to say –'

'You have things you would rather do?' said Mario. 'Your young friends?'

'No!' said Sep, too quickly. 'I was going to say I wasn't feeling too great actually. I think it's a bug.'

'There is one going about,' said Mario, nodding. Sep wanted to hug his big friend and explain, but knew it was impossible.

'You go,' said Mario, 'is OK. I see you tomorrow maybe? If you feel better? We can climb on to the roof and watch the comet? A special thing between pals?'

'Yeah,' said Sep, nodding, 'definitely.'

Mario winked as he closed the door, then turned back to the surgery, its interior lit with a green glow.

Outside, alone again among the crowds, Sep breathed out slowly.

Heading back to the pickup, trying not to draw attention, he thought again about the afternoon's revelations.

Mack.

Hadley.

The box.

And he realized there was only one way of throwing light on the situation – something that would have been unthinkable even an hour earlier.

'That was quick,' said Lamb, starting the engine and grinding the truck into gear. 'Right, if we take the forestry road, we should be –'

'We can't go to yours yet,' said Sep, closing his door with a thump.

'What? Look, we can hide there and figure out what we –'

'No, that's just it: we won't figure this out on our own. We need help – we have to go to the hospital.'

'What's wrong?' said Hadley, her tears dried in splotches around her eyes.

'Nothing's wrong,' said Sep, strapping himself in. 'It's visiting time.'

41

Guidance

Maguire opened gummy eyes. The room was hot, and she felt her back damp with sweat. She coughed, brought something jellyish and salty into her mouth, and turned her head to spit.

Sep was sitting at the side of her bed.

She coughed again and went to roll her eyes – but they felt like boulders, and it hurt.

'Hope?' she croaked. 'What on earth are you doing here?'

'I said you were my gran,' said Sep. 'I'm sorry, miss. I had to see you.'

She gestured at the steel water jug. Sep lifted it carefully, handed her the little cup and felt her skin on his. She was cold, even though her face glistened with the room's plasticky, clinical warmth.

She drank, little runnels falling from the sides of her mouth, then held out the cup for more.

'Well?' she said.

He flicked his eyes nervously at her as he poured.

'I wanted to ask about what happened to you.'

She scowled.

'This isn't the Hardy Boys. The police –' She broke off to cough and Sep steadied her shoulder, awkwardly supporting her bony joint as her eyes closed. 'The police are doing their jobs.'

'I'm not investigating, miss, I just –'

'Go,' she said, settling into her pillows and nodding painfully at the door. 'You shouldn't be in here and I don't want to have to call the nurse. Nice girl, I used to teach her. Very respectful.'

'I'm sorry, miss,' said Sep more firmly, 'but I *know* what happened to you.'

'I doubt that,' she said, and reached for the alarm.

Sep snatched it from her hand.

'Hey!' she said, grabbing his arm. 'Don't you –'

'Sadie,' Sep hissed urgently, his eyes bulging. '*Sadie.*'

She stopped pushing him away and her grip tightened.

'How can you possibly know that name?'

'Thom Roxburgh told us. She tried to strangle you. Well, my teddy bear tried to kill me – his name is Barnaby. I put him in the sacrifice box four years ago – but now he's back and we don't know what to do about it, so I need your help.'

They looked at each other for a long moment, and Sep didn't look away. Maguire's face – the same one that had glowered at him a thousand times, unyielding as a battleship – looked different, the skin around her eyes soft without the teacher's stare.

He nodded to show he was serious, then handed her another cup of water.

She drank it, still looking at him.

'What else did Thom say?' she said eventually.

'He told us this is worse than what happened to you, when you were kids,' said Sep. 'Sadie *chased* us today – she bit a chunk out of Thom's leg, then he shot her. And he said he saved you from her.'

She nodded.

'I knew it was him – that tobacco he chews. Did you say she bit him?'

'Yeah. And she tried to kill us too.'

'Jesus, Mary and Joseph,' she whispered. 'I assume someone broke the rules?'

'Mack,' said Sep, blushing as though he was grassing someone up in class. 'He broke, like . . . all of them.'

Maguire closed her eyes.

'He said he was lonely,' said Sep.

Maguire thought of the shade in the chair at home.

'Yes,' was all she said.

Sep wiped his face on his T-shirt, scraping the sweat from his eyes.

'Who did they choose?'

'What?' he said.

'The rules. Who did they come to?'

Sep met her stare. He felt like he could cry.

'Me,' he said, thinking back to the moment in his bedroom when the words had appeared without warning, like petals falling on his head. 'They just . . . came to me. It was weird.'

Maguire smiled.

'Like a dream?' She saw his face, and went on. 'They came to me too. We didn't know they really meant anything, of course.'

She took another drink, then set down her cup.

'What happens when you break a promise?'

'What?'

'People are hurt. Misery, pain, upset. That's what happens when you break a promise. Childhood is a powerful thing – there aren't many things in life as fierce as the bond between children. Between friends, who love each other.'

Sep remembered the vivid threads that had connected them that summer, how they had *felt* the connection. Each of them close. Each of them happy.

'Why didn't it keep us together then? If it's so powerful, how come we didn't stay friends?'

'Because you broke your promise,' said Maguire, 'and then you broke the rules. They are one and the same: the rules *are* your promise, to each other – and to the box. You gave it all that power, then corrupted it. And now you've taken the lid off it's returning that broken promise – all that misery and pain – to you.'

'I *knew* it,' said Sep, moving closer to the bed. 'Everything we gave it when we made our sacrifices is coming back and hurting us: me, Lamb, Darren, Hadley, everyone except –'

It'll always show the time of this perfect moment.

'– Mack.'

Sep pictured him stopping his watch, freezing time at the moment they all swore to be friends forever.

Mack.

It was his turn today, but nothing had come back from the box to cause him pain.

And, Sep realized, nothing would.

Because Mack had put his happiness in the box.

His watch was working again, now they were all back together. Sep pictured the big athlete snacking in the background, lonely every day since that summer – and himself, isolated behind his studies, rejecting Mack and the others and focusing only on escaping the island.

'That last time,' said Maguire, interrupting his thoughts, 'we knew we had to do it properly –'

'That's what Roxburgh said! What does that even mean, *properly*?'

A nurse looked over at his raised voice.

'The first time we made an offering,' Maguire whispered, 'we did it wrong. It was meant to be about our friendship, same as yours, but the others . . . didn't take it seriously. Only Thom and me. The other three took their sacrifices back straight away – so our promise was broken. It was bad. Morgan developed a lung infection. Lizzie couldn't eat properly. Shelley lost her hair.'

'Shelley who died in New York?'

She gave him a strange look.

'Aren't you sharp?' she said. 'That was Shelley, yes. Caught her hair in a subway train. Terrible business. I'd forgotten all about the offerings until Morgan died a few years ago. A crow came to the window that night, and I knew. Two came when Lizzie died; another yesterday, when Shelley . . .' She trailed off and nodded at the window.

Two crows were staring through the glass. One was badly injured, white bone jutting through torn flesh, and they watched the third join them in a flutter of wings – the pellet shining in its eye.

'And now it's my turn,' she said. 'I don't know why it's so much worse this time. Nobody died when we broke the rules. What offerings did you make?'

'My teddy; Darren put in some dragonflies; a watch; a mirror; a diary. And today we tried to put in new versions of the same stuff – like a new teddy, and Hadley put in the pen she wrote the diary with – but it didn't work!'

'That's it?' she said. 'Nothing else?'

'No,' said Sep, 'only –'

'Only what?'

'Blood,' said Sep.

'What?' shouted Maguire, smiling calmly when the nurse looked up sharply from her desk. She dropped her voice to a hiss. 'You put something *alive* in the –'

'No! It was Hadley – she dropped the lid and cut her hand; it was just a tiny bit.'

'Of her blood? Human blood?'

'Yes,' said Sep. 'What does that mean?'

She shook her head.

'I have no idea. But I don't like it.'

Sep edged closer to the bed.

'I can hear it now,' he said. 'And I can feel its noise.'

'Feel it? How?'

'I've got a toothache,' said Sep, touching his jaw, 'and the box's noise hits it like a drill. It's agony. Why is that happening?'

Maguire nodded thoughtfully.

'Have you smelled the things that come back from it?'

'Yeah,' said Sep, remembering Barnaby's stink. 'They're all damp, and old, and –'

'Rotten. Rot, corruption, decay: these are what it sends into the world, how it controls things.'

Sep bit down, thinking of how the pain clawed and pulled at him.

'So rot is the box's frequency, and my tooth's like . . . an aerial?'

She smiled, pleased.

'Such a bright boy,' she said.

'But how do we stop it?' said Sep urgently. 'The others are waiting outside and we need to do *something*. Roxburgh won't help us – he told us to stay away – but we can't just hide and hope it stops. It *won't* stop. Sadie, Barnaby – people could get hurt. Your friend's already dead! We can't go to the police; my mum wouldn't –'

'No, she wouldn't,' said Maguire, her face grim.

She took his wrist in her little hand.

'You have to focus, September. Think about why you made the sacrifice in the first place – why the box chose you five to make the sacrifice. Because it *did* choose you, make no mistake about that.'

'But I don't know *why* it –'

'– It's because you loved each other so strongly! Now you need to make a *new* promise to each other, another offering: of things that bond you together.'

'What do you mean?'

'Items you've given each other, tokens that make you think of your friendship. Give those to the box and you'll be giving it all the love you have for each other.'

'The love?' said Sep. 'I don't think we – we're not exactly close any more.'

'You are. You must be. It chose you all, just like it chose us.'

'Oh,' said Sep, understanding dawning. 'Roxburgh told us to forgive each other.'

'Right,' said Maguire. 'Forgive. Love. Make new offerings – offerings that show your love for one another. Thom *will* help you, but you must do what you can.'

Maguire smiled at him, and she looked in that moment like a completely different person to the corridor-stomping terror he'd known.

'We will,' he said. 'I'm sorry, miss. I'm so sorry.'

She nodded, and leaned forward to cup his face in her hands. They were warm now, and incredibly soft. Sep wanted to hug her – to let himself be held and kept safe.

'I know you can do this, September. You're a brilliant boy. Go. Be brave. And be careful.'

Sep nodded, then ran down the corridor.

Maguire gripped the edges of the bedclothes as his footsteps faded. She lay back as the daylight ebbed into pinkening clouds, and watched the crows outside her window.

—3

Love: 1941

The light on Aileen's skin dimmed as their fire died. The forest leaned in towards them with clawing thorns and the foliage rustled in the wind. The day was almost gone, and dusk's gloom was gathering around them.

Aileen looked down at the box.

'You all right, lass?' said Thom.

The others were watching her, their hats rain-flat to their heads, blinking drops from their eyes. Black feathers glittered in the trees, and the five felt their blood chill at the chatter of the birds' beaks.

Aileen straightened her back.

'Yes,' she said. 'Yes. Have you brought another offering?'

'The way you looked at me when I opened my door, I'd have brought my own mother in a bag,' said Thom. 'It's the ticket stub from the school play, that time they did *Hamlet*.'

She looked quickly at him.

'You kept that?'

He nodded.

'One of the best times we ever had, wasn't it?'

'But we didn't go to the play — we went to the pier and drank a bottle of cooking sherry.'

Thom nodded again.

'That's what I'm talkin' about.'

She smiled at him and squeezed his hand.

'We give these with love. Those other things were spoiled by our squabbling. We broke our vow – now we can do it properly.'

Morgan took a small object from his pocket, then turned it in his hands.

'I'm sorry about before,' he said. 'If I'd known it would –'

'It's all right,' said Aileen, giving him a soft, grateful smile. 'You're here. It's all this was ever meant to be – us together again, like we were before.'

Shelley, a sodden shawl wrapped tightly round her head, leaned down and dropped a cardigan into the box's shadows.

'This is one of the things Aileen brought me when our house flooded and my clothes got ruined. I'm glad to be here with you all, and glad to show it. I love you all. I'm sorry I ever forgot it.'

Morgan barked a loud sob and coughed into his hands.

'This was the hatpin Lizzie gave me to mend my bike, that time when I fell,' he said, a thick wheeze on his breath. He leaned down and dropped the pin inside. A few crows rose from their perches and fluttered through the clearing. 'You're my best friends,' he said. 'I'm glad to give this.'

Thom clapped a hand on his back as he straightened up.

Lizzie gripped her parcel with taut knuckles and shrunken skin. Her eyes, deep-set in black circles, burned with tears, and her face was set and firm.

'I did wrong,' she said. 'I curse nobody. I love my aunt. She took me in and she's kept me well. I'm giving this for her as well as you. It's the book Thom gave me when I moved here — it brought me comfort on lonely nights, and I'm grateful.'

Thom stepped forward and hefted the shovel on to his shoulder.

'Given for all of you,' he said, dropping the ticket on top of the rest, 'and for all of yours, hopin' they're safe until the end of this damn war, an' beyond.'

Aileen allowed a small cry to escape her lips as she went to her pocket and took out the little cross-stitch. Rain landed on the threads, spotting the image with dark wrinkles, and she held it against her chest. Behind her, the treelines skittered with animal feet, and she sensed the night-time forest waking up around them.

'I made this for all of you,' she said, laying it inside and stepping back, reaching for the others, 'and for everyone who needs it, even the Germans — they've got children and mothers and fathers too. If we could just love each other, maybe everything would be all right.'

They held hands and said the rules. Thom dragged the lid back into place and Lizzie hunched forward, shoulders heaving. Morgan wrapped her in one of his rangy arms and she buried her face in his side.

Aileen looked up, peering through the rain as the crows melted into the night sky, the gleam of their terrible eyes vanishing into the scattered stars.

Thom squeezed her hand.

'Well done, lass,' he said quietly.

Aileen breathed in the fresh green air, and smiled.

'Let's go home,' she said.

42

Bonding

'Hurry *up*, Sep!' said Arkle, leaning out of the window.

The truck was hidden in the trees at the edge of the hospital car park, its paintwork sticky with sap and seeds – and covered in the scratches of taloned feet.

'I'm coming!'

Sep jumped in beside Arkle. The truck stank even more strongly of mushrooms, and he wondered if they were growing under the carpet.

'Hi, Sep,' said Mack, twisting round in the front seat.

'Hi, Mack. You all right?'

Mack smiled shyly.

'Yeah,' he said. 'You?'

'Yeah.'

They nodded at each other.

'Good talk, guys – real deep stuff,' said Arkle.

'What did Magpie say?' said Lamb.

'That we need to make another sacrifice.'

Lamb nodded and took a deep, wobbling breath. 'I thought so. It didn't work last time – there's something we weren't doing right. I can't believe I gave it my mum's . . . and it didn't even work!'

Hadley squeezed her arm, and she shook her head. Then pointed at Mack.

'Did she say anything about why this asshole's had nothing happen to him, even though it was him who opened the damn thing?'

Mack bowed his head.

'Kind of,' said Sep.

'And?'

Sep looked at Mack, at the sorrow in his big, honest face.

'It's because we all accidentally gave it things that were hurting us, or that –' he saw Lamb's eyes flick up – 'had hurt us in the past. But Mack didn't do that. He stopped his watch because he was so happy that summer – just purely happy, and he put nothing in there *but* that happiness. Nothing's coming for him,' he finished as Mack turned to him with tear-filled eyes, 'because there's nothing there *to* come.'

Mack reached over to hold Sep's shoulder, then dropped his hand.

'That's what Maguire told me: the most powerful thing we did is make a promise to each other. That's what Roxburgh was talking about when he said to do it "properly". This time we've got to make sacrifices *for each other*. Maguire said we had to give it love. That's what they did last time.'

'How are we going to "give it love"?' said Mack.

'Well, Mack,' said Arkle, 'when a teenage boy and a sacrifice box love each other very much, sometimes they –'

'Shut up,' said Lamb, wiping the corner of her eye with a knuckle. 'But he's right. What does that even mean?'

'It means the things we give it can't just be random things, and they definitely can't be marked by any hurt or sadness. They need to be . . . connected. To us, and the bond we have.'

Arkle nodded quickly.

'All right,' he said. 'But I don't know about . . . you know, the love thing? I mean, I guess I could put in one of my socks, but –'

'Not *self*-love!' said Sep as the rest of them recoiled. 'Something about how you love *us*, as a group of friends! God!'

'You're a sick little dude,' said Mack, scowling at Arkle.

Clouds like fists had closed over the island, purple and orange with the sun's last glimmer at their heart, and the world prickled under the swirl of a pregnant sky.

'So we can't do it properly unless we're real friends?' said Hadley.

Sep nodded.

'Well, that's us screwed,' said Arkle. 'You can't stand the sight of me.'

'That's not true,' said Sep. 'Is it?'

There was a silence.

'Well, this is awkward,' said Arkle, his bottom lip curling.

'No, I think –' Lamb started, looking out the window – 'sometimes I think you're . . . kind of funny.'

'I didn't catch that,' said Arkle, leaning forward.

'Kind of funny,' Lamb said reluctantly.

'Oh. Thank you. I think you're good at lacrosse.'

She looked at him.

'I don't play *lacrosse*.'

Arkle hit the side of his head, then fumbled for his dental floss.

'I *know*, I meant ice hockey – field hockey! Oh my God, my brain is leaking! It's the box doing this. I . . .'

'I am enjoying this conversation,' said Sep, 'but we need to go. *Now*.'

'Why?' said Mack.

'Because Barnaby's standing on the bonnet.'

They turned and saw Barnaby standing stock-still – legs apart, elbows bent, ready to launch. His eyes glowed brightly in the trees' shadows, his mouth stuck in its chilling smile.

'*Shiiiiiiiiiiiiiiiiiiiiiiiiiiiiiiiiiiiiiiiiiiiiiiiiiiiii–*' shrieked Arkle as Lamb threw the truck into gear and leaped on to the road. Sep grabbed his deaf ear and roared, his rotten tooth suddenly on fire. A post van swerved wildly out of their way, horn blaring as it plunged into a ditch.

'*–iiiiiiiiiiiiiiiiiiiiiiiiiiiiiiiiiiiiiiiiiiiiiiiiiiiiiiiiiiii–*'

Barnaby grabbed the wipers, wedging his puffy little paws into the hinges. Lamb swung the wheel, throwing him to the side, but he held on.

'*–iiiiiiiiiiiiiiiiiiiiiiiiiiiiiiiiiiiiiiiiiiiiiiiiiiiiiiiiiiii–*'

'Get rid of him!' she shouted.

'Me?' Sep managed through his teeth, hanging on to his jaw. 'What can I do? It's not like he does what he's told!'

'Not you – Mack! Hit him with something!'

'I can't,' said Mack, shaking his pale face. 'I can't.'

Lamb rolled her eyes.

'Jesus, take the wheel!'

She wound open the sunroof and stood, lifting her hockey stick from the floor in a single movement. As she rose out of the truck Barnaby looked up, his eyes glowing on her skin.

'–IIIIIIIIIIIIIIIIIIIIIIIIIIIIIIIIIIIIIIIIIIIIIIIIIIIIIIIIIIIII IIIIIII–'

'Bye-bye, little bear,' said Lamb – and smacked the teddy square in the face, knocking him into the trees that lined the road.

She dropped into her seat and took the wheel from Mack's rigid hands, winding the sunroof closed as a swarm of dragonflies descended on the car, smashing on to the windscreen in a burst of yellow and black.

'–iiiiiiiiiiiiiiiiiiiiiiiiiiiiiiiiiiiiiiiiiiiiiiiiiiiiiiiit –'

They pulled free and drove in silence for a few seconds.

'That was the sexiest thing I've ever seen,' said Arkle, a string of floss hanging from his teeth.

'Yeah,' said Hadley, 'that was . . . badass.'

Lamb flicked the hair from her eyes.

'He'll be back. *Now* can we go to my house? I need to get this truck off the road – it's already scratched up, and the longer we drive around the more chance there is we'll be seen.'

'No,' said Sep, looking out of the back windscreen to check Barnaby hadn't somehow followed them.

'Are you *kidding* me?' Lamb shouted.

'We need to go to Roxburgh's house.'

'No way, man,' said Mack. 'He's mental.'

'Yeah,' said Arkle, fumbling at his dental floss, 'he nearly shot us last time!'

'No, he didn't! Maguire said we needed his help, and she's right: he knows the forest, and that doll would probably have killed us if he hadn't been there. So we'll need him next time.'

Lamb shook her head as Arkle began flossing frantically in the back seat.

'I don't like this. I want to go back to my damn farm, and I want to do this ourselves. I don't trust that guy.'

She was driving fast – too fast, Sep thought – and she touched her face as she changed gear.

'Look, Maguire said he would help us, and we have to try and get there while there's still a bit of daylight left – so we need to go, now!'

The turn-off for the farm was approaching.

'Lamb?' said Hadley.

Ptwing!

'*Aaaaaaaargh!*' shouted Lamb.

And she swung the truck off the road, on to the single-track path that led to the forest.

43

Storms

Bubbles broke on the milk's skin. Roxburgh stirred it briskly, thinking of the deaf boy and his friends. Chasing them away was the only thing to do, the only thing that would keep them safe – there was no warmth in their group, no real love; they'd nothing that might smother the box's anger, as *his* friends had managed all those years ago.

But they were headstrong kids, you could see it. And if they came back when he wasn't there . . . He nodded to himself, then grit his teeth and swore.

He'd have to track the offerings and destroy them. It was the only way to be sure. Somewhere out in the woods, Here'n'now would be waiting – and Roxburgh meant to be ready for him.

The wind was nudging the shack like the nose of some insistent beast, each gust the turning of a great screw – twisting the air inside until his skin felt too small and his head too tight.

He had sat and smoked through the receding daylight: wedged into the grimy chair, half listening to the radio's murmur, watching the sickly light of its display climb the walls and drinking enough whisky to float his teeth.

But still his leg hurt. His trousers were sticking to it.

He poured the cocoa, drank it – burned his lips.

'Goddamn it,' he muttered, startling himself with the noise.

Lundy whined and drew deeper under the sink. The little terrier had spent the afternoon chewing her paws, and had refused to leave her basket.

'It's all right, love,' said Roxburgh. His throat hurt from the pipe smoke and he coughed painfully with the unexpected movement of his voice. 'I've buried Biscay. She's not hurtin' no more.'

Lundy whined at Biscay's name and pawed the basket's empty half.

'You can't hide there forever,' he went on, almost willing the animal to speak back. 'You'll need to piss some time.'

Lundy stared at him. Her eyes gleamed in the radio's pale light.

'We won't hunt tonight, don't worry. We'll go in the mornin', when it's light.'

The sun disappeared behind the clouds and the gloom of evening came, licking at the shack and pouring under the door frame.

Roxburgh looked out of the window. The sounds of the forest had changed, as though smothered under cloth.

He reached for his mug again, and froze as he saw his hand trembling in mid-air.

'Goddamn it,' he said again, forcing his fist closed.

He reached under the sink to grab the dog's collar.

Switching off the radio, he opened the door and shoved Lundy on to the leaves, then stood in the doorway and scanned the woods, the feeble lamp in his small window casting a watery smudge on the ground. The forest was still, lit by the unreliable shadow of day's lurch towards night.

The lamp clicked off.

Roxburgh's head snapped round as though stung. The shack was still.

'Bloody electrics,' he muttered.

Lundy took a few steps – then froze, pressing herself to the ground, fur on end, staring back into the house. A low growl came from her belly.

'Don't be daft now. Come on –' said Roxburgh, biting off his words. The forest made his voice small, as though he was calling from inside a locked cupboard. 'Come *on*, dog,' he said again through his teeth.

Lundy urinated without moving. The water's rattle was the only sound for miles, and as Roxburgh waited for her to finish he saw that she was soaking her own legs.

'Damn it all,' he spat. He threw the cocoa on to the ground and reached behind the door for his shovel.

Lundy began to whimper.

'When I tell you to hurry up –' said Roxburgh, lifting her with his free arm and pressing his lips to the trembling head. He felt the little dog's body solid against his side, her wire-brush hair alert and stiff.

Away from his shack, even with his feet planted on ground he'd trodden a thousand times, the old gamekeeper felt untethered, like a sailor thrown overboard. He hefted the shovel in his hand and turned to the doorway.

Something moved inside it.

He tried to master his fear, tried to push himself forward – but he could not.

'Hello?' he said, into the dark.

Ahead of him, in the blind pit of his little shack, the radio clicked on.

Roxburgh's skin crept around him. He stood perfectly still, trapped in thin fingers of gooseflesh, unmoving while the music for the shipping forecast dribbled out into the world, reedy as an old gramophone.

Lundy began to tremble.

'Come on, lass, come on . . .' he managed as he forced himself to climb the steps of his home, turning the shovel's weight in his hand.

Dropping Lundy in her bed and raising his weapon, he felt the swirl of energy that comes from stillness being disturbed – from someone having just moved through a room.

There are warnings of gales at Viking, Forties, Cromarty and Tyne, said the radio in a tinny voice, as though it was shouting from miles away.

Roxburgh tasted blood, and realized that he had bitten through his lip.

. . . dangerous new low expected thirty miles west, easterly and cyclonic . . .

He walked towards the radio, sucking at the hot, coppery wound.

. . . of fifty miles per hour, though more for a time . . .

'These is my woods,' he said, his voice weak to his own ears.

He turned to look at the dog – saw his own face reflected in the window.

And a pair of gleaming green eyes behind him.

He spun round, swinging the shovel and smashing a lamp. There was a scrabbling at the back door, which swung open.

Biscay's body lurched into the shack, eyes green and bright, skin split by rot, her stomach open and heavy and stinking with worms. Lundy backed against the wall, howling and barking.

And Roxburgh felt that heat – of real, uncontrollable terror.

He screamed and fell, hands clawing at the dead dog's rotting skin, and then there was something else, something on his back: tiny hands, thin string that smelled of wet dirt, and a chittering laugh he thought he'd forgotten. *Here'n'now*, he thought as the string cut into his windpipe and stopped his breath – *Here'n'now*.

. . . *severe storms likely*, said the radio. *Extreme caution advised*.

44

Slipping

'Just calm down, Arkle,' said Sep. 'There's nothing to worry about – we're nearly there.'

'Yeah,' said Arkle, nodding, a piece of floss still in his teeth. 'Yeah, I guess, nothing to worry about; we're nearly in the scary-death-murder-forest looking for the man with the shotgun. Oh, shit shit shit shit shit shit, I'm losing my mind. Mack, have you got anything to eat? I need some sugar to calm me down.'

Mack patted his pockets. The truck buzzed over the cattle grid.

'No, I –' he said.

'Seriously? *This* is the *one* time you don't have anything? Can we put on some music or something? I can't cope with the silence.'

Mack leaned down to the stereo and turned a button. Shrill music filled the shadowy cabin, and they froze.

'Is that the freaking *Exorcist* music? What the hell, Lamb! Why do you even *have* that?' shouted Arkle. 'Turn it off, turn it off!'

'It's on the radio!' shouted Lamb. 'Stop it!'

Mack, panicked, pressed buttons as hard as he could. Hadley's cassette shot out, spilling tentacles of whispery brown tape on to the floor.

'Gah – have you got a pencil?'

'It doesn't matter about the mixtape!' Lamb shouted.

'Well –' said Hadley.

Lamb flicked on the headlamps as night bloomed around them and two pale circles appeared on the road ahead. They should have made the world brighter, Sep thought, but instead they made the evening seem darker still.

'I've got a pencil,' he said, reaching into his pocket. 'Let's everyone calm down.'

'Holy shit,' said Arkle, putting his head between his knees as Mack wound the tape back into the cassette. 'Holy shit. Something's happening in my brain.'

'What do you mean?' said Sep.

Arkle sat up, blinking quickly.

'My head feels leaky. My brain's full of leaks.'

'Your eye's twitching,' said Hadley.

'Well, maybe someone should put on some nice, happy music so we can sing along while we head towards certain death, all right?'

'We're not going to die, Roxburgh will –'

'Happy music!'

'All right . . . what about Bananarama?' said Hadley.

'Shit,' said Arkle.

She found another cassette.

'Wham!?'

'Double shit, that's why they broke up. Come *on*, people!'

'All right,' said Sep, opening his Walkman. 'The Smiths?'

Arkle knocked the cassette out of his hand and grabbed his collar.

'I am freaking *out*, September!' he said, eyes wide and twitching. 'Do you really think a *vegetarian* is going to make me feel better?'

'We're nearly there anyway,' said Lamb. 'Just deal with it and stop being such an asshole.'

Arkle began rubbing his arms as though trying to keep warm. He took out another piece of floss and worked it through his teeth as he stared at Sep.

'How ah you sho calm, Shep? Ah you 'ot shitting yo'shelf?'

Ptwing!

'Yes,' said Sep, and the thought made him grab for his Walkman. He clicked the play button and listened to Morrissey's tinny voice in the headphones round his neck. The insistent heart-like pulse of the box was swelling in his ear.

Lamb turned the wheel and guided them to a halt.

'We're here,' she said, killing the lights.

'I feel sick,' said Hadley, leaning against the back of the seat.

The colours had faded with the sunlight, evening coating the world in a shifting silver film. It seemed to Sep that none of the shadows were where they should be, and he fell as they walked, placing feet on stones that didn't exist and reaching for handholds that were only wisps of plant.

They moved without talking, lost in their own thoughts.

The noise of the box had remained steady in Sep's ear since Barnaby had landed on the car, and its ache had settled permanently into his tooth.

He looked back at the town. The storm was closer now, boiled up in the pressure cooker of summer heat. He could almost feel it glowing in his mouth, like blood from a bitten tongue.

Arkle moved closer to him.

'You called me Arkle in the car, you know,' he said. His eye had stopped twitching, but his pupils were glassy and wide.

'I know,' said Sep. 'I figured I don't like being called Septic, so maybe I shouldn't force Darren on you.'

Arkle grinned at him, then closed his eyes for a few seconds.

'Thanks, Septic,' he said.

Sep looked down at his feet. A dark stain was splashed over the earth – liquid made gummy and thick by the dust.

'That's blood, isn't it?' he said.

Arkle leaned down, his face inches from the mark, then swung up and fixed Sep with an uneven stare.

'Where?' he said.

Sep peered at the bloodstain. In the gloom it looked almost black.

'Never mind,' he said.

'Oh, look!' said Arkle. 'A critter!'

Smiling wildly, he scooped up something that might once have been a grey squirrel, but was now red, dead – and inside out.

'Put that down!' said Sep. 'Jesus!'

'No way, Jose! I'm keeping her,' said Arkle, cuddling the sticky lump.

Dark shapes fluttered and hopped between the branches.

'Arkle, that thing's probably full of bacteria –'

'Don't make this about *science*!' shouted Arkle. He started to dance with little wobbling steps, as though he was balancing on a couple of snooker balls. 'Just go with it, Seppy, come on. *Dear Mo-mee, dear Da-dee, you have plans for me* –'

'Darren, maybe it's not the right time to dance,' said Hadley unsteadily. She moved closer to Sep, and he caught her scent.

'It's always time to dance, Milky Bar Kid who's strong and tough,' said Arkle, his eyes closed. 'The rhythm's got me. You hear me, creepy-ass trees? It's GOT ME!'

'Arkle,' said Sep, moving to shush him as the box-noise began to howl, 'why don't we just –'

'Oh my God,' said Arkle, staring suddenly with wide eyes. 'Something bad is happening, isn't it?'

'Yes!' said Sep. 'Something very bad, that's why we need to keep moving, OK?'

A crow snapped its beak just above his head, and they looked up.

'Why are there four of them now?' said Hadley carefully.

'And why can I see one of their ribcages?' added Lamb.

Sep held his skull as though it might split and took a deep breath of fetid air, felt it shoot through his tooth in a white bloom of pain.

Arkle was nodding frantically.

'Right. Right right right. Shit. OK, let's go,' he said, then sprinted head first into a tree.

'Darren!' shouted Hadley. She dropped to her knees beside Arkle's prone body, her eyes half closed. 'What's *wrong* with him?'

'It's the box,' said Sep. 'He's been saying all day his mind is slipping. I guess it finally slipped.'

Lamb touched Arkle's neck, felt his pulse.

'He'll be all right. I think,' she said. Then she touched Hadley's shoulder. 'Are you OK?'

Hadley nodded, then climbed slowly to her feet.

'I'm fine. I just want to get this done.'

'Me too,' said Mack. 'You want me to carry him?'

Arkle coughed, sat up and grinned. There was a string of dental floss hanging from his teeth, and his mullet was askew.

'All right, Sep?' he said, blinking as though he'd just woken up. 'Everything good?'

'Great, thanks. How are you feeling?' said Sep, taking his hand.

'Oh, I'm good. *Sooooo* good – I just don't know what that weird humming is humming is humming for, you know? God, and my mouth is dry – it's so *dry*.' Arkle leaned over and gasped, his tongue pointy and long. 'Have you got any Spike?'

'We'll get you some when we get back. Are you sure you're feeling OK?'

'I think . . . maybe . . . But it's good good good. Thanks, Seppy Sep. You're such a pal, you know? I missed you . . . I missed you so much.'

Arkle threw his arms round Sep's neck.

'You're so clever,' he whispered, his breath hot. 'My Seppy Sep.'

'Break it up,' said Lamb. 'Roxburgh's house is this way.'

Sep prised Arkle's hands away, then checked over his shoulder. The others were standing together, ready.

'Let's go,' he said, pulling Arkle with him.

They went on, deeper into the forest, the wind whipping at them with growing strength, throwing the smells of dead things into their noses and tousling the feathers of the crows above.

45

Rosemary

The moon shone through the trees, scattering coins of light over their feet. The clouds above the gamekeeper's shack were a flat, tarnished silver, and the grass moved like a rippling pond.

Sep blinked his hair away as it struck his eyes.

'I thought you wanted to come here when it was light,' said Lamb, looking around nervously.

'Maybe you didn't drive quickly enough,' said Sep, snapping his head towards the sound of rustling leaves. 'Jesus, you can't bring that with you!'

Arkle was walking on lopsided legs, dragging himself along the hedge and hugging the inside-out squirrel. It hung wet and heavy in his arms, like a towel lifted from a washing machine.

'I'm going to call her Rosemary,' he said, a blissful smile on his face.

'I'm serious – you need to put it down,' said Sep.

'You're not my dad, shiny-shoes,' said Arkle, his nose in the air. 'And so, so, so what if I want a bagel?'

'Arkle, you're not making sense,' said Sep. 'That thing's all rotten, *and* it was probably killed by the box. Who knows what it might do?'

'You think that was the box too?' said Hadley.

Sep looked at her.

'What else would turn it *inside out*?'

'Well, she's mine now,' said Arkle, wobbling as he leaned away. 'I'm going to keep her forever, September October November December.'

Mack shook his head.

'Just let him keep it.'

'Come on, Rosemary,' said Arkle, holding the glistening lump against his chest. 'Can I have a bagel, though? For realsies?'

'Sure,' said Sep.

The forest's night-time whispers – the creaks of settling wood and the skitter of falling briars – surrounded them. The shack was dark, its doors and windows closed.

Lamb bit the inside of her bottom lip.

'Something's not right.'

'Well, we've come this far. We should –'

'Sep, we came to get help, but Roxburgh's obviously not here! This is too dangerous, it's too dark and we're too far from the truck. Let's go back.'

Sep looked at the little house. It was obviously empty. But something tugged at his thoughts, like clothes snagging on a thorn.

'But what if he needs *our* help?' he said. 'Like, he's lying in a pool of blood and can't reach the phone?'

'He probably doesn't even *have* a phone,' said Lamb.

'Whose point are you making?' said Sep. 'If he doesn't have a phone we *definitely* need to help him.'

She shook her head.

'This is dangerous, Sep – don't be reckless. He's not here. He's probably wandering around the woods, shooting things and spitting.'

'Me and Rosemary want to go to the car,' said Arkle.

'Fine. Well, I'm going to see if he's in there,' said Sep. 'Who's coming with me?'

Arkle tripped into Mack's arms.

'I'm going to take him to the car now,' said Mack, lifting Arkle over his shoulder. 'If something happens I don't want to have to run while I'm carrying him. You can catch us up, right?'

'Yeah. I'll be as quick as I can,' said Sep reluctantly.

Lamb shook her head, then followed Arkle and Mack.

Hadley looked agonized.

'You can't go on your own.'

A little knot tightened in Sep's chest.

'Thank you,' he said.

He helped her over a puddle, holding her hand a moment longer than he had to, then they stood in the darkness, listening to each other's breathing and peering through the gloom. The shack was square and black and surrounded by the stumps of trees.

'If he's really not there then we'll leave, all right? I promise,' said Sep. 'I just feel like something's happened to him.'

'It's so creepy,' said Hadley. Her voice wavered, and she moved closer to him.

'What?'

'I said it's creepy.'

Sep brushed against her arm. 'Are you all right?'

'Not really. I feel weak and dizzy, like all my energy's leaking out of me.'

'It's the box; it's trying everything it can to hurt us. That was something else Maguire told me: I was right about my tooth, but it's not the crows that are making it hurt – it's the rot.'

'What do you mean?'

'The box makes things decay, that's how it reaches into the world – all those dead things on the ground, and the stink that was on Barnaby. My rotten tooth is connected to that: I'm tuned to the box's frequency, and my tooth is dragging the signal through my deaf ear.'

'Bet you wish you didn't eat so much rock now.'

Sep laughed and, as they approached the shack on delicate feet, Hadley slipped her hand into his.

'How did you go deaf?' she said.

He looked at her. The gloom reduced her face to a flat mask, and he saw only her eyes, nostrils and mouth.

'You're asking me now?'

'I'm scared,' she said, swallowing hard. 'Tell me something that's not about this.'

Sep looked at Roxburgh's door. Instead of being shut, as it had appeared, it was slightly open. The frail noise of a radio came from inside, like a wasp in a jar.

'My mum was with this guy for a while when I was little,' he said. 'All I remember about him is that he shouted at her, and he was loud. One time he was so loud I started packing my ear with mud from the garden.'

'So your ear's full of mud?' Hadley whispered.

'What? No. It – it got infected.'

'Oh.'

They laughed silently, and the world seemed real again, just for a second.

'Are you ready?'

'No.'

'Well, let's go anyway,' said Sep, and he edged towards the steps.

46

Flight

The inside of the shack was lit only by the pale glow of the radio's dial, which hit the broken furniture and cast long, angular shadows. There was a pot on the stove, a wooden spoon leaning on its edge. Sep sniffed. Every wall and surface was made with cedar, and alongside the smell of its sweet resin was the odour of an old man's routine: tobacco and smoke, damp wool and muddy boots, and the steamy vegetable smell of soup.

And the forest, reaching into the place like a soggy fog, blanching everything with its damp green fingers.

'This is disgusting,' whispered Hadley. 'And he's not here. He probably hasn't even –'

'The radio's on,' said Sep quietly, reaching for the stove. 'And that pot's still warm. Something's happened.'

'*Sep!*' she hissed, pulling his T-shirt. 'You said we would go if he wasn't here, and –'

'Shh!' said Sep, tilting his head. He thought of the transistor scanning the frequencies in the air, and closed his eyes, trying to let his tooth find the box's signal.

'Oh,' he said.

'What?'

'Listen. Don't you hear that?'

She listened, holding her breath to let the silence fill her head. A tiny scratching noise, like a dry leaf caught in the wind, came from the darkness on the other side of the tiny living room.

'Sep!' she whispered. 'Let's go!'

He squeezed her hand, then tiptoed across the space and stepped over a chair into a well of blind darkness. His foot touched carpet, and he breathed out the tension in his belly.

'What are you doing?' whispered Hadley.

Sep moved over to the radio and turned down the volume, his hand throwing a huge, sudden shadow in the display's pale light. Hadley clamped a hand over her mouth.

The scratching noise continued. He followed it, moving further into the shack – when the radio winked out, smothering them in silence.

Hadley bit her lip, then followed him, walking as though the floor burned her feet, her eyes black with terror.

The scratching was coming from a small door beside a pile of clothes. Sep knelt and pressed his good ear to the wood.

Something on the other side was breathing, slowly.

Sep's heart crept into his throat. He listened as closely as he could with his deaf ear, but the box's noise was quiet.

He swallowed an acid-burp of fear, placed his hand on the door as softly as he could and turned to Hadley. She shook her head and waved wildly at him, but he nodded – and turned the handle.

Lundy spilled into the corridor, her fur spotted with crusts of blood. She scrabbled at Sep, trying to climb his legs with a desperate whine, and growling at the pile of clothes.

Sep fell backwards and held her trembling body, wrapping his hands round her chest.

'Oh my God,' said Hadley, her voice massive in the dead space as she sighed with relief. 'It's just the dog. Oh, thank God!'

Lundy growled a little, and Sep felt the movement of her lungs through his fingertips.

'She's terrified,' he said, leaning on the clothes as he stood. 'We need to take her with us, so we –'

His voice stuck tight in his throat. The wet smell in the cabin wasn't just the forest's heady bloom; there was something else. Something human.

It wasn't a pile of clothes. It was Roxburgh.

Sep stepped away, gesturing at Hadley to go – but she stood frozen to the spot, her eyes bulging in fright.

Run, he mouthed. *Run*.

She shook her head, tears shining in her eyes.

Sep raised his leg to vault the broken chair – when Roxburgh's body leaped and grabbed him, a sickly green light glowing in his eyes, his jaw hanging like a snake's, too loose and too wide and showing too much of his stinking mouth. The sharp fingers closed on Sep's leg and he heard a dry, dead growl beside him.

He turned to see the other dog – its body torn open, its guts dragging on the floor – burst forward and sink its fangs into the meat of his leg.

He screamed, ripping his leg from Roxburgh's grasp and leaving his skin in Biscay's teeth, then scrambled over the toppled furniture with the fingers grabbing at his shoes. He fell again, landing on his jaw and biting hard on his tongue, the sharp piece of rock in his pocket digging into his leg.

Roxburgh heaved himself over the chair, leaning down towards Sep with his mouth open.

Sep gripped the splintered rock like a dagger and brought it up into the Roxburgh-thing's face, driving the point into its pale, green-lit eye with a wet pop. The thing hissed and fell, and Sep pulled himself upright, tucked Lundy under his arm and ran, his torn leg screaming its agony with every step.

'Are you all right?' shouted Hadley, a few paces away, her hand out for his.

'Fine,' gasped Sep between quick lips, afraid of the vomit that was climbing his neck. The pain in his back tooth was excruciating, the box's noise whining into his gums like dental steel.

Something small and white and scorched appeared in the doorway, and Sep saw strings hanging from it like whispery tentacles. *Roxburgh's puppet*, he thought – and ran harder, leaning on Hadley's shoulder to keep his balance, his head swirling.

'Keep going,' she wheezed, taking a blast of her inhaler. 'We've nearly caught up with the others, come on!'

Sep followed her, grabbing at her shape like she was a mirage, fighting to keep hold of the slippery threads of his consciousness, and as the others came into view he fell again, landing on the little dog, who squirmed free, howling.

He heard their voices as his eyes began to close, letting the sound of bickering – safe, human bickering – wash over him.

'You're going on the flatbed,' Lamb was saying. 'That thing's getting nowhere near the seats.'

'Her *name*,' growled Arkle, hugging the furry mess and leaving a trail of watery dirt on his cheek, 'is Rosemary!'

Sep's eyes closed, and the last he knew was the bulk of Mack's arms beneath him and the sky swinging like a lampshade as he was lifted into the air.

die

But it wasn't him, it was . . . this

can't just keep the

But I couldn't leave

The floor was rocking under him, light was flashing in his eyes and Hadley was crying in his face.

'Sep!' she shouted, seeing his eyes slip open. 'He's awake! He's all right! Sep, can you hear me?'

'Urgh . . .' said Sep. 'Where are we?'

'We're nearly back on the main road,' said Lamb. 'You've been out for ages.'

Sep flexed his mouth. It tasted of vomit, his head hurt, and when he reached down he found his shirt was wet.

'Sorry,' he said.

'It's OK,' said Hadley, almost laughing. Lundy was in her arms. 'You're all right. My God, we were so worried –'

Sep realized his legs were over Mack's lap, and he tried to sit up.

'Stay still,' said Mack. 'Your leg's cut pretty bad. It's still bleeding.'

There was a knock on the back window and Sep jumped in fright – but he turned to see Arkle on the pickup's flatbed, cuddled into the inside-out squirrel, smiling and waving.

'Has he still got that thing?' said Sep. His mouth hurt too. He went through all his body parts, trying to find one that wasn't in agony, and decided his eyelashes felt all right.

'He wouldn't let it go,' said Mack, 'even when I threatened him.'

'Where are we going?' said Sep.

'My farm,' said Lamb. '*This* time we're going to my farm.'

'Sep needs a hospital!' said Hadley. 'He's bleeding so badly, it –'

'It's fine, it's getting better,' said Sep. It felt as though he was speaking with a mouthful of rocks, and he wasn't sure if the words sounded the way they did in his head.

Hadley's face blurred above him, almost pixelating, her movements becoming blocky and slow.

'How are *you* feeling?' he said.

'I'm fine. The minute we started heading away from the box I started feeling better! Sep? Sep!'

There was a massive bang, and they screamed as the truck veered over on its side.

The last thought Sep had as he slid on to the floor and out of consciousness was that they'd hit another car, and it was all over: they were caught; the truth would come out.

And it was somehow all his fault.

everyone OK?

My hand's cut but

Came out of nowhere, I didn't see it

all fine, everyone's fine

kill me, he'll actually kill me

Rosemary!

are we going to do?

Just leave it there

can do that, we have to

'Look at it, though, it's huge,' said Mack.

The front tyre was torn to shreds, but the engine was still running: its throaty rumble punctuated by a sound like popping plastic. Little jabs of pain knuckled into Sep's back and ribs, and he tried to turn on to his side, the stones shifting painfully under him. He'd fallen on the ground. The doors were open, and he was covered in fragments of broken glass. The others were talking. He heard Arkle laugh nervously, heard the *ptwing* of dental floss, Lundy's low growl and the rumble of Mack's voice.

His Walkman was lying beside him, shattered and broken, its silver insides spilling out. The tape had cracked in two, its label scraped away.

Sep realized it had been hours since he'd listened to it – since he'd felt the need to hide away behind his headphones.

Something groaned behind him, and he turned his head.

There was a stag lying a few metres away, its legs scratching at the track, its open mouth dark with blood. He breathed in, felt his lungs fill with its hot musk, and felt the darkness slipping into his mind as the creature bellowed into the night.

He tried to blink, tried to pull his mind back to wakefulness.

Then Hadley was there, and he opened his eyes.

'Sep! Can you hear me?'

'Where are we?' he said, the words all coming as one sound, the pain roaring through his body like a stifled scream.

'We hit a stag,' said Hadley. She had her hands on either side of his head and was looking at him upside down. 'Everyone's OK.'

She ran her fingers over his forehead, and despite everything – the screaming pain and the chaos and the heavy dregs of unconsciousness – he tingled.

He sat up and fell straight over, a weight like a steel ball rolling in his head. Mack steadied him, the big arms hooking into Sep's armpits.

'We need to get it to Mario,' said Lamb, kneeling beside the stag. Its legs were moving erratically in painful twitches, while the truck's exhaust puffed a murky, red-lit cloud over the scene.

'We don't have time,' said Mack.

The stag bellowed again, a massive, untamed roar that speared back into the woods and echoed through the trees.

'Listen to it! We can't just leave it here,' snapped Lamb.

Sep thought about Roxburgh, somewhere behind them, his little dead dog snapping at his heels.

'We need to be fast,' he said.

Lamb caught his eye.

'Hadley told us. Roxburgh's dead then?'

'Kind of,' said Sep, remembering the noise the thing had made when he stabbed its eye. 'Oh, Jesus. The box is killing people. And it's *our* fault.'

'It's my fault,' said Mack. His face was ashen, his eyes deep and red. 'Shit, I'm sorry. I never meant for any of –'

He dropped his face in his hands.

'We'd better get the stag on the flatbed,' said Lamb, flipping down the tailgate. 'Come on, Mack.'

'Are you kidding me?' said Mack, shaking himself and blinking away tears. 'Look at the size of this thing.'

'Don't give me that,' said Lamb, placing her hands under the stag's shoulders. 'I've seen you lift; you can manage this.'

Mack rolled his eyes, but squatted beside the stag and gripped its hindquarters.

'At least buy it dinner first,' said Arkle.

'Dude, shut *up*. Just grab something.'

309

Arkle reached out with his free hand.

'Not *me*,' said Mack. 'The deer!'

'*Oh*,' said Arkle.

He took his hand out of Mack's pocket, then put his arms beside Hadley's on the stag's belly. Sep grabbed the antlers as they swung towards Mack's unprotected side, and held on, teeth gritting with the effort.

'This thing is huge,' said Mack.

Lamb nodded at him.

'This is why you don't skip leg day. Ready?'

They heaved. The animal roared again, its weight hung between the stirrups of their grip.

'Nearly – there –' said Mack, veins sticking out on his forearms.

The stag roared again, and Sep heard movement in the leaves on the other side of the truck.

'We need to hurry!' he shouted.

The stag's neck was unbelievably strong, and he felt himself being pushed back by the antlers' white-tipped claws. He wondered what would happen if his hand slipped – how deeply the points would bury themselves in his neck.

'Done!' shouted Mack, and the truck's suspension buckled under the animal's weight.

There was a shriek from the darkness.

'Let's go!' shouted Lamb, banging her hand on the window frame and leaping into the cab. '*Not* you – you and that *thing* can get in the back!'

'With the stag? But – why?' said Arkle, holding up Rosemary's skin-peeled head to show off her cuteness.

'Get in the back! Now! We're not going to be able to go as fast with a flat tyre!'

Sep jumped in behind Hadley and slammed the door as Roxburgh's puppet leaped into the headlights – followed by a tide of dead animals.

'Oh my God!' said Hadley. 'What do we –'

'Smash them!' shouted Mack.

Lamb crunched the gears and the truck leaped forward as though stung, throwing the little puppet in the air. It landed on the bonnet and screamed, dragging its sharp little hands with a sound of tearing steel as the creatures spilled over the truck.

'The paintwork!' shouted Lamb.

'Forget the paintwork!' shouted Mack. 'Go!'

Here'n'now punched the windscreen – which cracked.

'Shit!' Sep shouted. 'What about Arkle?'

They looked out of the back window. Arkle was buried under a mountain of bloody fur, swinging his feet to keep the dead things at bay.

Another punch from Here'n'now made a bullet hole in the glass. The puppet reached into it and began tearing the screen from the truck like it was peeling an orange.

Lamb slammed down the accelerator and launched round a bend, tipping the truck almost on its side, the rubber of its shredded tyre flapping in mid-air as they screamed. The puppet's fingers snapped with the strain, and it flew into the darkness.

Sep heard a tap on the window behind him.

Arkle, tucked into the gap between the stag's front and back legs, gave him a thumbs up, then held up the inside-out squirrel. 'Still got her!' he shouted, trickles of blood on his hands and face.

Sep blinked slowly, trying to get rid of the spots dancing in his vision. The truck was rolling with a *budda-budda-budda* on its broken wheel.

'I'm hiding the truck in town once we've taken this thing to Mario,' said Lamb. Her hair was flying around her head, blown by the wind through the smashed windscreen.

'What good will that do?' said Mack.

'It's all smashed up *and* it's covered in blood! What else can I do but say it was stolen?'

'That's against the law,' said Sep. 'It could –'

'*All* of this is against the law!' shouted Lamb. 'Everything we're doing is crazy. The truck won't last much longer with three tyres – we're ditching it. There's a tarpaulin in the back. I'll cover it with that.'

'And then what?'

'Go home and get your bikes, then come to my farm and think about what we're going to do next.'

Arkle rapped on the back window again and waved at them with one of Rosemary's little legs.

'Where are we going?' he shouted.

'Town!' shouted Hadley. 'We're ditching the truck and taking our bikes!'

'That's cool,' said Arkle. 'Cool cool cool.' He shook his head. 'I think I feel a bit better.'

He vomited over the side of the truck.

'Why do we need bikes?' said Sep. He thought of his Chopper: never idle during the summer of sacrifice, and never used since.

'What if something happens?' said Hadley. 'Bikes would be better than running.'

Sep closed his eyes again. The truck's soggy smell was adding to the rolling vomit in his belly, and he felt the contents of his stomach slosh against its sides as Lamb turned another corner and headed for the row of shops. The sky was swirling with electric heat as the storm neared boiling point, and when he looked out the window he saw its fierce energy had emptied the streets.

Lamb brought them to a neck-snapping stop behind the vet's surgery and killed the engine. The truck sagged in exhaustion, and fluid pattered from its guts.

'Right. Sep, you need to go in and make up some story about how we found the stag.'

'I'll help you get down,' Hadley added.

'Oh, God –' said Sep.

'What is it, Sep?' said Mack.

'Just . . . I said I was sick. If I go in he'll know I lied to him. I've never lied to him before.'

'But you are sick,' said Lamb, 'I mean, you look like shit.'

'Thanks,' said Sep.

He climbed down after Hadley, holding her hand to steady himself, focusing on the fabric of her sodden, bloodstained glove to stop his head from rolling about.

'What if he's not here?'

'Then we're in even bigger trouble,' Hadley said.

Sep stared at her. 'You look better. Stronger.'

'I *feel* better. I'm –'

'Wait,' interrupted Sep. 'You've felt better each time we've left the box. And worse as we got near it. And you've been feeling weak since yesterday.'

Sep took her hand and turned it over. The wound shone in the truck's door light.

'This isn't healing properly,' he said as the others craned their necks. 'Jesus, Hadley: *this* is what the blood you dropped in the box is doing – it's making you weak! You've given it that part of yourself – your blood, your strength – and now it's hurting you with it.'

'Oh my God,' said Lamb.

'It's taking my strength?' asked Hadley.

'To make itself stronger,' said Sep, nodding at the smashed-in windscreen.

Hadley pulled her hand away. Her face was pale.

'I'm fine,' she said. 'Go on, we can't stay here.'

'But –'

'Go!' she shouted, and pushed him towards the surgery door.

Sep looked down the row of shops. Being back in the midst of civilization seemed too big a jolt, like the bin with the crisp packets and the puddles of ice cream had beamed down from an alien ship. It seemed impossible that he could close his eyes after being bitten by a zombie dog, then be chased by a murderous puppet and *more* zombie animals – and open them to find a poster for a bake-off.

He knocked on the door. Nothing happened for a moment, and hope rose inside him for just a second before a light clicked on inside and Mario said:

'Hello? Who is this?'

Sep swallowed a sharp, bloody ball of spit. A swell of noise made him look around, wondering if Barnaby was close, invisible in the shadows behind his closed green eyes.

He gritted his teeth, chewing his bad tooth deeper into his gum.

'It's Sep, Mario. Could you –'

'September? What is –' Mario's face, sweaty and pale, appeared between the blinds. 'My God! You are hurt?'

The door swung open. The surgery was lit with such brilliance that it hurt Sep's eyes and he turned away, exposing the deep cut on his head and the vomit on his T-shirt.

'You *are* hurt! Oh my God, my Sep, come in. I will –'

'No,' said Sep, taking Mario's hand from his shoulder, 'it's not me. I – we –'

'We?' said Mario.

The stag bellowed a long, mournful bark that split the sky.

Mario bustled past Sep and approached the truck. He nodded at the others.

'Hi, Mario,' said Arkle. The effects of the box seemed to have worn off. His eyes were glassy and wide, but he was still clutching Rosemary to his chest.

'We must get him inside,' said Mario, ignoring Arkle and pressing his hands on the stag's heaving side. 'I will fetch the trolley. Open the gate – and be careful; he is badly hurt.'

'Mario,' said Sep, reaching for his arm as he returned to the surgery. 'I'm sorry, I didn't know what else to do.'

'Is OK,' said Mario. He wiped his face on his T-shirt, exposing his great stomach for a moment. 'Animal is hurt, of course you bring him to me, of course.'

'No, I mean earlier, when I said I was ill, I —'

'Oh, my Sep, is fine, is fine,' said Mario, and he gripped Sep's arm, lowering his voice. 'You have friends to go out with — is good. But is bad that they drive without licence: be safe, always, be safe. You are my best boy.'

He mussed Sep's hair, then disappeared into the surgery. By the time he re-emerged, the stag had begun to slide off the end of the truck. Mario ran over, the trolley rattling on the stone, and helped Mack pull the stag on to the stainless steel, its hot reek splashing on to the pavement.

Gesturing to the others that he would catch them up, Sep went to follow Mario as he rolled it inside. Lamb raised her hands in question and Hadley bit her lip, her hand gripping Lundy's fur.

But Mario pushed him away.

'No,' he said firmly, his hand on Sep's chest.

'What's that?' said Sep, touching the butterfly stitches on Mario's puncture wounds.

'Is nothing,' said Mario, waving his hand lightly. 'A dog, today.'

'Isn't it always a dog?' said Sep, and he smiled weakly.

Mario smiled back — but to Sep's eyes it was a strained and painful grimace.

'You *must* be going to the hospital now,' said Mario.

A dark little figure dropped unseen through the open skylight behind him – its glowing eyes fixed on Sep.

'But –'

'You must! Look at your face!'

Sep stood back, hiding the blackened wetness of the jeans sticking to his wound. Its agony had subsided to a sharp throb, and he felt his pulse beating through it. His deaf ear sent familiar shards of pain into his back tooth, and he looked around, expecting Barnaby to flicker out from the darkness beyond the street lights.

He looked up at the sky – the hurtling comet hidden by thick cloud. He thought of the plans he and Mario had made to watch it together.

'I can help,' he said. 'I'll stay with you, Mario! You might be in –'

'No – hospital! I am vet, I know what I am doing. You go, go with your friends.'

The last words twisted in Sep's heart as the door closed in his face. He stepped back into the swirling stormlight, the stag roaring its deep, broken agony as Mario wheeled it away.

'Get your new sacrifices and your bikes, then meet at my farm,' said Lamb.

They each turned and ran towards their houses, Sep hobbling as best he could on his ruined leg – and hiding his face, so the others wouldn't see.

47

Fox

The squad car was in the drive. Sep swore under his breath and crept as soundlessly as he could towards the house.

Something moved at him from the darkness. His heart leaped and he cried out before he could stop himself.

'Oh thank God, it's only you,' he whispered, his heart pounding.

The fox hopped a little in expectation.

'I don't have anything. Go! You'll get me in –'

'Sep?' said his mum, opening the screen door.

'Hi, Mum,' he said as casually as he could. 'I was just getting –'

'Where have you been?' she said. She'd been making a sandwich, and a slice of ham was still clutched in her hand. 'I've been so – oh my God! What's happened to you?'

'Ah,' said Sep, remembering his bashed-in face and bloodstained clothes. 'I . . . fell. Over. From a tree. I fell over a tree.'

'You're *covered* in blood! And you've been sick! Are you all right?'

'I'm fine, Mum. Honestly I am – it's not my blood. *Or* my sick.'

She pulled him into a hug, then shook him hard.

'Where have you *been*?' she said again. 'I told Matt to keep you in –'

'Oh, he told me. I went to Lamb's house instead.'

She let him go and stepped back. Candlelight from the porch surrounded her body, its shadows hiding her expression – but he could see her skin was waxy and grey.

'*I* told you to stay in school,' she said evenly. 'It doesn't matter that it was Matt who gave you the message – it came from me and I expect you to do what you're told. We haven't found who assaulted Mrs Maguire, and until we do I need to know you're safe. I came home for a change of clothes and something to eat, *and* to see if this was where you'd gone. But I'm going back to the station now, and you're coming with me. Go and get cleaned up, and we'll –'

'No! I'm not going there!'

She turned and looked at him.

'Excuse me?'

He took a step towards the garage.

'I'm not going with you. I'm – I'm going with my friends.'

'Your "friends"? And who are they?'

'The ones you asked about yesterday: Arkle, and Lamb, and Mack. And Hadley,' he finished, taking a deep breath.

'No,' she said, shaking her head.

'I am!'

Sep ran to the garage, pulling open the door with a screech.

'You're – wait, Sep!'

She grabbed his arm as he fumbled for the light switch.

'You're to come with me, right now! I can't deal with you as well as everything else. I just –'

'You don't have to deal with me, honestly. I don't mean to make you feel any worse. I just – you have to trust me. I know how to make this go away.'

He found the switch, and clicked it back and forth. The bulb sputtered, then winked out. But in the half-second of light he'd seen his old yellow Chopper, tucked away behind the lawnmower and the charcoal, its frame buried under years of neglect.

'Go away?' his mum said. 'Make what go away? What are you talking about?'

Sep grabbed the bike, shaking the worst of the dust away.

He looked around, trying to find something that connected him to the others, that could convey the strength of the bond he'd rediscovered in the last twenty-four hours. But there was nothing in the dirty garage, and he knew there was nothing in his room either: no photos, no mementos. He'd buried his life in schoolwork and thoughts of escape, and he saw now how stark his life had been – how he'd shut out the happiness he might have had.

An old notebook and pen lay on a shelf. He grabbed them, tore out a blank page and wrote for a moment, then folded the scrap of paper into his back pocket.

His mum was talking.

'– don't feel good just now, Sep, but that's not anything you need to worry about. You've got so much going on:

school and your scholarship and everything, and once the sickness passes –'

'But what if it doesn't?'

'What? But, Sep –'

He put his hands on her face.

'Mum,' he said. 'Have you ever known me to misbehave – or let you down?'

'No,' she said after a moment.

'So trust me. All right? *Trust* me.'

He hugged her. Her hair tickled his nose, but he let it sit there as she cried, thinking of the times she'd held him, in the quiet space that was only theirs.

'Everything's OK,' he said quietly. 'I promise.'

'No, no, I –' She wiped her face. 'I need to go back on shift, so –'

'So I'll stay at Arkle's. You like Mrs Hooper, remember?'

She laughed a little – and he knew it was going to be OK.

'You be careful then. I trust you, my brave boy.'

'I will,' said Sep.

They held each other's eyes.

'I will,' he repeated, then he wheeled the bike into the driveway.

In front of him were two shining eyes – little specks of light in the dark. His mum gasped, her hand on her chest.

'That bloody fox,' she said. 'I nearly had a heart attack.'

The fox pawed at the path and moved forward.

'Can I have that ham?' said Sep.

'No,' she said, shaking her head. 'No, you know what I think about you feeding that animal – they're vermin, Sep.'

The fox padded another step forward, then scampered back. It yawned – a wide stretch of pink and white – then licked its lips.

'Please?' said Sep. 'I've been feeding him for ages. He's my – he's my friend.'

He kept his hand out.

She rolled her eyes, but gave him the ham. It was slimy and cold, and Sep tossed it on his hand as he held it out.

The fox came forward, slowly, reached out and took the meat. Sep held on tight, just for a moment, just long enough to run his hand through the animal's fur. It was soft and warm and thick, and he felt the life inside it, hot and sharp, felt the animal jump at his touch.

'Shh,' he said, 'it's OK . . . it's OK . . .'

'Sep?' whispered his mum.

Sep moved the fox's fur again, letting it flow through his fingers, watching how the moonlight caught the layers of colour; then he tickled its ears and it rubbed against his hands. He felt his pulse thudding as he tried to contain the surge of excitement – then the fox backed off, its eyes flashing in alarm.

'I'm sorry,' he said again, smiling. 'On you go.'

The big amber eyes blinked at him for another second – then the fox ran off, sprinting into the trees, prize gripped in its teeth.

Sep breathed out, felt his heart slowing down, and looked around his garden, at all the safe little spaces he'd made here over the years, behind the bushes and in the trees.

'Never do that again,' said his mum. She climbed the steps into the house. 'Phone if you need me,' she added before she went inside.

'Your number still 999?' said Sep.

She laughed, then blew him a kiss and closed the door.

Sep climbed on to his bike. Rust covered the frame like blisters, and when he settled into the saddle it whined shrilly. He kicked the pedals.

The chain was solid.

He stood up, forcing the greaseless wheels to turn and climb the hill, and, as he swung towards the farm and away from town and school and human life, he looked up at the sky and wondered how, on a spinning ball of rock, this madness had found *him*, now, at this exact moment in time.

He looked for the comet, but could not find it in the clouds. As his torn leg shot a white noise of agony into his brain, he wondered how he could ever have thought anything other than the sacrifice box was to blame; how he could have imagined this chaos could have come from such an earthly concern as space dust or fallout when it was focused on the five of them – that special five who'd filled one summer with so much happiness.

He swung off the road, the bell chiming on his bike as he rattled on to the pavement – unaware that the fox was ghosting through the shadows behind him, its soft paws silent on the ground.

48

Autopsy

Mario fixed the mask to his face and turned his lamp towards the stag. The animal's breath came in quick bursts, and its heat shimmered in the cramped air. But the swivelling eyes were unresponsive, black and huge and bulging.

'My great friend, what are we going to do with you?' he said, swinging the lamp closer. The air was too heavy to reach the skylight, so the day's heat hung around him like a wet curtain, pointed with the stag's panicked stench. He wiped his sleeve across his forehead and blinked away the sweat.

The bite marks itched on his hand. Barkley and Mr Snuggles had been locked up in the chip shop's cold store, hidden from sight in case Sep had come into the surgery. They were bound with surgical tape, but had been working at their bonds even as he'd carried them through, and they'd been tied in a hurry. He would be careful when he opened the door, he decided. And he *would* open it, soon – he was no closer to discovering the source of their strange re-animation.

He picked up his Dictaphone and leaned in close to the stag, steadying the rolling wedge of its head and keeping the antlers' forks away from his face. The big neck moved at an odd angle, and he clicked on a little torch, shining it into the eyes with a yellowish glow.

'Victim of crash with truck, red stag, fully mature: at least three legs broken and possible skull fracture,' he said, a faint tremor in his voice.

He ran his hand gently along the stag's flank. Its wail of pain pressed like thumbs into his ears, and when he lifted his hand he saw a stub of white bone, like a fresh bud, poking through a tear in the skin.

'Has broken rib also,' he said. 'I am sorry, my friend, sorry,' he soothed, wiping his sleeve across his forehead again. The stag bleated, mournful and low.

Mario put his lips to the microphone and was surprised to see his fingers shaking as he pressed the red button. The stag's noise had been shockingly loud – and so *angry*.

He puffed out his cheeks and blew out two sharp breaths before leaning over the body again.

'Shape of torso indicates spinal damage or major damage to shoulder blade,' he said. 'There is injury mid-thorax and denuded bone protruding through left side of chest. The skin is teared and ribcage is visible, also organs . . .'

He turned the lamp so the light sliced through the ribs. Under the glisten of tissue and fat the big heart was thudding in bursts of dark, twisting muscle, like a living fish tied in a knot. Behind it, the great bags of the lungs crashed against the bone.

Mario felt the animal's power like an electrical charge in the room. The stag was huge, immense, and although he had worked with large animals in the past, he realized he was profoundly, deeply frightened. Something was not as it should be, and the wrongness of it jarred in his bones.

He felt the world shrink to his dark little room, with nothing beyond the circle of light in which he sat – nothing but himself and the beast.

He looked at his empty hand, saw four dark crescents had been dug into his palm. There was blood under his fingernails.

Mario blinked, tried to focus, and sucked at the boiling air.

'One of antlers is cracked along base of pedicle. Neck seems potentially broken, is loose, maybe vertebrae dislocated.'

He peered more closely at the stag's neck. The thick mane was dark and wet, and smelled coppery and warm. Mario parted the fur with his gloved hand and saw a wound about the size of a coin, gently burping bright blood like a hot spring.

'Carotid artery appears to be damaged, maybe severed,' he said, his voice shaking. The blood was coming faster now, a knuckle of it welling through the mane. He wiped his forehead with his sleeve.

'This bleeding,' he said, 'we must stop it, my friend. Here . . .'

He lifted a scalpel and turned the stag's neck by pushing the antlers away, and as the blade broke the skin the animal wrestled against him with staggering power.

Mario eased another syringe of anaesthetic into its neck – felt its muscles relax under his hands. When it was still again he reached into the burning incision and forced an aluminium clamp on to the flesh, tightening it against the arterial flow, its quick pulse matching his own.

'We will fix you,' he said. 'Your carotid artery is sealed, but is more perhaps in the chest – damage to torso means also artery broken here.'

He slit the stag's skin further, lifting the thick, hair-plugged layer with his fingers and peering into the oozing mess below. The thick crimson pencil of the carotid artery was torn and punctured, like a burst fruit. He set to work with more clamps, finding the worst damage in the glare of the lamp, all the while maintaining a steady commentary into the Dictaphone.

As the stag moaned again he heard something else behind the sound – a soft movement, like a falling cushion. It came again, urgent and quick, the way a trapped bird moved.

He strained his ears into the silence. There was nothing except the bottle-top whisper of wind over the skylight, and the gentle sound of the sea beyond as the tide broke over the shore.

He realized his fingernails were digging back into their crescent wounds.

The light went out with a thump.

Mario leaped in fright and his scalpel tore the length of the exposed artery. As he stumbled in the dark, a burst of hot blood slewed across his face and hit the floor with a noise like tearing paper.

'Oh!' spluttered Mario, slipping as his heel streaked through the puddle, and knocking his head on the trolley's steel leg.

Lights flashed in his vision. Above him the deer began to bleed out a warm stream from the tabletop that pattered on to his skin and splashed into his mouth. It landed in a halo around his head, tinkling lightly on the linoleum.

He counted silently, waited for the room to stop spinning.

The soft noise came again, louder. It was closer this time, and he felt a puff of air cool the blood on his face.

'Hello?' he said, fumbling for his surgical torch and casting a bright disc of light on to his cabinet. He climbed to his knees and moved the light over the shelves, the silhouettes of books and mugs twirling in the shifting beam, filling the room with thin fingers of shadow that gathered into a fist around him.

'Hello?' he said again.

The stag breathed out, heavily and finally, as though it was blowing out a candle.

His torch flickered and died.

'*Skatá*,' said Mario.

Something moved in the shadow. Instinctively, he moved to corner it as he'd cornered gerbils, cats and rabbits – when shining green eyes peered up at him.

Then leapt.

As Barnaby climbed on to his face Mario screamed, his howls of panic muffling on the bear's stuffed fur, until after a moment's agony the little bear vanished, and the big man was still.

Beside him, its casing split by the fall, his Dictaphone clicked off loudly as the tape ran out.

49

Pliers

Hadley was cycling into the farmyard when Sep arrived. Roxburgh's little terrier was in her basket, wrapped in a shawl.

Sep squeezed his reluctant brakes as hard as he could, but nearly crashed into her before he stopped. She held his handlebars to steady herself, and they both laughed nervously.

'Very cute,' said Sep.

'What?'

'The dog,'

'Oh,' she said, and blushed. 'Yeah, she is. I'm going to call her Elliot.'

'Isn't that a boy's name?'

The storm began to break, its energy tipping over with an almost audible sigh and speckling them with the first drops of rain. Hadley tucked in the shawl more tightly.

'I like boys' names for girls.'

'Elliot,' said Sep, holding a finger on the dog's wet nose. She licked his hand and whined happily. 'How do you feel?'

Hadley turned over her hand so they could both see the cut on her palm. It was as vivid as ever.

'Not great,' she said, her hand trembling. 'Scared.'

'We'll beat it,' said Sep. 'I swear.'

Hadley flicked her eyes at him, and Sep leaned in, eyes closing as his lips parted.

Then the farmhouse door opened behind them and he jumped a foot in the air.

'Scare you?' said Lamb.

'Yes,' said Sep. 'Thanks.'

She turned back into the house.

'Hurry up. Leave your bikes in the hall.'

'Why are there only two? Who's not here?'

'Nobody, chill out – Darren stashed his beside the barn.'

They followed Lamb into the kitchen, where Mack and Arkle were already sitting, their faces shadowed by the low-hanging light. Arkle blinked slowly at them, his sombre expression reflected in the vomit he'd left on the table that afternoon.

'Sep and Hadley,' he said, then, spying the dog wrapped in Hadley's arms, 'and E.T.'

'You don't look good,' said Sep.

'That's genetic – I have ugly parents.'

'Does the box make you feel *that* bad?'

Arkle nodded slowly.

'It's like . . . you know when your mum wants some peace and quiet, so she gives you more Calpol than you really need?'

'No,' said Sep carefully.

'Oh. Well, that.'

'Have you been sick again?' said Hadley.

'I wish,' said Arkle, closing his eyes as though contemplating nirvana. 'That would be amazing. I'd hurl up all the dragonflies and Spike in a big technicolor yawn and I'd never feel sick again. By the way,' he added, 'this is spreading over the island now. It's out of control. When I went back for my bike, all the power had gone and a dead cat was chasing my parents through the house.'

'Where's Rosemary?' said Sep.

Arkle sat up straight.

'Oh, *no*! I left her in the truck – is it well hidden, Lamb?'

Lamb popped open a can of drink and rolled her eyes.

'It's under the willow tree. But I'm more worried about the damn car than your dead lump.'

'She's not a lump,' said Arkle, taking a sip of Spike. 'She's my fluffy cuddle monkey.'

'Can I borrow, like, a T-shirt or something?' Sep asked Lamb.

'You want to wear my clothes?'

'No, it's just –'

He pointed at the vomit and blood on his T-shirt.

Lamb rolled her eyes.

'There's a basket with clean laundry beside the door. Take one of my dad's tops – and don't look at my underwear.'

'I'd wear *that*,' said Arkle.

Lamb hit his arm.

'Right,' she said. 'How are we going to do this?'

'We're going to go back and make proper sacrifices – for each other this time,' said Sep, rubbing his jaw as the pain moved back into his teeth. 'Did you all bring something?'

He began to change self-consciously, hoping Hadley wouldn't look at his topless body as he pulled on a white vest.

'Of course,' said Mack.

'Yeah, yeah. Can I smoke in here?' said Arkle.

'Whatever,' said Lamb, 'my dad smokes constantly.'

'Magic,' said Arkle, sparking up and leaning back in his chair.

'I brought a proper sacrifice. It was easy really,' said Hadley, coughing. 'Doesn't it feel like this is what we should always have been –'

Her eyes rolled up into her head and she slumped over the table.

'Shit!' shouted Arkle, jumping to his feet as Sep reached for Hadley's face.

The light went out with a bang, scattering hot glass on to their skin. They leaped back, their chairs toppling, and stood in frantic silence, only the glow of Arkle's cigarette lighting the room.

'Shit shit shit shit shit shit –'

'Give me your lighter! There's a candle on the windowsill,' said Lamb.

Hadley stirred, blinking in the darkness.

'Oh, God,' she murmured, 'I feel terrible –'

'Shit shit shit shit shit shit,' said Arkle, the red ember of his ash trailing across the room.

Sep tried to breathe, but the box's voice was screaming in his ear – and his tooth had exploded. He pulled at his face, as though he could tear out the pain with his skin, and he howled in agony.

'Sep!' shouted Hadley, forcing her head up. 'What is it? Oh, God, someone help!'

Mack grabbed Sep's shoulders and held him against the tabletop.

'My – tooth –' said Sep. 'The box – it's in my tooth!'

Lamb spun the ignition of Arkle's lighter, aiming the flame at the fat candle on the sill, but as it flared they saw the press of bloody flesh outside, the teeth and tongues of all the forest's dead creatures working on the handles and frame, the slime of long-dead skin like slug-trail on the glass, and they screamed.

Lamb dropped the lighter in the sink, and the carnival of gore disappeared.

'Oh my God,' she said. 'Oh my God.'

Sep arched his back with the pain. His rotten tooth had burst in his gum, and he bit down on it as hard as he could, squeezing out the agony.

Mack and Arkle were each holding down a shoulder.

'Give him this!' said Lamb, holding out a wooden spoon.

'What's he going to do?' said Arkle. 'Make cupcakes?'

'No – he can *bite* on it! You need to force his jaw open!'

Sep writhed again, spots flashing green and yellow behind his eyelids.

'Take – it – out –' he managed, hissing the words between clenched teeth.

'What? The whole tooth?' said Hadley.

The window frame leaned in with a crack and the walls of the farmhouse thumped as more creatures joined the press on its sides.

Sep nodded sharply.

'Have you got pliers?' said Hadley.

Lamb was staring, dumbstruck.

'Lamb! Have you got any pliers?'

She nodded, pulled her eyes away from Sep and pointed.

'Y—yes, in the drawer there.'

Hadley pulled open the top drawer in the huge, antique dresser.

'It's full of rubbish!' she said. 'There's just paper, and tape, and a square battery, and –'

'You can never find a square battery when you need one, can you?' said Arkle, puffing maniacally.

'Shut *up*, Darren! Just help me look!'

'I'm scared!' shouted Arkle, throwing piles of cardboard and junk on to the floor. 'There!' he shouted. 'Aha! Pliers!'

He handed them to Mack, still pressing Sep's wriggling shoulders to the table, wide-eyed with fright.

'You need to do it, Golden Boy – you're stronger than me.'

'I can't!' said Mack.

A thin ribbon of white twisted down the centre of the glass as it began to split. Teeth clicked against its surface.

'You're his friend!' shouted Hadley.

Lamb grabbed the pliers.

'You hold him,' she said. Then, looking at the others: 'Force open his jaw.'

She leaned down to Sep's good ear.

'You need to help me, Sep,' she whispered. 'When they open your mouth you need to point to the bad one with your tongue, all right?'

Sep grunted, the tendons in his neck as taut as pulled rope.

'You ready?' said Lamb, raising her voice over the racket outside. 'One, two – *go*!'

Hadley and Arkle pushed down on the wooden spoon, forcing Sep's jaw to open and sending a wave of fire into his brain. He felt his body seize up, a lump of stone pinned by Mack's weight, and as Lamb shoved the oily-tasting pliers into his mouth, Sep used every shred of strength he had to point his tongue at the back tooth around which the storm spun.

Lamb locked the pliers around it – and pulled.

The seismic crunch of the root shook through Sep's skeleton, and he heard its crack echo in the chambers of his head – but as the red, fresh, *good* pain filled his mouth the agony and the noise ebbed away and he opened his eyes, leaned forward and dribbled hot, spitty blood on the floor.

'Thank you,' he said, and took Lamb's hand.

The window caved in.

50

Barn

A river of flesh and fur spilled into the kitchen, mouths and claws tearing at the worktops as the rain howled in.

Hadley heaved at Sep as they ran, Lamb slamming the kitchen door behind them.

'The sideboard!' she shouted.

She and Mack pulled it over the door just as the things inside smashed into it, dark claws reaching round its edge.

'Slam it!' she shouted, and they all leaned on the door at once, chopping the claws like carrots.

'Shit shit shit shit shit shit shit —' said Arkle.

'Where do we go?' said Hadley, holding Elliot's head as the dog whined.

'The barn,' said Lamb. 'We need to cross the yard, but it's got the strongest door and stuff we could use as weapons.'

'Have you already thought about this?' said Sep.

'Of course,' said Lamb, pushing him down the hall. 'You haven't thought about where you would go in your house in a zombie apocalypse?'

'No,' said Sep.

'I didn't know girls thought about that stuff too,' said Arkle. 'Marry me, Lambert.'

The kitchen door cracked.

'Go!' shouted Lamb.

The top half of the door broke and the dead animals tumbled into the hall, their green eyes swirling in the dark as Lamb sprinted across the yard.

She pulled open the side door on the massive barn, and the others ran after her through rain that fell like steel cables, the barn's trembling frame matching the roar of the thunderous sky.

Sep slipped on the shining cobbles and turned in horror to the toothy mass behind him. He saw some flesh-stripped cats reaching for him and kicked out, scrambling backwards – when strong hands grabbed him and dragged him quickly along the ground.

As the creatures fell away a badger-faced thing burst forward, locking its mouth on to his shoes and tugging him back with terrifying strength. He yelled as the bones popped in his feet, and as he kicked off his baseball trainers a high-pitched, motorized whine screamed past his ears and Lamb struck at the creature with a lawn-strimmer, its whirling blade tearing the skin from the creature's forehead and flaying its bright eyeballs like peeled grapes.

Sep was dragged into the barn and Lamb followed, swinging about her with the strimmer, a welder's mask covering her face – then she slammed the door, dropping a sleeper-sized bar across it as the creatures battered on to the other side.

Sep coughed and spat, leaning forward to drool on to the barn floor. He turned to thank whoever had saved him.

Hadley was kneeling beside him, Elliot tucked under her arm, her face tight with concern.

'Hadley?' he said.

'God, that was close,' she said.

He looked at her slight frame.

'You nearly lifted me off the ground,' he said.

She smiled.

'You're not so heavy.'

'So what do we do now?' said Arkle, shouting over the thumping door.

'We wait it out,' said Lamb.

'How? They're not vampires; they won't vanish in the morning.'

'Well, maybe they'll go after someone else when they can't get in!'

'We don't *want* them to go after someone else,' said Sep, 'we don't want them to go after anyone! And –'

Sep moved his jaw. The noise had disappeared. Even though the creatures were on the other side of the door, a few feet away, there was nothing in his head. Lamb had pulled the rotted thing out of his body, and now the box couldn't get to him. Which was good, except . . .

The world outside seemed suddenly draped in blindness, as if a thick fog had come over the island. It was as though Barnaby had been fitted with a bell, and now he was out there, somewhere – silent and invisible.

Sep looked around the barn. They'd played here, that summer, swinging on a tow rope from a sagging beam. It had been full of old farm equipment: pieces of rusted iron sharp enough to cut flesh; the engines, shells and tyres of vehicles put out to pasture; boxes of dangerous-smelling powders beside viscous bottles with yellow, crossboned labels. And a back door.

'The other door,' he said, dribbling blood on his chin. 'Does it still work?'

'What do you mean?' said Lamb. 'It's a door – what's to work?'

'I mean, it's not blocked or anything? We could get out that way?'

Understanding dawned on her face.

'Yeah, we could,' she said.

'But those things are outside,' said Arkle. 'Why would we go out there if we could stay here?'

'Yeah,' said Mack. 'He's right; it's safer in here. We should stay for now. Maybe we can get out later.'

'But what if *they* were stuck inside?' said Sep. He stood up and, balancing against Hadley's shoulder, raised his voice over the snare of rain on the tin roof. 'If we go round the back they'll follow us through here – then we close the door and trap them.'

'And we'd be even safer,' said Lamb.

'Exactly. Especially if –' He sniffed the air. 'You've got fertilizer in here, right?'

Lamb rolled her eyes.

'It's a *farm*,' she said, 'of course there's fertilizer.'

'What about antifreeze?' said Sep, looking at the looming hulk of a tractor parked in the shadows.

'Yeah, but –'

'Oh, *shit*!' said Arkle. 'You're going to blow the barn up!'

'No, I'm not,' said Sep. 'You are.'

'Oh my God.' Arkle bit his lip. 'This is my dream. I mean – a large-scale detonation. I don't know what to say –'

'Don't say anything,' said Lamb. 'You're not doing it.'

Sep tongued the pulpy space where his tooth had been. 'We have to,' he said, 'otherwise we'll either starve to death or they'll break inside eventually and rip us apart. We have to do something.'

'But not blow up my barn!' yelled Lamb, grabbing Arkle's collar as he started to rummage on the shelves for antifreeze.

'I think Sep's right,' said Hadley.

'Geek-on,' muttered Arkle.

'Mack?' said Sep.

'We are *not* taking a vote,' said Lamb.

The things hammered on the door and it shook on its hinges.

'I'm with Sep,' said Mack. 'He's right most of the time, so he's probably right now.'

'Four to one,' said Sep. 'I'm sorry, we have to.'

'Come on,' said Mack as he lifted Lamb away. 'It's for the best – this thing's about to fall down anyway.'

'My vote counts for five!' she shouted. 'It counts for a hundred! Sep!'

'Wait for us at the back door!' called Sep. 'We'll be as quick as we can!'

Lamb's howls of protest were snuffed out as they reached the door, and Sep looked at Arkle as he bent to examine the sinister-looking tubs and cans.

'Can you do it?'

'Hell, yes. It's trying to stop myself that's the hard part.'

'How long?'

Arkle shrugged.

'I've got plenty of galvanized buckets here so, I don't know . . . Four minutes?'

'Brilliant,' said Sep, wiggling his bare toes. 'Then I'll create a diversion.'

'What are you going to do?'

'Distract them, like, divert their attention.'

'I know what a diversion is, dickhead,' said Arkle, heaving a tub of green pellets on to the steel table. 'I meant *how* are you going to divert them?'

Sep handed Hadley a strimmer, then picked up the hedge-cutter and swung it like a bat.

'Just a bit of gardening,' he said.

'Wait –' said Hadley.

Sep pulled the switch and the cutters leaped into life. Hadley looked at him.

'We can't do this,' she said. But she put Elliot on the workbench next to Arkle, and gripped the strimmer's handles.

'Just for a few minutes,' said Sep, lifting the bar from the door. 'We run through them, lead them to the top of the path, then run back, right? By the time they've followed us, Arkle will be ready and we'll be straight out the other side. You *will* be ready, won't you?'

'Defo.'

'This is crazy,' said Hadley.

'It won't take long,' said Sep. 'Just pretend it's field hockey – only the ball is a zombified badger's face.'

'This is *crazy*!'

'Good luck,' said Arkle.

He watched them run through the door and made sure it had slammed back in place before he returned his attention to the buckets he'd set out in a neat row. Elliot watched him carefully, her head cocked to one side.

The strimmer and hedge-cutter roared with reedy fury until the actions of their parts were stoppered by a wet, tearing sound – like a race car slowing on treacle.

Arkle delicately tipped bottles into the buckets, letting their contents fall gently. He stirred and prodded, and as bubbles broke on the surface and the smell began to sting his nostrils the sound of electrical motors returned.

'Magic,' he said, and the door burst open behind him.

Sep hobbled through, blood on his feet.

'What happened?' shouted Arkle as he rolled out the taper.

Sep gritted his teeth.

'I cut my feet.'

'Holy shit! Are you all right?'

'I'm fine,' said Sep. His vest was stained with mud and splashes of gore.

'That thing would have killed you!' said Hadley. 'I just bumped into you – if you'd had shoes on then –'

'I'm fine, just keep moving!' said Sep, throwing the hedge-cutter on the floor as Hadley grabbed Elliot and ran.

'Will I light it?' asked Arkle.

Sep heard the sprinting claws approaching the barn.

'Yes! Now!'

Arkle flicked his lighter with a damp scratching noise – but no flame.

'Come *on*, you've never let me down yet,' he said to the little silver box, 'don't start now.'

He flicked the wheel again.

'Sep!' he shouted. 'It won't light! *It won't light!* Lamb must have got it wet when she dropped it in the sink!'

He spun the wheel again and again, but no sparks came.

'It's OK,' said Sep. 'Try again.'

Arkle flicked his thumb.

Nothing.

The noise of the creatures echoed in the cavernous barn, drowning out the noise of the storm. Sep grabbed the lighter from Arkle's hand and blew on it to dry the flint, spun the wheel.

Nothing.

'*Shiiiiiiiiiiiiiiiiiiiiiiiiiiiiiiiiiiiiiiiiiii—*'

Sep pulled the lighter apart, ripping out the fuel-soaked cotton and grabbing two stones from the floor.

'You always made fun of me for being in the Scouts,' he said.

'It was the *woggle*!' said Arkle, panicked tears streaking his face as the creatures burst through the door. 'It's such a funny word!'

'Well, woggle this!' shouted Sep, and struck the stones together.

They sparked, and the ball of cotton burst into flames.

'Yes! Yes! Oh my God, how are you better at starting fires than me?' said Arkle, touching the flame to the taper and breaking into a run, Sep following as the claws of the box-creatures ticked on the concrete floor.

They threw themselves through the door on to the cool, wet grass, and Mack slammed it behind them.

'How long do we have?' said Sep. He opened his mouth, letting the cool rain fall on his tongue.

'Oh, like, six seconds,' said Arkle.

'Shit,' said Lamb.

They ran together, across the yard towards the farmhouse, jumping over the low wall as the barn exploded in a fireball of brilliant orange, panels of corrugated iron scattering like seeds, streaming with smoke and spotted with tiny fires that hissed out in the torrents of freezing rain.

The barn collapsed, the roof thudding on to the flames inside.

'Oh, *shit*,' said Lamb, watching the smouldering wreckage. 'The barn, I – I – what the hell am I going to tell my dad?'

Arkle lit a cigarette on one of the small fires that had landed around them, then exhaled smoke through a massive grin.

'On the plus side,' he said, 'it'll really distract from you smashing up his truck.'

51

Crabs

'I'm just saying: maybe it would have been nice if someone had reminded me my bike was there before I blew it up.'

Arkle was pacing in his socks: a trace of his explosive had burned a hole in his Converse boot and left a scorch mark on his ankle.

'It was *you* who left it,' said Mack. 'I don't see how this is our fault.'

'Don't give me your shit, Golden Boy,' said Arkle. 'And, oh! Great! This is my last fag! Isn't that just *peachy*?' He tapped it from the packet and pulled it away with his lips. 'Why do the worst things happen to the best people?'

'You know,' said Hadley, 'Roxburgh's dead. You just blew up Lamb's barn. The box is draining my strength. Sep's had a tooth ripped out, his feet all cut *and* he was bitten by a zombie dog.'

'Yeah yeah yeah,' said Arkle, lips tight as he leaned down to light his cigarette on the gas ring.

'We need to go back to the box – now,' said Sep. 'We have to finish this.'

Lamb was staring into space, her face blank.

'He just . . . blew it up,' she said, then made a popping-bubble sound.

'Seriously. We need to get out of here,' said Sep. 'Do you think there's any chance someone didn't see that fireball?'

'We're definitely doing this now?' said Mack. 'I mean, it's dark, and the rule says –'

'The rule says not to *open* it after dark, right?'

'Right, that's what I'm –'

'But you didn't close it last time, did you?'

Mack furrowed his brow.

'No,' he said after a moment, 'that doll came, and we ran away.'

Sep nodded.

'That rule doesn't apply to us now, does it? So we're doing this on our own terms – tonight.'

They looked at each other. Each of them appeared scorched and bruised, and their singed eyebrows gave them an air of considered surprise.

'Your new sacrifices, then,' said Sep. 'What have you got?'

Mack went to his pocket and produced a tight triangle of plastic.

'Garbage?' said Lamb.

'No! It's an empty popcorn packet.'

'So . . . garbage,' said Lamb, narrowing her eyes.

'It's not,' he said, holding it up. 'Look at the stripes – it's Wilko's popcorn!'

'Dude,' said Arkle.

'You can't even *buy* this any more! This is from that summer – it's the popcorn wrapper from our movie night! I kept it!'

'That's perfect!' said Sep. 'Jesus, Mack, I can't believe you did that.'

Mack shrugged, smiling happily.

'I told you. I missed you guys.'

'All right, what else have we got?' said Sep.

Lamb dropped a pebble on the table.

'It's from the time we went swimming,' she mumbled, avoiding their eyes.

'What?'

'I said it's from the time we went swimming!' she shouted.

Sep gave her a huge smile.

'You big softy,' he said.

'Don't –' she started.

'This is Sep's book,' said Arkle, reaching for his back pocket. '*The Shining*. I – I couldn't read it. It was too scary and too long, but he gave it to me that summer, and I've always thought of him when I saw it under my bed.'

They looked at the crumpled paperback, sitting on the edge of the table.

Sep laughed.

'I didn't give you this,' he said. 'You must have taken it without asking me. I've actually been looking for it. Like, a lot.'

'Well,' said Arkle, stubbing his cigarette into the sink, 'that act of casual theft made me think fondly of you for the last four years. I'm glad to sacrifice your property.'

'Hadley?' said Lamb.

Hadley stood with difficulty, leaning on her chair.

'The mixtape from the box,' she said.

'What? It has to be something to do with each other,' said Mack. 'About how we're friends.'

'This is!' she said. 'I was surprised no one recognized it before.'

She pulled it out of her pocket and showed it to Sep. 'Don't you remember? The handwriting's smudged, but you can still tell it's yours.'

They all looked at him.

'Mine? But –'

He picked up the cassette, reread the label.

'I made this for you,' he said, remembering. 'We listened to it –'

'On the beach. We toasted marshmallows.'

'All right,' said Arkle, puffing out his cheeks. 'Last one. Sep, what have you got?'

Sep went to his pocket, felt the piece of paper inside.

'No,' he said. 'I don't think I should.'

'Come *on*,' said Lamb. 'It can't be any more lame than my swimming pebble. Show us!'

Sep shook his head, backing away from the table.

'I can't. I've written something –'

'What? That's like a home-made Christmas present!' said Arkle. 'You can't give it that!'

'Yeah, that sucks,' said Lamb. 'You're the one who said it's all about love. How can you just write something?'

'I know, but . . . I didn't keep wrappers or pebbles or tapes – *or* steal things from your houses. Everything I feel about you guys is just . . . in my head. In my heart. All I could do was try and make that into *something* I could hold in my hands. It says everything I've ever wanted to say. Do you trust me?'

'Are you going to cry?' said Mack, looking at the ceiling. 'Because if you are, that would just set me off, man, and I don't think I can even –'

He broke off and fanned his eyes.

'OK,' said Arkle, 'OK. Yeah! I trust you! I trust you! Let's do this!'

Lamb looked at Hadley. She nodded.

'We trust you,' she said.

'Good,' said Sep, smiling gratefully at them. 'Because we need to go now. Like, *now* now.'

'Right,' said Hadley, making a fist with her uncut hand. 'Let's do it.'

'Well . . .' said Sep.

'What?'

'Just,' said Sep, looking to the others for support, 'it might kill you, Hadley – you could die just by going near it. Maybe you should –'

'You're not serious?' said Lamb.

Hadley shook her head. 'You need me.'

'Yeah, Sep. If we're going to make sacrifices for each other we *all* have to be there,' said Lamb. 'We have to do it together, or not at all.'

349

'But she might –'

'I can look after myself,' said Hadley. 'It's my own fault I gave it blood. I'm going to do what I can to stop it, same as the rest of you.'

She pulled back her shoulders and gave him a defiant look.

'All right,' he said. 'But you have to tell us if you need help – even if it means we go back and try another time.'

'Fine.'

Lamb looked Sep up and down, then shook her head.

'The state you're in.'

'I'm OK,' said Sep, examining himself. His feet and the bite wound in his leg had stopped bleeding, but his white vest was spattered with gore, and he was covered in mud and scratches.

'Wait!' said Arkle. 'What am *I* going to do?'

'What do you mean?' said Hadley.

'Well, I've got no shoes, my clothes are covered in fertilizer and I blew up my bike.'

'What shoe size are you?' said Lamb.

'Wait, can I have shoes too? I'm an eleven,' said Sep, turning back from the doorway.

'I'm a five,' said Arkle.

'A *five*?' sniggered Mack.

Arkle gave him a warning stare.

'Yes, Macejewski. A five.'

'Darren I can help,' Lamb said. 'He can wear my hockey boots. Sep, my dad's only a nine. I'm sorry.'

'So I need to go barefoot?'

'Class!' said Arkle. 'What about the other things?'

'Borrow some more of my dad's gear from the basket – *don't* look at my underwear – and you can take my sister's old bike. I'm pretty sure it's in the shed.'

'You've got a deal,' said Arkle, lifting the lid from the basket. He nodded. 'I'll take these clothes, your boots and your sister's bicycle.'

As he was changing, the others gathered in the courtyard. Sirens sailed through the sky, their alarms mangled by the rain that lashed the ground and splashed in the wet earth.

'Are you all right?' Sep asked Hadley.

She tucked Elliot into her basket and tightened the dog's shawl.

'Yes,' she said. 'It's kind of gone past that, hasn't it? I mean, it doesn't matter how we are – look at everything that's happened because of us.'

'I know.'

She pointed at his feet, slashed and bare.

'Will you be OK?'

'Like you said – I'll have to be.'

She looked up at the stars, visible through a torn strip of cloud. Raindrops beaded on her glasses.

'Do you still feel insignificant?' she said.

Sep allowed the way she made him feel to flow over him in heady, perfumed waves, washing away all the stains of the past and leaving him whole and clean and strong. He smiled.

'Not really.'

Arkle emerged from the house, clacking on the stone with Lamb's studded boots, the sleeves of her dad's rugby shirt rolled to doughnuts around his wrists.

'I'm shitting myself,' he admitted as they looked over. 'If I die dressed like this they'll think some buff guy shrunk in the wash.'

'Well, saddle-up, short-ass,' said Lamb, wheeling something round the side of the house.

'Wait,' said Arkle, 'isn't your sister older than you?'

'Yeah, she moved to the mainland, like, five years ago.'

'So what is she, a pygmy?'

Lamb handed him the little pink bike.

'She took her racer with her. This is her old one.' She put her head on one side and smiled at him. 'I used to be so jealous of the tassels.'

'This isn't funny,' said Arkle as the others laughed. 'You know I saved our lives by blowing that thing up, right? I should be celebrated, not slagged off!'

'That's all there is. You want to walk?'

'*No*,' said Arkle, climbing on to the little bike and pushing off, pedalling twice as fast as the rest of them. 'I just wish the basket didn't have a pony on it, that's all.'

'He could have taken my dad's bike obviously,' whispered Lamb as she passed Sep, 'but this is *way* more fun.'

The sirens had grown louder by the time they reached the gate.

Sep looked down towards the town. The tide was in, the water tight around the island. From here the bay looked closed and sharp. Like a claw.

He turned towards the forest track, and lightning split the sky with a jagged pink fork. They froze.

'It's dangerous to be near trees in a storm,' said Hadley.

'It's dangerous to stay here,' said Sep. He nodded to them and pushed off, ready to fight through the pain in his leg and his mouth to lead them against the box.

The treeline blew apart.

At first he thought it was a landslide, and fear sped his heart – then he saw the pincers, and terror stopped it.

'Go!' he shouted, stamping on the pedals and shooting off down the hill, away from the battalion of crabs, and he turned and saw the others doing likewise, even Arkle speeding away with a tinkle of his bell. All except Hadley.

Her chain had slipped. She'd climbed from her bike and was keeping the frame between her and the crabs, Elliot clutched in her arms.

Sep jumped clear, leaving his wheels clicking backwards, and ran at the horde, lashing out with his feet and knocking away their terrible limbs.

'Sep!' she shouted, backing away down the path.

The sirens were closer, almost at the bottom of the hill.

He reached her, grabbed the bike and pushed it at the nearest crab. It backed off, moving its pincers like a lofted blade.

'If we push them with the bike they'll keep backing off!' he yelled.

He stepped the bike forward, the wall at their backs, making a safe barrier between them and the grabbing claws.

'Sep!' shouted Arkle. 'Are you all right? Did you get Hadley?'

'We're fine!' shouted Sep, moving the barrier another step, 'we're coming back out!'

'Hurry up! The police – your mum, she's almost here! I can see the lights!'

'We're nearly at the top,' Sep grunted. 'Be ready to run.'

Hadley nodded, holding the dog against her chest.

'Run!'

Sep shoved the bike on to the crabs' massed spikes and turned, watching Hadley bolt past the last crab's desperate snap, and as he went to follow he felt a pull, and turned to find his jeans snagged on the chain.

The first crab cut his chin. The second cut his arm. The third pulled out a chunk of his hair, and then he heard only the snap of their claws and Hadley's distant cries as the weight of them tumbled over him, the stink of the sea thick in his nose.

He gritted his teeth, waited for the claws to find his throat, and thought of his mum arriving in her squad car to find him, bloodied and torn and still.

But then something else was there beside him, something small and strong, pushing snarling past him; and he grabbed the thick, warm fur of the fox, *his* fox, as it leaped in among them, its quick jaws snapping at their shells and legs.

He held on to it, pulled himself to his knees and grabbed the next pincer that came at him.

It closed violently, slicing off the top of his index finger.

Sep roared, tore the claw in half, then lifted the crab and swung it at the others.

But as he ran free he saw them crowding instead round his fox, their claws already stuck with its fur as it leaped once – then fell back.

'No!' he shouted.

Hadley grabbed him.

'The sirens, Sep, we have to go!'

Sep turned away, closing his ears as they tore his fox apart.

Hadley stowed Elliot in Arkle's pink basket, then jumped on to the back of Sep's bike. They took off again, tears streaking across Sep's face as they swooped away from the flashing blue lights and into the cover of the trees.

52

Surgery

They were deep in the trees that led to the forest. Rain had filled the land, stirring up the odours of earth and wood, and the stones gleamed with the clean smells of slate and moss.

'Wait,' said Sep, rolling to a halt. 'What about Mario?'

'What about him?' Lamb shouted over her shoulder.

'I've just realized – we've left him with a dying animal.'

Arkle jingled up beside Sep.

'So?' he said. 'He's a vet.'

'Don't you see? We keep getting *attacked* by dead animals – what if the stag dies then comes back to life? He'll be trapped in there with it!'

'Oh,' said Hadley.

'I need to warn him,' said Sep, wiping his brow. Blood from his severed finger spilled down his face.

'Holy shit!' said Arkle. 'Are you OK?'

'Yeah . . .' Sep blinked slowly. 'But I probably need to wrap this up before I pass out. I can get a bandage in the surgery.'

'You're going on your own?'

'I won't be – Mario will be there. Then I'll come and meet you at the edge of the wood, just before the ravine.'

They looked uneasy.

'You want me to come with you?' said Arkle. 'In case, you know, you pass out again.'

Hadley nodded.

'I'd come, but you'd have to carry me twice as far then.'

'She can ride with me,' said Mack, and even in the throes of everything Sep felt a stab of jealousy in his stomach.

'Cool,' he said as Hadley climbed from his saddle and up behind Mack. 'I'll check on Mario, bandage this, and come straight after you.'

He tried not to think of his fox, but hoped, *hoped*, that it was dead and quiet, and wouldn't open glowing eyes once the crabs had finished.

'This way's quickest; it'll only take a few minutes.'

'For you maybe,' said Arkle, angling the tiny bike downhill. 'I'm riding Twinkle Snowdrop here. That's got to be tough,' he added once they were away from the others, speeding towards the back of the town.

'What?' said Sep.

'Watching your girl ride off with another man?'

'She's not my girl.'

'She is – she's got a geek-on for you. I told you.'

'Shut up.'

'Dude, I'm –'

'Shut *up*.'

They rode in silence for a minute, picking their way carefully between the roots and stones, until they emerged on to the road beside the graveyard.

'It's so creepy. Jesus, it's so creepy,' said Arkle, crossing the street on to the other side, away from the tall dark gates.

'There's nobody here,' said Sep, 'don't worry.'

'Nobody *alive*!' said Arkle, looking through the dark layers of neatly stacked headstones. 'What if, you know, like Roxburgh, or –'

'It's fine – the gates are locked.'

'What if they're gate-opening zombies?' said Arkle, the tassels on his handlebars fluttering as he sped up.

'Stop saying –' Sep began.

He looked into the darkness of the graveyard and felt the vast pull of its reservoir of decay. He imagined what might happen if the box was to grow further in strength – if it could reach its vile power into this space – and felt a surge of deep dark sadness overwhelm him.

He pedalled after Arkle as fast as he could, and a moment later they arrived at the little row of shops, leaning their bikes silently in the shadows.

'I'm cacking myself,' said Arkle matter-of-factly. 'Like, seriously – I think my guts have given up. I can't hack this. I know you're a crab-fighting zombie-whisperer now, but some of us have delicate bowels.'

'I'll be quick, then we'll get to the box as fast as we can,' said Sep as they tiptoed towards the surgery's front door.

The blood was running freely from his finger. He breathed in, and felt light-headed, as though he was being carried in strong hands.

'Wait here,' he said.

Arkle grabbed his arm.

'Here?' he whispered. '*Here?*'

'Yeah. I'll only be a minute.'

'But – the –'

'You need to keep an eye on the bikes – if anything happens to them we're screwed.'

'God, I wish I had another cigarette,' said Arkle, kicking the fence and wrapping his arms round his chest.

Sep crept inside the silent, pitch-dark reception, ghosted across the floor and tentatively edged open the door to the surgery.

He strained his deaf ear, pressing his tongue into the bloody space in his gum – but there was nothing. No noise, no breathy whisper.

But the door had been open, and Mario always locked up. Always.

So he was still here.

With a sickening twist in his stomach Sep took a deep breath and moved into the room.

The stag was on the table. Its enormous legs were spindling off the sides, bones splintered like wood, hooves resting on the floor. The room was boiling, and Sep gagged on the hot stink of fresh blood, dark puddles of it pooled on the floor.

His finger was throbbing, waves of pain roaring through his arm with pressure and heat, the severed tip burning in the air. He fought back a swell of nausea. He had to cover the wound, get some kind of antiseptic on it before it became infected – if an infection moved into his blood he could get septicaemia. Fever.

Death.

Swallowing the lump of his fear, Sep tried the light switch, easing it over noiselessly, and then flicking it up and down with despair when it clicked emptily, leaving the surgery drenched in shadows that were large and dark and altered beyond recognition. He looked, concentrated: the cabinet, the scales, Mario's chair, the drawers of paper files; the shelves of tinctures and medicines on the wall.

And the stag, gigantic in the small room — a part of the outside world brought where it didn't belong, the edges of its bulk bleeding into the darkness. Beneath the sharpness of its blood it stank of sweat and a dirty, wild musk, and Sep felt an ancient terror creep through his bones as he approached it, screaming at him to run.

But he felt more blood drip from his wound.

It needed a dressing, otherwise he'd eventually lose consciousness. He spotted the little box — top shelf on the other side of the room — and took a step towards it. The shadows moved as he did, turning round him in the dim glow from the street.

The stag's ears shifted suddenly in the lights of a passing car, and he leaped back, thinking for a moment it had cocked them with living instinct. But as the lights spun away the giant ears remained still, and he breathed again.

Pocketing the antiseptic, Sep moved until he was level with the animal's head. Its eyes were huge, bulbous and dark, and still shiny. The tongue was stuck out between the teeth — a great curtain of stinking meat from which hung thick drool in a stalactite of grey thread. Close to, the antlers were enormous, a bark-textured cage of short points, like blades sprung from the boughs of an oak.

Fascinated, he leaned towards the animal, for a fraction of a second forgetting where he was and why, fear nudged aside by the creature's immensity and presence, and as he crouched down he noticed the other shadow, the one that wasn't visible from the door, the one that didn't fit into his memory's roll-call of fixtures and furniture. A motionless body, huge and round, face up and still – one hand still reaching for the table leg, the other clasped to its throat.

And a huge mop of dark, curly hair.

'*Mario?*' he breathed. 'Oh – oh my God, Mario, oh Jesus Christ, no –'

He grabbed the table for support, then staggered back, blinked away tears and took a deep breath of the stinking air.

The throat under Mario's hand was grossly distended, like a stuck frog bubble, and the veins along its side were dark and vivid and thick as worms. Blood had spilled from his mouth.

Fighting against his own body, Sep forced himself up and reached for his friend.

The stag bellowed and rose from the table, its shattered legs scrabbling for purchase. It swung its head around, catching Sep's shoulder with the spike of its antlers and knocking him into the glass cabinet, which fell on to Mario's prone corpse. Sep cried out as his skin burst on the antler's points, then dived away and backed into the corner.

The stag reared up, its broken bones splintering like glass, and Sep looked at it in horror: its chest cavity was gaping and wide, split open and glistening, the little clamps on its severed arteries chiming as they swung. The animal was dead, torn open and empty, but it lashed wildly at him and howled in rage.

It reared again with a sound like tearing meat, and as he ducked from the antlers Sep realized the animal was splitting further apart under its own weight.

He heaved until he saw spots and lifted the cabinet away, but was caught again by the stabbing antlers, and as he fell backwards the cabinet landed on Mario again with a metallic crash. A drawer slid out, fluttering index cards on to the congealing blood, and as Sep watched their paper darken he felt his head spinning with nausea once more, the pain from his finger lighting his arm with bursts of fire.

The stag was between him and the door. Mario's body was crushed. There wasn't anything else he could do but run.

He grabbed the points of the antlers and held them as far from himself as he could. The stag roared, throwing back its head so that its mouth was in Sep's face, the air of its throat hot in his eyes, flecks of blood pattering his cheeks. He pushed back, driving the animal's head away, shocked at the strength of its neck and its kicking limbs, and it bellowed as it tried to reach him.

Sep slipped in blood, righted himself and slipped again, holding the antlers above his head like a trophy – when something at ground level caught his eye.

Mario's mouth was moving. First a twist of lip, then a burst like pus from a wound, leaving the skin suddenly loose beneath the packed thing that had spilled outwards: a dark shape, cloaked in a sac of glistening mucus.

Sep screamed.

Barnaby unfurled on Mario's chest, his little limbs popping back into shape as he stood upright and turned to Sep with shining green eyes.

He had climbed inside Mario's throat and choked him to death. Mario, Sep's protector and friend; Mario who had nothing to do with any of this.

Sep screamed again as the little bear ran towards him, and as he stood up to flee the stag pulled back its head, readying the antlers to strike. But as the deadly points swung towards him he ducked, saw them swipe past his head and catch Barnaby like a fly in a web.

Sep landed on something hard and square, and rolling away saw it was Mario's Dictaphone.

He grabbed it and turned to see Barnaby writhing in the antlers' cage as the stag tossed its head again, its eyes like green fire.

And just as he gasped with relief, he saw Mario's ruined body shift on the floor, the green-eyed head turning to look at him.

Sep threw himself into the chip shop, away from the trapped, bloody heat of the surgery and towards the only door that wasn't locked with a key – the cold store.

But the slick blood on his hands made his fingers slip from the numbers on the little lock, and as he wiped his fingers dry on his jeans to try again he realized his mind was blank – he couldn't remember the code.

The door to the surgery opened behind him and Sep saw two green, glowing specks of light reflected in the brushed steel of the door.

'It's your *birthday*,' he said under his breath as the Mario-thing shuffled towards him on heavy, dragging feet. 'We stayed late and had pizza; we *always* have pizza on your birthday –'

The thing moved round the counter –

'And it's *Greece's* day –'

He gasped as thick fingers touched his bare arm – and remembered –

'The twenty-fifth! Your birthday is the twenty-fifth of March!'

He punched in the digits and ran inside, felt the wind of the grabbing arms brush his skin and, as Mario's body thumped loosely on the door, Sep covered his face with his hands and wept.

The cold store was dark but for the dim glow of street lights coming through the old window in the roof, its glass shrouded in a thick fabric of cobweb.

'Mario,' Sep whispered, listening to the big hands move on the door and looking in despair at his cell. 'Jesus Christ, Mario . . . Jesus Christ, I can't –'

Then he remembered Arkle, sitting cross-legged in Lamb's living room. He turned up to the skylight and took a deep breath.

'Mario goes bad,' he said. 'The hero escapes by climbing.'

He put a foot on the empty bottom shelf to haul himself up.

Then realized it wasn't empty.

A dog, green eyes slitting open, had shifted its head to look at him and there were countless more eyes – smaller and sharper and rounder – behind it.

The door thumped again.

'Oh, come *on*!' Sep shouted, kicking away the lunging mouth and scrambling on to the next shelf.

Teeth locked on his jeans, and *something* – some long, cold thing – began to drag itself slowly up his leg. He looked down and saw a pair of the tiny green eyes inching towards his face and felt long-toed feet drag over his legs. With a sinking heart Sep recognized the shape of Mr Snuggles.

The iguana hissed, and Sep realized that not only would he die if he stayed still, but his death would be slow and painful.

And his body would be eaten by a costumed, zombie iguana.

'Bollocks to that,' he said, and heaved up with all his strength, touched the window and pushed. It was locked fast by paint and time and rust. He pushed harder, hammered with his fist, heard it begin to give.

The door cracked with the force of Mario's weight.

Sep hammered again, harder and harder, until the glass shattered and fell and he pulled himself through the empty frame, knocking the lizard to the floor just as the Mario-thing roared into the dark space behind him.

53

Footprints

Sep slathered the antiseptic on his severed knuckle, tore a strip from his vest to bind the wound, then he and Arkle watched the movement behind the graveyard gates, Arkle rubbing Sep's back as he wept. The faces on the other side of the bars were slack, the dark clothes were torn, and pale hands shook the padlock's chain.

'There's so many of them,' said Sep, his thumb on the Dictaphone's play button – unable to press it, knowing what was trapped inside. 'It's so sad. It's not even scary, it's just sad. Look what we've done.'

They held each other until their strength returned, then pedalled in silence through the rain, watching lightning strike the forest.

By the time they'd reached the woods Sep had stopped crying.

'Thank God,' said Hadley when they arrived. 'We've been so worried.'

'Have you seen anything?' said Lamb.

Sep looked at Arkle.

'What?' said Lamb.

'Mario's dead,' said Sep. 'It was Barnaby – he must have been looking for me. Now Mario's dead. And it's our fault.'

'Oh my God,' said Mack. He coughed and gasped for breath, sticky spit catching in his throat as tears welled in his eyes. He reached for Arkle's shoulder to steady himself.

Lamb dropped to her knees.

'Are you OK?' said Hadley, blinking through tears. 'We didn't know –'

'Mario's dead,' Sep said again, and the weight of it hit him in the chest.

Lamb bit her lips.

'Let's end this,' she said.

Sep nodded, looking at his hands, imagining the rain that soaked them as splashes of crimson from Mario, Roxburgh and his fox: all dead at the hands of their stupidity.

'Now,' he said, and he led them into the forest.

The path, like everything else – like their clothes and skin and hair – was soaking wet, and the rain drilled into the ground and hissed in the puddles. The world was an explosion of damp, running soil, and they fell again and again, Sep's bandages plastering coldly to his skin as they pressed further into the trees.

He felt Hadley's hand slip into his, and he squeezed it gratefully.

'Not too tight,' said Arkle.

'Dude!' said Sep, dropping his hand. 'Come *on*!'

'I'm freaked out! Please, I just can't – what's his name again? The big guy?'

'Mack?'

'Mack! Oh my God . . . my brain, I can't –'

Arkle's face was wide and frightened. Sep took his hand again and helped him forward.

'Just for a minute, all right?'

'Thanks, Seppy.'

The ground underfoot was slippery and spongy, oozing over Sep's torn feet whenever he found softer turf. He felt the texture of the forest's skin on his, and remembered, with the soles of his feet, running barefoot with the others over this path.

He balanced on a tree trunk, swore as the bark peeled off in his grip – and landed beside an unmistakable shape: the enormous, round-toed boot-print of Roxburgh, pressed deep and wide in the soft earth and filling with water that glowed silver in the moonlight.

Arkle helped him to his feet, and Sep found another print beside the first. It had looked – and *sounded* – as though the gamekeeper's legs had broken when he fell from the shack, but the prints were close together, and deep. So he was walking, slowly, and – Sep stepped back – walking *out* of the woods.

'Look,' he said, pointing.

'Look at what?' said Arkle.

'Roxburgh's footprints!'

Mack leaned down and ran his finger round the lip of the boot's impression.

'Pretty recent,' he said.

'How do you know that?' said Hadley.

'The edges. The turf hasn't sprung back yet, so it's not been there for long.'

'What are you, the Lone . . . Star?' said Arkle.

'Ranger,' said Mack.

'We've been here for a while,' said Lamb. 'If he'd left the woods we'd have seen him.'

'But look – he's been this way!' said Sep. 'That's brilliant – one less thing we need to worry about. Let's keep going.'

He turned to Hadley, standing beside him, shining in the wet.

'I don't feel well,' she said.

She looked even more drawn than before, her eyelids and skin shrinking against her skull.

'I know,' he said. 'We'll be there soon, and we'll fix it, I promise. We'll –'

And as he spoke his eyes refocused, past her face and into a pool of moonlight that hung, bright and heavy, in the mist.

Roxburgh's corpse was walking towards the box, a shambling, slow, unyielding step that dragged him through the forest's knots without pause.

Sep's body ceased to function. He felt his blood stop, and his lungs froze as he looked down.

Roxburgh's legs were broken and splintered, grinding shards of bone protruding from the feet: feet that were on backwards and making – with a soft, sucking sound – backward footprints in the mud.

Hadley stifled a scream, and Sep started to back away as silently as he could, millimetres at a time.

The two of them turned back to the others as Roxburgh reached the edge of the puddle of light and moved into the shadow of the trees.

'Did you see him?' whispered Sep, though he knew by their faces they had.

'Holy shit,' said Lamb, almost breathing the words out. 'What do we do?'

'Go the long way,' said Sep. He wondered whether a gamekeeper's ears would be as keen when they were undead, and added: '*Quietly.*'

Hadley nodded, and they turned to go.

Ptwing!

Sep saw Arkle anxiously rethreading his floss, and before he could grab him he'd fixed it in his grip and pulled.

Ptwing!

Roxburgh's ruined body turned slowly towards them.

'What?' said Arkle. 'It's making me feel better – I can remember how to floss, even if my mind is –'

The forest exploded in eldritch shrieks and green light as the Roxburgh-thing screamed – and they ran again, agony filling every part of Sep until it took him over completely and he didn't know, couldn't imagine, where it might end.

They ran through thickets of whispery thorns, tangled their hair in spiders' webs and cut their faces on the trees' hanging claws, and the thing kept gaining on them, scrambling across the ground on its hands and knees and the splintered bone of its feet, the shard of Sep's stick of rock glinting in its dead eye.

A buzzing storm of dragonflies fell on them from the trees, and something white and scorched dropped on to Hadley's head. She fell, clutching at strings. A lump of bloody fur flew into Lamb's face and she staggered back, hands flailing at her face, Mack hauling at the green-glowing thing and throwing it against a tree before spiking it through the head.

Sep ran along the ravine – a hundred-metre drop on to slippery rock – and fell to his knees.

Then Roxburgh was on him.

His skin had been rebuilt by animal fur, his face studded with too many eyes, and he gnashed at Sep's throat with teeth that were not human.

Arkle grabbed the thing's jacket and it rounded on him, falling and landing on his face, its fur-patched chest bursting open. Sep kicked it and saw the dark, tarry bags of the old gamekeeper's lungs drag over Arkle's gurgling mouth.

As Lamb tore Here'n'now from Hadley's face and threw him into the darkness, the Roxburgh-thing leaped once more at Sep. He heaved back against the stinking deadness of its hands on his neck, pulling against its fierce strength, but its muscles were no longer human and they knew no weakness, no mercy – only the crushing anger that closed on Sep like a steel trap, pushing him to the edge of the cliff.

Sep battered on the stick of broken rock in the thing's eye until his skin broke – and still the thing pushed, its leering mouth dribbling sulphurous bilge.

A branch swung in and knocked its head away, splitting the neck in a shower of blood and – as Sep dragged himself

371

from the ravine's edge in a mess of knees and elbows – the Roxburgh-thing slid into the darkness, the lights of its eyes winking out as it fell.

'Is everyone OK?' said Sep. Blood flowed from the space in his gum, and he swallowed it.

'No,' said Lamb, throwing the branch to the ground. She was holding her eye with both hands. It was swollen closed, and already purple. 'That bloody thing nearly burst my eyeball.'

'Where's Arkle?'

'*Smoker's lungs,*' said Arkle's voice from a nearby shrub, '*smoker's lungs . . .*'

Mack was vomiting on a tree. His leg was buckled beneath him, his lip split by a trickle of blood.

'Hadley?' said Sep. 'Hadley!'

He saw the glitter of her shoes first – she was lying in a sweep of giant roots, her arm twisted behind her, the thin scores of string visible across her neck.

'Hadley!'

He ran to her, lifted her head and held it in his lap.

'Can you hear me?' he said, touching her cheek. 'Hadley?'

'She's so pale,' said Lamb, dropping on to her knees. 'Why's she so pale?'

'It's killing her,' said Sep, pressing his fingers into her neck. 'It has been since it took her blood. I can't find a –'

Hadley's pulse flickered weakly against his skin. He ground his teeth and sucked more blood into his mouth.

'We shouldn't have brought her here.'

'But we needed her to –'

'Well, we need to think of something else now!' said Sep. 'Hadley? Hadley, can you hear me?'

Her eyes peeked open and found Sep's. He leaned in closer.

'Why are you looking at me like that?' she said.

Sep almost laughed with relief.

'It helps me think,' he said. He watched her eyes close again, then turned to the others.

'You've got blood in your teeth,' said Arkle. 'Want some floss?'

'I'm going after it,' said Sep. He swallowed.

'What are you talking about?' said Lamb. 'What are you going to do?'

'I'm going to the box alone.'

Lamb shook her head.

'I didn't tell the truth before, about the mirrors,' she said, holding Hadley's hand in both of hers. 'It was only one that broke – I said it was all of them, but it was just the one on her dresser. That morning, when it was my turn, it had a huge crack . . . and when I looked in it I looked like *her*, and I – smashed the rest of them, all of them. I couldn't – I had to tell you –'

'It doesn't matter now,' said Sep, gripping her shoulder. 'I'm going to kill it.'

'Sep, no!' said Mack. 'We'll all go, we'll all do it – together!'

'You can't even stand! Lamb can't see. Hadley's unconscious –'

'I'll come,' said Arkle, rising and falling in one movement. 'Or maybe not. Sep, I'm sorry – I can't stand up.'

'How's your watch?' Sep asked Mack. 'Is it still working?'

Mack nodded.

'Then it'll be all right, won't it?'

'Here,' said Mack, taking the watch off and holding it out. 'Take it.'

'Thanks,' said Sep. He strapped it to his wrist, three holes up from the groove worn by Mack.

'Wait, Sep,' breathed Hadley, her eyes flickering.

He leaned in and kissed her, pressed his lips into hers so that she might know his feelings and read his thoughts; tasted her breath in his mouth and let her fill him up inside, the glorious sense of her shining like sunlight in his heart.

'I'll be back soon,' he whispered.

She nodded, then slipped into unconsciousness again.

Sep took the scrap of paper from his pocket and pressed it into her hand, then ran into the darkness.

'Check out the bold Sep,' said Arkle. Then he vomited behind a bush.

54

Sacrifice: 1986

As he ran Sep reached into the forest with his deaf ear, searching for the whisper of the box's noise.

But there was nothing. Now the rotten tooth had gone he could no longer find its corrupt frequency.

He cursed the blind darkness, empty now of warning, peering into every shadow as he found himself pulled back to all his resentments, to the small, selfish, lonely thoughts he'd hidden from himself for so long. He leaned against a tree, closed his eyes and fought back against the tide of self-loathing; focusing on how his empty world had exploded with voices and laughter, on everything his mum had done for him, on the warm glow of friendship the others had re-kindled in his heart; and he thought of Mario, his great friend. Always patient. Always kind. Always on his side – murdered by the box's anger when Sep had led Barnaby to the surgery.

He felt the memories of Mario giving him strength, and he reached for the Dictaphone, his bare feet skidding on more slick wood.

Mario's voice, whispering like a ghost through the rain, found his good ear.

. . . antlers is cracked along base of pedicle. Neck seems potentially broken, is . . .

He rewound further.

. . . dead tortoise, is been maimed by cat, eyeball torn out and is missing . . . most likely eaten by cat who also is dead . . . the intestines of the tortoise have been . . .

He wound it forward, just for a second.

. . . ripped apart, kidneys dangling from wound under shell, and all other major organs have been torn from . . .

He wound it forward again, laughing painfully at Mario's frankness, then found what he was looking for.

. . . are my great friend, September. Mario loves you. And he knows you will do brilliant things, because you are clever and brave. The bravest person I know . . .

Sep sobbed into the night, rewound the tape and played it again and again as the clearing's open, moonlit space came into view.

. . . friend, September. Mario loves you. And he knows you will do brilliant . . .

. . . September. Mario loves you. And he knows you . . .

. . . Mario loves you . . .

'I love you too, Mario,' he said aloud, looking up to see a column of dark cloud twisting towards the sacrifice box. And in a tiny gap of clear night sky he saw the comet – a piece of distant magic he should have been watching from the chip-shop roof, sipping tea with his great friend – hurtling, indifferent, over all this chaos.

He took a deep breath, felt the hot coal of Mario's love burn in his chest and pulled himself over a fallen log.

Barnaby leaped from inside the cavernous trunk and Sep fell, landing in a huge puddle of deep, slick mud. A fork of lightning slashed through the sky, illuminating the little bear's antler-torn, terrible face as he bore down on Sep, his stuffing bursting out from the side of his head.

'I know what you are now!' Sep shouted.

Barnaby's bright eyes stared into his, and Sep realized he was staring into his own soul.

'No! I *know* what you are!' he shouted again. 'You think you can hurt me, but you can't! I *own* you! Everything that's in you!'

He threw a stone. Barnaby ducked, closed his eyes and – without their light – vanished.

Sep scrambled to his feet and ran into the empty space the teddy had filled moments before. He peered through the forest's murk, through the shifting leaves and the fists of thorns, searching for movement.

'I know you're here!' he called, swinging his head under a low branch. 'I know everything that's in you, and I'm not scared of it!'

He moved deeper into the darkness.

'You're her sickness,' he shouted, 'and my guilt for wanting to leave, even when I thought she might die! I had those thoughts, but I'm still a good person – I love my mum and I love my *friends*, and I'm not scared of any of that shit any more! I own it, all of it: all the bitterness and the guilt and the regret! They're mine! I *own* them! *And I own you!*'

Glowing eyes rushed at him from the branches' depths.

377

Sep aimed a kick at Barnaby, who grabbed his foot and ran up his leg, his soft limbs squelching with rain and mud. Sep beat at him, grabbing the ears and the neck, and gagging on his stink. With all his strength he prised the teddy away from his chest and held him in mid-air, locking his hands round him and squeezing, the pain of his severed finger roaring like a bright fire.

'I *own* you!' he shouted again – and squeezed again, watching the bear's defiant glare ebb away as the light died in his eyes.

Barnaby went limp. Sep dropped him on the ground, and turned to the clearing.

The box had gathered the forest like a protective cage. The clearing was barred by trunks that leaned and coiled together, knuckles of yew embroidered with birch and twisted with oak. Tangles of twigs and leaves had meshed high above, making an urn of shimmering, greasy air.

Sep squeezed through a tiny gap in the trees, angling his body through a spider's web of sinew and skin. His torn leg snagged on it with an explosion of pain that flashed lights in his eyes, and he roared, grabbing at the air around the wound.

Bones popped beneath his feet with tiny, wet sounds as he stumbled over the roots that fell into the box. Its stone shone like licked skin, its open mouth blacker than night, larger than before – larger than it had ever been.

Large enough for a person. Sep nodded in the shadows.

It was waiting for him.

The sacrifice box's terrible pulse beat through him, through the soles of his feet and the pores of his flesh, the vibrations of a drumbeat he could no longer hear, but which hammered at him with all its strength. It flickered with a pulse that filled his head with hot tin, and he fell face first on to the mud and roots, shaking as he remembered the moment he'd wondered about his mum dying, wondered for a split second what would happen afterwards – whether her death would mean he'd get to leave the island.

'No!' he roared, dragging himself up and crawling on his knees towards the box as the roots grabbed at him. 'She's going to be fine. I love her, and I know myself, I know who I am – all my weakness and my strength, all the selfish thoughts *and* the love. I claim it, all of it! The misery *and* the light! It's mine, not yours – *mine*!'

He saw Here'n'now's eyes glinting like stars on the edge of his vision; heard the buzz of insects' wings and the slip of feathers.

Sep counted the birds.

Four.

'You don't scare me,' he said aloud. Then he threw back his head and screamed it, screamed it at the sky and the sacrifices and into the box's void: 'You don't scare me – I scare you! I scare *you*!'

He reached down, picked up a slick little skull and crushed it in his hands – threw the shards at the crows as they came at him.

And climbed inside the sacrifice box.

55

Love

It pulled at him like a magnet – drawing his blood against his skin and filling his eyes with stabbing pain as his ears, both his ears, roared with the pressure in his veins.

He had only one thought, but it beat at him like a hammer – that his mother and his friends were waiting for him.

'I love you,' he said, his mouth open in silent agony.

And as he spoke he was taken by the roots, his flesh filling with thorns as the box's solid, even strength gripped him like a fist.

Sep screamed at the force of it – screamed until he felt the fibres tear in his throat and blood run from his broken lips – and a time passed around him that could not be measured or understood, leaving him hovering in a light that froze his skin and boiled his guts.

I'm dying, he thought – a formless notion spoken not with his mind, but with his soul.

He stopped screaming.

His fears and worries drifted from him like falling blossom. Sep laughed, watching them twirl.

That's all there is, at the end, isn't it? he thought. *People, and what you've shared.*

He thought of them all. Lamb. Arkle. Mack. Hadley. His mother. He leaned back against that swell of happiness – and felt the box tremble.

'Oh, you're scared of *me*,' he said, and reached with all his strength into the roots that held him, found the evil the box had cast into the island and held it in his grip, pulling it back like a net from the sea, dropping the reanimated dead where they stood, the glow dying in their eyes as the box's power began to shrink.

As he withdrew the box's poison he absorbed the wonder of his world: the crackle of growing grass, the pull of the tide and the soft breath of the people in their beds, their beating hearts like raindrops on a pond; he found his mother – and reached out his love towards her.

And found something else. He'd thought her sickness had returned, but she wasn't *sick*.

She was pregnant.

Sep felt joy wash over him as he listened to the tiny heartbeat thumping alongside her own. A little girl, curled and growing.

His *sister*.

The sacrifice box struck back, crushing him, breaking him, killing him.

As his consciousness ebbed away Sep saw the means by which he would live forever, dancing as a speck in a sunbeam, or growing in soil; sparkling in the wings of dragonflies or glittering in seawater; and he sensed his distant body falling apart until he was dust, the golden thread of his consciousness dissolving until he was nothing but the matter that had once been rock and starlight.

Mum. Mum. I'm sorry. I'm sorry, Mum.

Hadley.

Her name struck him like thunder, and with it came the awareness of himself, of *himself* and all the happiness that was his to claim. He felt a tug from the world and knew that the others – his friends, his *friends* – had made it to the box, were speaking over it, making *real* sacrifices, little pearls of love; and calling him back, saying not the rules but a single word.

His name.

Light, white and blinding, filled him, and he was once more bones and muscle; once more a heart and gasping, wet lungs, lying in skin that was cut and bruised and cold. Something else came to him, something silky and light. He reached out, felt the pull on the other end . . . and then he was awake, the watch on his wrist ticking, the crows exploding from the trees in a silent constellation, drifting as feathers to the earth and filling the sky with the gleaming specks of their eyes.

Sep gulped at the beautiful green air until his breath was taken by the force of Hadley's lips – firm and soft and tasting of *her*, of her breath and her skin and her spirit – and they held each other, the rain washing them clean, each with the other's heart beating in their chest; the headscarf gripped in his fist, a scrap of paper in her hand.

56

Mainland

August

Sep leaned over the railing and watched the jellyfish spinning like ghosts through the ferry's wash. The sea was slate black and glassy, the sky the colour of polished brass – bright and pulsing with heat. He closed his eyes and turned his face to it, felt the light kiss his skin.

The island was shrinking as the boat neared the mainland – already so small he could cover it with his hand. But even at this distance he could see the tide's retreat from the island's glorious, barnacled bones.

And he could see the forest. He shuddered as he thought of the wet stone and the blood-black soil, remembering the smell of Barnaby's fur as he'd wrung it in his hands.

Here, surrounded by the laughter of day-trippers, it seemed impossible, but he squeezed the bandage on his finger and felt his pulse throb through the half-healed scar on his leg. He finished his soda and watched the island vanish into the haze.

'You look serious,' said Arkle, leaning in beside him. 'You changing your mind? Cos, you know, if you wanted to stay that would be, y'know, cool.'

Sep smiled.

'No, I'm still taking the scholarship.'

'You sure? I mean, you've got the little Tenchling on the way, your mum and him are moving in together . . .'

'Dude –'

'I bet Magpie would like it if you stayed. Daniels might be less keen. You know he blames you for the whole "pellet-eyed crow" thing.'

'I know.'

'He's seeing a counsellor about his nightmares.'

'I *know*, Arkle.'

'I was at the last match of the season: Daniels missed two penalties, *and* got sent off. He's lost it.' Arkle's eyes misted over. 'It's beautiful, man. You all right?'

'Yeah, I'm just . . . thinking about everything.'

'You think too much, Sepster. Take a leaf out of my book – it's got cardboard pages and loads of pictures. And talking of pages . . .' Arkle shuffled closer and lowered his voice. 'What did you write on that piece of paper?'

'What?' said Sep, frowning.

'The . . . *paper*,' whispered Arkle. 'The one you were going to sacrifice. I *saw* you give it to Hadley. And she's had it ever since.'

Sep laughed. 'Why do you even care?'

'Just that once you gave it to her she, you know. Kissed you. With tongue. I was thinking if I could get a similar message to Anna Wright then –'

'I'm not telling you,' said Sep, grinning. 'Here, what did you do with Rosemary? You didn't burn her or anything, did you?'

'No way! I mean, I can't believe I was *cuddling* that thing, but I buried her in the garden. I'm growing up, like.'

'Good,' said Sep. 'Wait – whose garden?'

Arkle winked at him.

'Never you mind. But listen, you'll come back for holidays, right?'

'These still *are* the holidays. I've not even left yet.'

'I know, but you will, right? Cos Lamb's getting *Legend of Zelda* and I thought –'

'I promise. I'll even be back at weekends.'

'And not just to French kiss Hadley?'

Sep rolled his eyes.

'I thought you'd be happy for me.'

'I am,' said Arkle. 'How's your hand?'

Sep held up the enormous bandage.

'Not great.'

'It looks sweet,' said Hadley, appearing beside them, 'like you've got one of Mickey Mouse's fingers.' She took a quick photo of her friends, then reached into a carrier bag, balancing Elliot in the crook of her arm. 'The ferry's shop isn't great, but here you go: one stick of rock and one Milky Bar.'

'Aw, Milky Bar Kid! You got it!' said Arkle, beaming as he blinked away the camera's flash. 'Did you get my –' Hadley passed him another box – 'nicotine patches? Thanks, I'm gasping.'

Sep turned over the rock, looked at the words on its edge.

'Hill Ford all the way through,' said Hadley.

Sep nodded. He felt a tremor of recognition inside himself – a sense of place that ran up from the soles of his feet.

'Thank you,' he said, taking Hadley's hand and turning it over. The cut had begun to fade.

'It's fine,' she said.

Sep nodded. He checked Mack's watch, ticking steadily on his wrist.

'How long till we dock?' said Arkle.

'Not long. Half an hour.'

'Do you ever hear things with your deaf ear any more?' said Hadley.

Sep shook his head.

'Not since Lamb pulled out my rotten tooth. You want to try – see if anything gets through?'

He angled his head. Her lips brushed his skin, and sent a shiver through his body.

'I love you, Sep Hope,' she whispered.

Sep smiled.

'That's my good ear,' he said, squeezing her hand as they went to join the others.

. . . so you can understand that leaving Hill Ford has been a very difficult decision to make.

Madam, the act of applying to your prestigious establishment caused me to reflect on the nature of my life – and I found it rich in ways I could not have imagined.

I know that I am loved. My life to this point may have been defined by my academic achievement – but my future will be shaped by the love I have for my family, and for my friends.

Sincerely yours,

Sep Hope

Acknowledgements

Nobody writes alone, and I was supported in the creation of this book by many wonderful people.

Thank you first to my darling Julie, for listening to a thousand hours of out-loud thinking, for reading and re-reading endless paragraphs, and for agreeing to marry me – you've made me happy and proud beyond measure. Thank you to Tessie, for bouncing on my knee as I finished the manuscript, and for filling my heart with joy. To my extended family, as always, for your support through difficult times. And to my friends, for giving me a template by which I could measure Sep's growing friendships (Nicolas Anelka?)

Thank you to my UK editors for their enthusiasm for this dark little story: Shannon Cullen, for guiding me through my first book and the early drafts of this one; Natalie Doherty, for your vision and patience as I wrestled the story into place; and Tig Wallace, for getting me over the finish line. To my American publisher, Ken Wright, and my editor, Leila Sales, for your guidance, and for believing in this book from the very beginning. To my agent, Molly Ker Hawn, for securing another unusual deal and for continuing to work magic with my career. To my copy-editors and proofreaders, Jane Tait, Frances Evans, Sarah Hall and Mary O'Riordan, for catching all the many errors that slipped past my eyes. To my publicist these past two years, Clare Kelly, for all your help, organization and enthusiasm; and to Harriet Venn, for your work in support of this book. To my young reader, Evie Baird, for your time and insight.

The Isle of Arran has always played an important role in my life. All our family holidays were taken there, and its elegant silhouette is my constant companion when I run on the beach, weaving stories in my mind. Arran is where my imagination lives – the town of Hill Ford is a composite of Brodick and Lamlash – and I'd like to thank the island and its people for having inspired me to such an extent.

Thanks also to the pupils and staff of the schools I both attended and taught in: Carolside, Williamwood, James Hamilton and Kyle. My memories of you helped Hill Ford High come to life. A special mention must go to my old history teacher, Lawrence Curran – my favourite of many brilliant teachers – immortalized here as Sax Solo, the music teacher.

And finally, to my mum and dad, Ellice and Chris. Thank you for everything you've given me, without which none of this would have even seemed possible. I love you both.

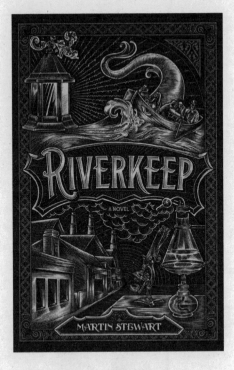

Fifteen-year-old Wulliam is dreading taking up his family's
mantle of Riverkeep, tending the river and fishing corpses from
its treacherous waters.

But then everything changes.

One night his father is possessed by a dark spirit, and Wull
hears that a cure lurks deep within the great sea-beast known as
the mormoarch. He realizes he must go on an epic journey
downriver to find it – or lose Pappa forever.

**'Startlingly original . . . It would be an extraordinary
book by any author – but this is Martin Stewart's first'**
Spectator